Fic
  Bromell, Henry.
  The follower.

  Putnam, 1983
    223 p. ;

THE FOLLOWER

THE FOLLOWER

Henry Bromell

G.P. Putnam's Sons
New York

Designed by Dorothy Wachtenheim

Library of Congress Cataloging in Publication Data

Bromell, Henry.
The follower.

I. Title.
PS3552.R634F6   1983   813'.54   83-10930
ISBN 0-399-12863-8

Printed in the United States of America

1

The day began with a late breakfast at Mosby's Drugstore on Forty-ninth Street.

"What'll it be, darling?"

The blue-haired woman behind the counter smiled, her broken red nails and stub of a pencil poised above her pad. I never knew her name. She always called me darling, as she did everyone else who came in and sat at her counter.

"Eggs and coffee. And bacon," I said, deciding to splurge. "Crispy bacon. It has to be crispy or I can't eat it."

"Crispy bacon," she slowly wrote, underlining crispy.

A customer farther down the counter called for more coffee.

"Coming, darling," she sighed, giving me a wink and waddling away.

While I waited for breakfast, I thought about my parents—guilty thoughts, because I'd just told them I wasn't coming home for Christmas. They live in Springfield, Massachusetts, where I grew up. I had lied and told them I had a part in a play that ran through Christmas Eve and started again the day after Christmas. In fact, I hadn't been able to get a part, any part, in over three months. I was afraid to go home, afraid that I might say yes when my father tilted toward me over brandy and suggested, gently and needfully, as he had done at least once a year since I graduated from Brown, that I consider forgetting the acting business and instead stay and help him run his Chevy dealership. Whenever I went home in those days all that happened was that I felt like a failure.

I was still sitting there waiting for my breakfast when
Henry appeared, conjured from nowhere, a smiling black
man on the stool next to mine, leaning forward with his
elbows on the greasy counter and grinning at me conspiratorially, as if we'd once done something extraor-
dinary together. "Hey, man," he chattered. "How's
things?"

"Okay, Henry. How about you?"

"Oh, pretty good, pretty good."

Henry was a pimp, a short, compact, muscular man
wearing the pimp's uniform: a pink suit, a dozen gold
rings, a wide-brimmed white hat, and a luxurious fur coat
that almost reached his ankles. He had an impish smile
and the glassy-eyed composure of a well-fed junkie. I had
met him a few months earlier, when I was sitting in
Mosby's after work one night. Henry liked to hang out
there, making phone calls from one of the three booths at
the back. The place was open twenty-four hours a day,
and nobody bothered him. "My headquarters," he called
it with pride.

Now he leaned closer. "You look like a sad and lonely
man to me. Why don't you let old Henry help you ease
the burden? Huh? How about Darlene? I told you about
Darlene?"

I'm sure I didn't look like much of a john, no money in
my clothes and face, but he tried me anyway. Maybe he
tried everyone. He was an ambitious hustler, working day
and night to find work for his girls.

"No, thanks, Henry," I said.

My breakfast arrived. Henry ordered coffee, then
started talking about his girls, their various virtues, their
nimbleness, and the stock market. "I got investments," he
assured me. "Substantial investments." His talk shifted
easily back and forth between his girls and the stock market. For every cunt there was a proxy, for every blow-job
a split.

"Know what I think?" he asked, spooning sugar into
his coffee. "I think this country's in big trouble. I mean
big trouble. And you know why? Because people don't

know how to pray no more. That's right. They just plain forgot how to pray. Me, I pray. Oh, yes, I do. I pray my investments won't die in a crash, if you know what I mean. I pray my girls won't get no diseases. And you know what? It works. The Lord hears. 'Henry,' he say, 'I hear you,' and he lets me alone. That bacon looks like shit, man."

"I like it this way."

His eyes wandered around the drugstore, looking for potential clients. "You sure you don't want to celebrate the evening with beautiful Darlene?" he asked me again, without much hope.

"I've got to work, Henry."

He nodded. "Yeah, me too. That's the way it is. Can't stop working."

He gave me a pat on the arm and slid from his stool and started to fish out change to pay for his coffee. "Someday I'm gonna take a vacation. Yes, sir, a vacation." Two quarters rolled onto the counter. "Gonna fly me down to Bermuda and lie on the beach all day and get me a suntan."

Laughing, he moved away toward the phone booths at the back of the drugstore. He fascinated me, Henry did, because he seemed to know nothing of guilt. For that reason, I didn't trust him. I was wrong. He was a friend. A very good friend.

2

I finished my coffee, then wandered over to Fifty-eighth Street, thinking I might go see a movie at the Paris. When I got there, all I found was a long line and the latest sentimental comedy from France. It was cold out, five days before Christmas. The Plaza was busy, patriarchal doormen helping people from their limousines and taxis. Bright Christmas lights framed the tall windows on the first floor. I had stayed there once as a kid, with my mother.

I couldn't remember much about it, except that a piece of mint candy was left on my pillow every night—just for me, I'd thought. Carriage horses shivered in their halters on the Fifty-ninth Street curb. Behind them, the thinning afternoon light spread sadly across the treetops in Central Park.

That's when I heard her singing, a high, pleasant voice on the other side of Fifth Avenue. Looking, I saw a girl in her early twenties, playing a guitar. A small crowd had gathered around her in a semicircle, quiet with respect, as New Yorkers are in the presence of music. She was wearing an old coat, too big for her, and she held her head high as she sang, a blue knit cap covering her short hair. I waited for the light, then crossed the street to listen.

I'd heard plenty of street singers before, but none with such an easy, mournful voice. She sang from her belly, and so the song seemed to rise from deep within her, personal enough, strong enough, to stop passersby and make them linger, huddled in the cold. Beneath her huge, frayed overcoat, she wore two layers of gray skirts, mismatched high wool socks, and workboots. Her hands were protected, sort of, by fingerless gloves, and she strummed her guitar lightly, picking at the strings with delicate precision. The music didn't support her singing, it floated around it. Some of her listeners moved their bodies in time to the song. New Yorkers not only respect music, they want to be part of it, and they were enthusiastic when she finished.

She accepted their applause with careful indifference, an actress too proud to take her third-rate audience very seriously. They asked for more, but she demurred, collecting the coins from her guitar case and packing away her guitar. Finally she straightened, holding her back with her left hand, and started slowly down Fifth Avenue. She looked straight ahead, never meeting the curious glances of people on the sidewalk.

Having nothing better to do, I followed her. I often followed people in those days. It was a way to get through the long afternoons before work, and sometimes the night hours, after work, when I couldn't sleep. I suppose I was lonely. I hadn't been in New York very long. I didn't know many people. I certainly meant no harm. I'd simply pick someone who interested me and follow him, and in the course of watching him live his daily life start to feel more alive myself. An innocent enough habit, I thought, like my collecting model soldiers. There was no way I could know then that it would almost get me killed.

Fifth Avenue was packed with Christmas shoppers, all the windows of the fancy stores filled with jewels and expensive clothes. Elegant women in fur coats, trailing perfume, strolled through doors held open by more uniformed doormen into Cartier's, Gucci's, and Tiffany's. They say there are more suicides in New York during Christmas than any other time of year. I believe it. Those windows make you feel bad if you don't have any money. They make you feel stupid.

When she reached Forty-ninth Street, the girl turned right, heading west. I kept a good fifty yards between us, not wanting her to realize I was following her and get scared. I knew she'd get scared. I already knew that much about her. She held her head high, all right, and she moved along the sidewalk as if she didn't care, one way or the other, what people thought of her, but I knew she was scared and that the indifference was a pose. It masked her face, so I still didn't have a good idea what she looked like, up close anyway. She sent out a protective aura, an invisible circle of air, that kept her safe. People sensed it, and though they stared at her, they also gave way to her.

We crossed Times Square together, sidling through the crowds, past a thousand blaring radios. During my first few months in New York, I'd never understood why all the people in Times Square didn't just walk over to Fifth Avenue and trash the place. Later I understood that most New Yorkers don't resent Fifth Avenue, they only want to get there themselves. That's the city's secret drama, the engine that keeps the whole thing running. *Believe in hope all ye who enter here.* Those store windows back on Fifth Avenue were filled with hope, positively shining with hope, and the suicides who littered the Christmas season probably saw everything they didn't have and thought it was their fault.

Black pimps like Henry in tight white suits and wide-brimmed hats surveyed Forty-second Street with the eyes of lizards, looking for prey, their ticket to the good life. Boys walked along the sidewalk in groups, walked as if they were dancing. A nervous sexual energy seemed to lift them a few inches from the concrete. Outside the theaters, people stood before small television screens, watching scenes from the movies playing inside. The air smelled of skin, skin and a sweet mixture of hot dogs and marijuana. Whores, up early, lounged in doorways or sat in McDonald's eating breakfast, their wigs askew, the newest layer of makeup transluscent in the unfair daylight, so that they seemed to be wearing faces within faces within faces, a Chinese box of identities.

Above us all, the huge neon signs were already blinking in a trance, and around the top of the Times Tower ran a line of news: ... UNEMPLOYMENT UP ... REAGAN DE-CLARES ......

I followed the girl all the way down to Thirty-ninth Street, where she stopped and opened her guitar case. The sidewalks were less crowded here, fewer shoppers in this part of town. I stayed back, leaning against a phone booth across the street. Even from a distance, I could see that she had to force herself to sing, that she was tired, and cold, and wanted to go home. Where was home? I wondered. Where did she live? Does a girl like that even have a home? Or did she sleep in the streets, or abandoned buildings, or Salvation Army barracks? There was something pathetic about her now, singing alone. No one stopped to listen, except an old man and his wife, arm-in-arm, who hesitated, gazing at her, and then shuffled on, leaving her behind.

Three kids approached her from Sixth Avenue. They were young, around fourteen or fifteen. One of them, the tallest, who moved with the sly, cocky self-assurance of a leader, was an albino. All three were dressed in suits and ties, and all three wore similar overcoats, long trenchcoats with winter linings.

They stopped when they reached the girl. The albino said something to her. She immediately stopped singing and started to pack up her guitar. The albino stepped closer, and touched her with an obscene familiarity, as if he knew her. She seemed to shudder, and pulled back, withdrew even further into herself, while he continued speaking. He didn't hurt her, but she was scared of him. She fumbled and dropped her guitar case before she'd completely clasped it shut. Gently, he stooped and picked it up, securing the clasps and handing it to her.

Later, I was to wonder why I didn't help her. It might have saved me a lot of trouble. But I rationalized. They weren't, in fact, doing anything to her. So I stayed put, practically hiding behind the phone booth, and watched as she retrieved her guitar case from the albino and hurriedly took something from her coat pocket and handed it to him. He was still staring at it in his hand when she turned and left.

He looked up and stared after her, then said something to the other kids. They all laughed, three high, thin voices in the near-empty street. Pocketing whatever she had given him, the albino led his friends away, toward me. They didn't see me, thanks to the phone booth. I caught a quick but clear look at the albino's eyes. They were pink, and they gleamed in his pink face.

I slipped out from behind the phone booth and down Seventh Avenue, cutting across town on Thirty-eighth Street until I reached Sixth, just in time to see the girl start downtown on the other side of the street, in the sunlight. There was nothing nonchalant about the way she walked now. She moved as fast as she could, the awkward pull of her guitar case making her sway from side to side.

The sun had started to sink in the west, throwing long shadows from the buildings across the street. The girl moved ahead of me, into shadow, into light. We passed old granite office buildings, the kind with brass doorways and green marble lobbies inside. We passed a dress shop, and a toy store where I had once bought a Napoleonic soldier, a two-inch lead soldier cast from a good mold and painted perfectly by the Armenian I could see through the glass window, hunched above his bench, a jeweler's glass squinched in his right eye and a small brush in his hand.

Up ahead, the girl turned west and continued for a block, then turned downtown again. A seagull flapped slowly above our heads, wheeling and dipping in the high eddies of air, cold air rushing in from the Atlantic. As a kid, I had broken my arm jumping from the roof of the garage, hoping to fly, convinced I could fly. That was when I was about the same age as those kids, the albino and his friends. Watching the girl bob along in front of me, I wondered who they were. What had the albino said to her, and what had she given him?

We reached the Garment District, streets crowded with black kids and Puerto Ricans pushing tall carts of clothes. Trucks were backed up, loading and unloading bales of brightly colored materials, rippling stacks of corduroy and cotton. This was an even older world than Times Square, an immigrant's world, the crimped streets dark and damp and the four-story buildings encrusted with fussy scrollwork. Voices chattered, mingled, called back and forth like echoes in a canyon. There was no gaiety here, only work, the feverish struggle to make money, to escape. Old men in black suits watched the chaos, lingering only briefly on the girl as she pushed through them. A few of the black kids, huge combs sticking from the back pockets of their tight jeans, looked up and said something to her as she passed, teasing her, no doubt, then getting back to work pushing their carts.

One of the carts cut me off, blocking the way. Through the hanging clothes, I could see the girl stepping into an alley across the street. The kid pushing the cart, a tall, skinny mulatto, had stopped to light a cigarette, sneaking a rest. I tried to step around him, but another cart was there. A truck, also stuck, honked its horn, impatient to move. Lazily, the kid looked up, slowing down even more.

I scurried like a crab, sideways along the sidewalk, until I found an opening between two parked trucks. I slid through, dodging more carts in the middle of the street, and finally reached the other side. The alley was empty.

About two hundred yards long, it didn't go all the way to the next street, but ended in a warehouse and a wide loading platform. Very little sunlight penetrated the narrow passageway. All the windows facing the alley had been painted black, except for the ones on the ground floor, which had been bricked up. Large dumpsters, spilling rejected cloth and soggy cardboard boxes, sat at twenty-foot intervals.

I walked slowly down the alley. The girl wasn't there. When I reached the loading platform at the end of the alley, I climbed up onto the concrete lip and tried the double doors into the warehouse. They were locked from the inside.

A magic trick can make you feel crazy, and this was a magic trick, because when I returned along the alley and tested the other three doors that she might have used, they were all locked, too. After a complete circle of the alley, I stood again at the entrance, staring along the length of dumpsters and broken glass at the platform.

She had vanished.

3

I wandered back up to Fifth Avenue in the cold twilight, still feeling pretty crazy. The sky was dimming to orange, a dull hue beyond the buildings. Cold blasts of wind howled along the streets, so that people had to lean forward to walk, holding on to their collars and hats.

I had followed grandmothers home to Queens. I had followed suburban housewives in town for a shopping spree. I had followed high school kids from video arcade to pinball machine to deserted docks, where they sat smoking joints and skipping stones out to sea. I once followed a businessman from skyscraper to skyscraper, meeting to meeting, trying to imagine what it would be like to be so purposeful. Another time, I followed a social worker past mounds of garbage on his rounds through Brownsville, a land of rubble, abandoned buildings and broken windows, acres of waste, no people in sight. I had followed dozens of people all over New York, but I had never followed a street singer before, and I had never seen anyone vanish like that.

She wasn't beautiful, but something of her lingered in my brain, just behind my eyes, like a blurry double vision. I could see her and I couldn't see her. Her face was vague, a white emptiness. It was the way she moved that I remembered, her vulnerability. Was I just feeling sorry for her, this poor girl my age who had to wear rags and sing on street corners? Yes, I decided, reaching Rockefeller Center. It was Christmas, and Christmas tends to make me feel sorry for everyone.

I decided to go watch the skaters for a while, then stop by a place I knew on Fiftieth Street and get a cup of coffee.

Walking through Rockefeller Center, I passed secretaries hurrying *click-click-click* down to the basement post office with their Pitney Bowes machines. Guys in green suits with wide, puffy bodies clutched their briefcases and kept their eyes on middle distance, unfocused. You can feel like a zombie in New York. The dark Deco lobby of Rockefeller Center looked like a tunnel, the two escalators carrying people silently up and down, only the kids rambunctious enough to cause a stir, to enliven the deadly sliding silence. The kids squealed and shoved, their voices high-pitched and excited.

Outside again, I stood by the wall looking down at the skaters. It was getting dark quickly, and there was a cold flat smell of snow in the air, a dry, metallic sting. The Christmas lights shined, red and green and white. Below, behind the glass windows surrounding the skating rink, people sat sipping tea, bundles of Christmas presents piled on vacant chairs.

Around and around the skaters swirled, laughter rising

up into the gathering dark. I had to hold the collar of my jacket closed to keep the wind from whipping down my neck. I kept thinking about that girl, the singer. Where did she go when it got dark and the cold wind lashed against her throat? She couldn't have just disappeared. I remembered her fingers, knuckles red, plucking the strings of her guitar, and I heard her voice, clear and strong as she sang. What a life, going out each day and singing on street corners. How much did she make? Was it enough to live on? Probably not, though she lived. That was the miracle. She probably made less each day than those people behind glass had spent on their tea and pastries.

I thought, briefly, of calling my parents and telling them I'd changed my mind, that I'd catch the next train to Springfield and be home for Christmas. A momentary tug—and then I remembered my father's silent, wounded solicitude, my mother's patient worry, the smells of the house, my bedroom unchanged since I left, childhood books and baseball pennants mocking my return. I remembered the thin gray light on the empty factories, rows and rows of huge red brick buildings deserted and covered with tuneless graffiti, windows shattered. It was too depressing, too much of my own life rising up to stare me in the face. And yet the scene below—the cheerful skaters, the people eating and talking inside the restaurant—suddenly filled me with such a horrible feeling of detachment that I almost hurried right to Penn Station. It was as if I couldn't convince myself that I had anything to do with those people down there. They looked so small and far away.

A pretty girl wearing a long green scarf fell on the ice. A dapper old man, gray hair neatly brushed, eyes serious with unconcern, skated haughtily by, hands clasped behind his back, each step a casual, pushing slide. Everyone was sliding, up, down, around.

A heavy weight settled on my chest, making it hard to breathe. As I crossed Fifth Avenue, the office lights and the Christmas lights in the store windows and the looming dark stones of St. Patrick's all seemed to curve over me and press down, trapping me like an elevator, a small box.

A taxi, brakes shrieking, almost hit me. The driver leaned on his horn, glaring at me as he swerved by.

"*Asshole!*" he shouted.

I stopped at Harvey's newsstand on the corner and bought a paper. The headlines announced MASS MURDER IN DETROIT.

"What's the news today, Harvey?"

"Never read the damn things," he muttered inside his little temple, surrounded by porn magazines. "Aggravates my ulcers. You just get up?"

Harvey wore old-fashioned rimless army glasses, and his hands were so black from ink he looked as if he were wearing gloves.

"Up and out by one today, Harvey."

He shook his head. Harvey thought that my life— working at night, sleeping all day—would get me in trouble. "It ain't natural," he said.

"Nothing's natural, Harvey." I took my change. "Thanks."

Harvey stared at me. His old-man eyes—was he sixty? seventy? a hundred?—were moist and unhappy.

"Get *married*," he growled. "Be *normal*. What's wrong with you kids you can't be normal?"

"Good night, Harvey."

4

This Side of Paradise was on the first floor of a three-story brick rowhouse on East Fifty-fourth Street. A pink neon sign above the front door was the only clue that the place wasn't just a house. The noise of the music didn't hit you until you stepped inside and found yourself in a large room filled with drunks and dancers. There were tables set up on one side of the room, each with a candle in a red bowl. In the middle of the room, facing the dance floor, stood a 1948 Ford pickup, just the frame, no wheels. Inside the cab, instead of a dashboard, were two turntables, tended to by a tall, wiry kid wearing dark glasses and a Yankee baseball cap. His name was Two—the first digit of his Social Security number. He refused to be addressed by anything else. His job was to administer the music, the loud rock and roll blasting through huge speakers suspended from the ceiling. At the far end of the room was a bar, and behind the bar stood Alex Hagen, dispensing drinks. It was his nightclub.

Besides myself, there were three other waiters: George and Lewis, two gay guys in their early thirties with identical thin mustaches, both of them also unemployed actors, and Sandy, a pretty nineteen-year-old from New Jersey. She wanted to be an actor, too. America's the only country I know whose theater schools train waiters.

Work that night did not go well. I couldn't concentrate on what I was doing. Twice I mixed up orders, carrying hamburgers to a table that wanted sole and a medium steak to a woman who wanted rare. Her date, a belly in a suit, made things difficult. He was trying to impress her, I think.

"This is ridiculous!" he shouted pompously, fighting the music. "We've been waiting half an hour for the wrong food? Who runs this goddamned place? I want to see him. *Now.*"

Alex had to bite the bullet and placate them with a free steak and a bottle of wine.

Then he pulled me aside, back by the kitchen: "What the fuck's wrong with you?"

Alex frightened me. He was a long-haired, thick-shouldered Vietnam vet with a way of drifting back into his head when he talked to you, behind the tight, abstracted smile of an assassin. His left arm, from the elbow down, had been blown away by a booby trap, and instead of a hand he had a shiny hook, which he used with dexterity, as if he'd been born with it.

He tapped it lightly on my chest, just below the neck.

"One more time and you're out. I can't afford fuck-ups."

I returned to my tables, determined to stay on top of things, but I still managed to screw up a few more orders. I brought one man a Scotch instead of bourbon, and another time I simply forgot that someone was waiting for an Irish coffee. Sandy was helping Alex behind the bar, so she covered for me.

The room was smoky, hot from so many bodies pressed together, sweating, grinding. Their smell and the sour reek of beer thickened the air. I don't know if you can call what they were doing on the dance floor dancing. It was more like a group throb. It wasn't hard to imagine everyone deserting the streets, crowding down to dance, happier in that cave than ever up above. Soon there'd be no one left in the city. They'd all be underground, dancing. Skyscrapers overgrown. Streets as grassy as Roman roads.

> *I want to touch you*
> *I want to kiss you*
> *James Dean, who can we be?*
> *Who can we be?*
> *James Dean, who can we be?*

Two was blowing it. The energy was sagging too low. Dancers had started to settle at their tables. This was the wrong song, a depressing song, a hopeless song, a boring song. He sensed it, too, and tried to shift the mood by sliding into Pat Benatar, but that was too quick, it just confused people. He fumbled on, peeking out the windshield to see how things were going. He'd lost the heartbeat and now he had a roomful of individuals, lost souls, each heart beating on its own, alone. Even the talk was beginning to sag.

I usually loved rock and roll, but that night it depressed me, because it seemed, suddenly, such a hopeless celebration, such a cheat, like a hymn without a religion. I'm too reticent to dance myself, I do all my dancing in my head, but I can soar sometimes, the burden of consciousness lifted, my separateness gone. Rock and roll had always

helped me fly, but not that night. That night the pounding, pulsing noise was just that, noise. It meant nothing, it
offered nothing.

Looking around me at the dark, throbbing room, the
faces waiting so eagerly for pleasure, I thought I was
going to faint. Blood left my face, my hands tingled. I almost fell. You're just tired, I told myself, trying to get my
breathing back to normal. Not enough sleep, not enough
food. The faces whirled and dipped, a mad swarm feeding
on the music, the solid repetitive beat and the volume, as
Two slowly worked everyone back onto the same track,
pulling all those heartbeats together again and urging
them toward the dance floor, that little square heaven of
purple lights.

When I was sure all my tables were happily stocked, I
told Sandy I wanted a drink of my own, a whiskey, and
nodded toward the kitchen.

She looked surprised. I usually didn't drink.

"Are you okay?"

"Sure," I said. We were both shouting, like everyone
else in the room.

I liked Sandy. She was a full, soft girl, with a fine map
of freckles around her green eyes. We had gone out together a few times, and we even slept together once, neither shy nor in love. As I walked back to the kitchen to
wait for her to bring me my drink, I realized she was the
last woman I had slept with. Five months ago, I calcu-
lated. Last August. Five months since I'd slipped into a
woman's warm body.

The kitchen was small, a deep sink and two stoves and
three refrigerators crammed together between the sweating gray walls, the sagging shelves of cans and spices.
Raoul, a fifteen-year-old Haitian, washed dishes. Suto, a
mild, slow-moving Korean, was the cook.

Sandy came in with my drink. "Here you go."

"Thanks."

She smiled, hesitating before leaving, waiting for me to
say something. "You've been hiding."

"Not really." I lit a cigarette.

"Then how come you won't talk to me anymore?"

"I talk to you."

"No, you don't." She was concerned, and maybe a little hurt.

She took a sip of my whiskey. "I'm not making it up. We really don't talk anymore. Don't you know that?"

"I'm sorry." I couldn't think of anything else to say.

"What're you doing for Christmas?" she asked.

"Going home." I was getting good at lying.

Both Raoul and Suto were watching us, listening.

Sandy lowered her voice. "You look terrible, Gregory. That's all. You won't talk to *any*body. What's the matter with you? You look so sad."

Quickly, softly, she said, "You can come back to my place later, if you want."

Why wasn't I attracted to her? It hit me then, a fist in the gut, that breathlessness again. I wasn't attracted to anybody. I'd forgotten how. I'd drifted so far away from humankind that the closest I could get to people was following them. But I couldn't tell Sandy that. I could only stand there, letting her smile wither and fade, until finally, with a small shrug, she turned and left the kitchen, leaving me alone with my fear.

After the last drunken, stumbling customer had gone and Alex had locked the door behind him, we had to clean up before going home. Sandy counted tips at one of the tables, stacking the coins into separate piles of quarters, nickels, dimes. George and Lewis gossiped as they worked. Two was still in his cab, putting away records and dusting the turntables.

Alex pointedly ignored me, withdrawn into his world of work, the steady, practiced motion of washing glasses, rubbing the bar clean.

"Business is hopping," I said, idiotically. I was trying to make up for my mistakes. "Must feel good."

Alex held his glass up to the light, wiping away a streak with a towel clasped in his hook. "What?"

"Business. You must feel good, it's going so well."

"You can always make a living selling booze."

Alex lived alone on the third floor of the building, renting out the rest as offices. He never left the place. He was either upstairs, doing whatever he did up there, or he was down in the nightclub, working. He smashed his hook into a huge block of ice in the aluminum sink and lifted the ice deftly to the shiny industrial refrigerator he kept in a nook behind the bar.

I persevered. "Doesn't it bother you, never getting out of here?"

"Nowhere to go." He returned to the glasses. His eyes, avoiding mine, were angry. The muscles in his forearm tightened. "I got everything I need." He paused and looked at me significantly. "From where I'm standing right now I can reach a .357 Magnum in three seconds."

A hole blossomed in my belly. "A Magnum? Here?"

"Bet your fucking ass. You gotta be able to defend yourself. You know what I do in my free time, Hartz? I practice. So I'm ready." He smiled. "Trouble with you, Hartz, is you got no idea what's going on around you. You got your fucking head in the clouds." He spoke to the bottles, or his own reflection beyond the glass shelves.

Behind me, George called, "Sandy, you finished yet?"

"Give me a second," she said wearily.

"Will you please hurry up?" George nagged. "I want to get out of here."

Sandy exploded. "Now you made me lose count! Now I got to start all over again!"

"None of you guys are ready," Alex continued, facing me now, leaning close across the bar, his cold hook touching my chest again. "You're all fucking useless. You gotta be ready. You don't get a second chance. There's just survivors and dead people, Hartz."

Again, the smile, only this time he leaned even closer and brought his hook up to my face. His voice was soft. "Did I turn in my M-16? You think I'm fucking stupid? I took it down and smuggled it in." He waggled his hook before my eyes. "Carried the barrel back in here. Now I got that baby greased and loaded right by the side of my bed."

"I give up!" Sandy cried, exasperated, flinging coins onto the floor. "It comes out different each time! My feet hurt! *My feet hurt!*"

I wasn't the only one with problems.

5

It was after two in the morning by the time I left the nightclub, but I knew I wouldn't be able to sleep yet, so instead of heading home I walked around midtown for a while, observing my fellow night people, the taxi drivers, and the whores on Forty-second Street, beautiful black women in red wigs, and the occasional drunk, a guilty businessman, hurrying to safety. Everyone was waiting. I could feel it in the air. Something had to happen. The city was going to explode. People would turn on each other some night, or wake to find a prophet in the streets.

I walked through Port Authority, that deadly white light, past rows of silent faces, men and women sitting on benches waiting for buses to Kansas and Florida. They held suitcases and paper bags on their laps, and they all stared straight ahead, as if there were a movie on the opposite wall.

Coming out the main entrance, I nearly bumped into a cop. I almost reached out and grabbed his gun. I don't know why, but I always have that impulse when I see those revolvers glistening on a cop's big hips. Grab it and what? Shoot somebody? Get shot myself? It's like going to the top of the Empire State Building, something I only did once, because of the temptation to jump, not a need, but a fear that drew me closer and closer to the edge, as if someone were pushing me gently from behind, gently but firmly.

I crossed back to the East Side, still too wired to go

home. The wind blew hard, cold, right at my face. Rats scuttled in an alley, knocking off the top of a trash can. Steam rose silently from manholes in the middle of the street, the smoke of subterranean campfires.

There seemed to be a music, an order, behind it all, a rhythm running under the streets, vibrating up through the soles of my feet. There seemed to be a beat in the throb of a million generators, even a melody, the little patches of light glowing in the tall buildings. But in fact the city was out of control, like the dancers that night. No one was in charge anymore. The city just ran on its own energy, on the bodies consumed, on the heat given out, the combustible tension of desire trapped, rage trapped. I tried but couldn't ignore all those other lives jostling against me, everyone competing, struggling to raise himself higher on the shoulders of a dead man, climbing, kicking, to the top. The city was a battlefield. A hundred different armies roamed the streets, lawyers here, junkies there, doctors and pimps, white folks, black folks, Puerto Ricans, fags, rich and poor and everyone in between squinting down the barrel of a shotgun from each barricaded home. Only the prowling blue police cars were left to stitch the whole thing together, gleaming as they slid beneath the streetlights.

I moved across Madison and the wide calm of Park Avenue, Christmas trees dark at that time of night. As I walked, I tried to understand what it was that we all wanted, what it was that the city teased us with and then withheld. Alex and his guns, his paranoia a kind of drug to keep him happy. Sandy inviting me back to her room. She was lonely, of course. Just like me. Harvey the newsdealer said get married. Be normal. Maybe he had a point. And the girl, the singer—I pictured her again, holding that beat-up guitar, reddened fingers touching the strings, her head held high and her voice reaching out clear and strong. What did she want? Money? Escape? What did *I* want?

The streets on the East Side were empty, everyone comfortably in bed, dreaming of Martha's Vineyard. Another police car cruised by, slowing to check me out, keeping pace for half a block before speeding away into the night. I didn't breathe until it had disappeared from sight. Even in the cold, cops made me sweat. It was as if I walked around convinced I'd committed a crime.

Then I saw the kids.

I was just about to cross to the east side of Lexington. The avenue was empty, a long, undulating stretch of darkness broken only by the diminishing line of streetlights hanging over each intersection. One by one, the lights turned yellow, then red. A block south, materializing from the shadows, stepped a group of small human figures, and I recognized the albino, the one I'd seen earlier, talking to the singer. His white hair glowed beneath the red traffic light. Behind him trooped maybe a dozen more kids, all about his age, between thirteen and fifteen, though a few could have been as young as twelve, I couldn't be sure from that distance. They moved silently, on sneakered feet, walking south. They looked like animals on a hunt, tense, compact bodies sliding stealthily along the sidewalk. They frightened me, like Alex.

I stepped back until my shoulders touched the wall of a florist's shop. It was almost three in the morning. What were they doing up? I wasn't tired anymore. Adrenalin pumped through my arms, my legs. The traffic light turned green, and as if that were my signal, I started following the kids. I wondered where they might lead me. To the girl? I felt a little foolish, though. Didn't I have anything better to do than follow a bunch of kids down Lexington Avenue at three in the morning? No voice, no thought, answered. I followed people, that's all. I really was curious. Who were these kids? Mole-man following mole-kids, that's what we were. Linked together by the string of streetlights mindlessly clicking from red to green, through yellow back to red, then green again. Dawn wasn't too far away, and I sensed, or imagined, a pearling gray in the east, a faint salty sun that would soon blanch the streets and send us mole-people scurrying blindly for the shelter of darkness.

The kids continued south for ten blocks. They walked as if they owned the night. The streets were empty. Only an occasional taxi shot down Lexington, rattling and jolting over bumps, running with the lights. Most of the buildings were dark, shops on the ground floor shuttered behind roll-down grates, and above them apartments reaching high into the darkness. I tightened my shoulders against the wind. It was whistling now, straight off the sea and into my face, as if Lexington were a tunnel. One of these days, I promised myself, I'm going to buy a winter overcoat. My windbreaker, and that's all it was, couldn't have broken a breeze. It was a black satin jacket, lined for warmth, trimmed in red and backed with a bright red decal of Mickey Mouse. I'd bought it at a sleazy boutique down in the Village, my first week in New York. This was my only effort at style. The rest of my clothes just found their way into my life. I couldn't remember buying them.

I shivered and hunched, my eyes on the kids up ahead. Sometimes they disappeared into the shadows, and I had to stop and wait for them to appear again, afraid I'd walk right up against them in the dark. I stayed a hundred yards back. There was no one else around, nobody on the streets, nothing for camouflage.

We passed dark pawn shops and beauty parlors, we passed dry-cleaning places with plastic flowers in the windows, we passed coffee shops and hamburger places and small boutiques that displayed their expensive nothings on skinny cream-colored manikins, dead eyes smiling out into the street, green lights turning orange reflected in their pupils, as if they were having an idea.

The kids took their time, the albino always a few feet in front, that white hair and pale pink skin making him look like a photograph in reverse, something that never quite got developed, stuck forever on another plane. The other kids followed in a tight bunch, almost in formation. I half expected the albino to raise a sword and sound the charge. Instead, they quietly turned the corner onto Forty-eighth Street, heading toward the water.

I stopped and lit a cigarette. It took a few tries, with the wind, and I had to face the building, protected by the recess of a doorway. I can remember the white lettering on the rippled glass: DR. JOSEPH FRANKENHEIMER, CHIROPRACTOR.

I turned around and faced the empty street. There was the corner, Forty-eighth and Lexington. Just another street corner. So why was I playing this little game, stopping for a cigarette? I wanted to give them plenty of time to get ahead. That was the logic. I smoked half the cigarette, slowly, before grinding it out with the toe of my sneaker. Then I approached the corner. When I got there, I dropped to my hands and knees and peeked around the corner, my right cheek brushing the sidewalk.

Forty-eighth Street was empty, dark except for the pools of light cast at fifty-foot intervals by the old-fashioned rococo streetlamps. I could make out the black metal railings, the front stoops of the brownstones, the neat window boxes blooming with black flowers. Cars were parked along the south side of the street. I could hear electricity sparking and hissing in the lines above me. That was the only sound. Except for the scream.

At first I thought it was a siren wailing, far away but coming closer, wavering on the wind. But it wasn't. It was a woman's voice, the cry of an animal defending itself, a high, terrified screech cut short by silence. The silence was even worse than the scream. It questioned my sanity. Had I even heard a scream? I'd already felt crazy once tonight, and this time I didn't want to see things, too. Casual as could be, I stood and dusted the knees of my jeans. I'll just go home now, I told the street. Thanks for the offer. But then the street said, *Listen.* And I remembered. I'd heard the scream bouncing between houses. An echo— the scream had echoed. Can an imagined scream echo? I wasn't that crazy, was I?

I took the corner and started up Forty-eighth Street, straining to hear another scream, or voices, but nothing came. Just the electricity and the gentle squish of my sneakers on the pavement. There was a dry taste in my mouth, bitter. A woman had screamed. She was in trouble. The sound had come from the end of the street. I moved on the balls of my feet, ready to run.

I finally reached First Avenue. Ahead of me, across a large, open square, rose the curving dark glass of the United Nations. It looked like the remains of a future ruin stranded in darkness. I remembered film clips I'd seen of that building, from the early sixties, when the United Nations still seemed inviolably secure, a hospital for international politics, staffed by good, even-tempered doctors who would never let the situation get out of hand. Now it squatted in silence, the few lighted windows glowing dimly. As I watched, one of the lights winked off.

I was staring so hard everything blurred. I moved my own eyes quickly, scanning the plaza, trying to pick out any movement. The wind had more room here, and blew in cold, quick blasts, scattering bits of newspaper and tugging at the awning of the nearest apartment building. Even in the dark, it was an elegant building, sleek and safe. Johnny Carson had lived there before he went to Hollywood. Truman Capote still lived there. If there was a doorman, he was inside, in the warmth of the lobby, asleep probably, leaning back against the wall, his mouth open, his folded racing form forgotten on his lap. But I never got a chance to find out, because I heard footsteps running toward me, fast quiet footsteps, a muffled stampede pounding up at me.

I looked around for someplace to hide. All I could see was a depression next to the brownstone behind me, short concrete steps, surrounded by a railing, that led down to the basement. Vaulting over the railing, my hand slipped, and when I came down I twisted my ankle and nearly fell on my ass. I had to stick my fist in my mouth to keep from yelping, for the footsteps had reached me. Looking up, I saw a dozen shadows running by. I dragged myself up on one of the bars that guarded the basement window.

It was the gang of kids. The albino was leading. He held a long fur coat above his head. It fluttered behind him like a cape. The light wasn't too good, but I thought he was grinning. The kids disappeared around the corner, back onto Forty-eighth Street.

I hobbled over the railing and limped in the direction they had come from, into darkness, my left foot shattering every time I put weight on it. I forced myself to use it, and after ten yards the shards of glass in my ankle started to melt. I massaged it. Fifteen yards, and I could stand on it. But it would be swollen and sore in the morning.

I was looking for a woman, a woman who had screamed, and finally I found her. She was lying face down on the sidewalk, at the entrance to an alley, her legs twisted beneath her. She had long, dark hair that merged with the dark sidewalk, and her back was bare. She was wearing a long evening dress. Evening shoes rested at her feet, as if she'd just stepped out of them to go to bed. One of the heels was broken. Her right hand had folded beneath her when she fell. Her left hand stretched out, oddly tranquil, and seemed to be pointing after the kids. I thought at first that the long, thin sliver of darkness that perfectly mirrored her outstretched arm was a shadow.

Stepping closer, I saw that it was blood.

6

The woman stirred. A soft moan floated into the cold air and was blown away. She wasn't conscious, but she was struggling to get there. She had a wide, pale forehead that tapered down like a heart to high cheekbones and a small, delicate chin. Her mouth was also small, a red slash of surprise in her white face. I guessed her to be in her forties, though she may well have been a youthful fifty. She was obviously a woman who had the money to take care of herself. Her slender body belonged to an eighteen-year-old. The kids must have jumped her from the alley, taken her mink coat, her purse, and fled. What had she been doing out there alone so late at night? She was a setup, a walking target, an invitation to violence.

I moved as if drugged, or dreaming, or both, my hands thick and slow, my feet glued to the sidewalk. I knew I shouldn't move her, that I should run to the apartment building and bang on the glass doors until the doorman woke and called an ambulance. But part of me didn't yet understand that this was real. I stood there mesmerized by the dark hair splayed on the sidewalk, the human body so inhumanly sprawled. I was dazed, as if I were the one who'd been attacked. I watched myself from a distance, grew furious with myself for not moving, not acting. The wind swept across the plaza, lifting her hair, delicately. Far away, a ship's horn blurted warning.

Something glinted near her head, on the sidewalk. I bent over and picked it up, then startled myself awake by screaming. The shiny object was a pair of scissors, heavy silver scissors, the kind they use to cut thick cloth. It was covered with warm, sticky blood.

My scream must have woken her, too, for her eyes opened and looked right at me. Our faces were almost level on the pavement. Our eyes met, and briefly she smiled, like a girl waking up from a long, pleasant nap. Then she saw the scissors in my hand, and simultaneously the pain must have hit her, she must suddenly have remembered who she was and where she was and what had happened, for the smile faded and was replaced by a look of pure terror, so fast it was like watching a metamorphosis.

She started screaming at me in Italian.

"*O Dio mio!*" Her mouth, dry with panic, worked for words. "*Aiuto!*"

She was shrieking now, trying to roll away, untangling her legs from beneath her and hauling herself up into a sitting position. Her bra had been ripped and her breasts jiggled in the dim light.

"Lady, I—"

Her English came as a second thought. "*Leave me alone!*"

"Lady, please, I'm going to help you."

"*Assassino!*"

"You don't understand."

Her voice, growing in strength, smothered mine.
"*Killer!*"

"Please, listen to me."

She was pushing herself backward along the sidewalk,
her eyes fixed on the scissors in my hand. I stared down at
them. How had they gotten there? I tried to drop them,
but they wouldn't fall. I had to shake my hand, hard, to
get rid of them, and even then it was more like peeling
them off. Finally the scissors clattered to the cement.

She reared back and roared into the night, panic pushing her voice higher. "Help me! *Help me!*"

I reached for her, to calm her. She jumped, pumping
her legs, her scream a pure, unmodulated shriek now, no
words, just a shriek piercing the silence of the street. I
heard a window slide open somewhere above us.

I was fighting my own panic. "Please, don't scream, I'm
not going to hurt you."

My words were lost. They couldn't compete with her
fear. She kept her mouth open and took deep, sobbing
breaths, voicing every agony she'd ever felt, a long, shattered keen that seemed to fill the street, the open, empty
plaza, rebounding and doubling in force until the scream
could be heard in Harlem. She must have been in shock,
for she didn't realize what had happened to her hand, anymore than I did, until she raised it to shield herself, finally
remembering that she had arms that could fight.

Her ring finger and her index finger had been severed
just below the knuckles. The open stubs squirted blood. I
felt my head go hot and prickly. I had to hold on to the
sidewalk to keep from swooning.

Finally it registered. "Oh my God! My hand! *My
hand!*"

"Let me help you." The words rolled out of my mouth,
separate and unrelated concepts.

Nearby, another window slid open, and a voice called
down, "*The police are coming!*"

It was a man's voice, a civilized voice edged with unac-
customed fear. "Do you hear me? I've called the police!
They're on their way! *Leave that woman alone!*"

The woman gulped and gagged, then retched all over herself. She could die while the brave man above us, invisible in the darkness, called down.

"Don't worry!" he consoled. *"The police will be here any minute!"*

The woman seemed to have forgotten me. She was sitting cross-legged, her breasts glistening with vomit, staring at her hand, as if it were a dead bird she'd found on the sidewalk. Her glazed eyes held no recognition, only a vague curiosity. Slowly she looked up at me.

"Please believe me," I said. "I didn't do it. I was just following those kids. *They* did it."

Survival instinct broke through her false calm, and she let out another scream, mixed with tears, a heaving, gasping cry. "Help?"

It was a question, addressed to the anonymous buildings.

"Please don't scream."

"Help?" She gazed around her, pleading.

I took a step closer. "Just don't scream. Let me help you."

That did it. She must have thought I was going to kill her. Using a strength she shouldn't have had, desperate to escape me, she rested all her weight on the heels of her stockinged feet and pushed herself backward, so hard she left the ground and flew a yard or two, landing on her shoulders, her head snapping back and hitting the pavement. All the while, she screamed, the same high wail I had heard from Lexington Avenue. Only this time, when she paused for breath, the wail really did continue, and it wasn't an echo.

Looking south, I saw whirling blue police lights speeding toward us. More sirens sounded nearby.

Suddenly the night itself was wailing.

I tried one last time. "Will you believe me, please? *I didn't do it. I didn't do anything!"*

"Killer," she wept. *"Killer!"*

The sirens were getting closer.

* * *

I turned and ducked into the alley and made my feet, which felt like they were wading through surf, move me toward the next block. I could hear the woman still screaming behind me. I kicked a trash can out of my way, bruising my knee. The alley was dark. I had to feel my way along at full flight. My ears buzzed. My body had taken over and was just trying to save itself, much as the woman back there had screamed when she saw me. She didn't *think* I was her attacker, she *knew* I was her attacker, just as I *knew* the cops wouldn't believe me. My fingerprints were on the scissors. My hand was pasty with the woman's blood. I felt the night whistle past me as I ran. I was part of the night, and it carried me to the end of the alley.

A police cruiser, lights flashing and siren howling, screeched around the corner toward the United Nations. I waited ten seconds, looking for more police cars. The street stayed empty. I left the alley and ran as fast as I could to the next alley, through it to Third Avenue, then north for a block. My head hammered. I thought my heart was going to fly out of my mouth. My legs kept working. I dodged onto Forty-ninth Street and ran until I reached Park Avenue.

A street cleaner was moving slowly up the east side of the street, brushes whirring. I sprinted to the meridian, the island of bushes and trees that runs up the middle of Park Avenue, and dove into one of the hedges. Branches scraped my face and my palm hit something hard, cold, that hurt. Crouching into as tight and small a ball as possible, I held my hand up. There was a piece of glass, broken bottle, wedged in my palm. I yanked it out and sucked the wound. My ankle was throbbing.

I sat there, listening to the sirens. They were fainter now, and no more seemed to be coming. Park Avenue was still. The street cleaner, orange light revolving over my head like a searchlight, lumbered past, the whirring *shhh* of the brushes receding north.

I sat in the hedge for about five minutes, catching my breath. There was no way the woman or the cops could identify me. All I had to do was get home without getting caught on the streets. I wanted to stay and rest, but I knew the police would start fanning out soon, maybe even bring in more cruisers. I had to get to the West Side, and fast, before they spotted me. Once there, I'd just be another degenerate straggling home. There were thousands of them. Dawn on the West Side was often crowded with as many people coming home as going to work. I could merge, vanish. But first I had to get there.

I decided to try for the subway stop on Broadway and Fiftieth Street. That meant three crosstown blocks. I wondered if my lungs could take it. They did.

I took the steps down three at a time, stumbling because of my ankle. I grabbed the railing to keep from falling, and remembered the blood. It covered my fingers, both the woman's blood and the fresher blood from the cut in my palm. I noticed a page of newspaper—the sports page, I thought, irrelevantly—brushed up against the side of the white-tiled tunnel that led to the subway. Stooping, I picked it up and wiped my hand clean as best I could, then crumpled it up and tossed it into an overflowing trash can, the kind with a swinging door at the top. I had to push the newspaper in among the soda bottles and wet Kleenex.

Limping, I hurried down the tunnel, my sneakers squeaking. Keep calm, I told myself. You're doing all right. You're a survivor. I think I even grinned. *You're a survivor.* Then I thought of the woman, lying on the sidewalk, and felt sick again. I saw the stubs of her fingers raised at me in accusation, squirting blood. I saw those gleaming guns jiggling on the hips of running cops.

When I reached the ticket booth, I slowed down, trying to control my panting, sauntering up to the window as if I were just another late-night customer. The black woman behind the grate stared at me. I fumbled for change, dropping coins that rolled and clinked on the floor. Finally I managed to get three quarters into the smooth lip under the glass. She took them and slid me a token, still staring. I was careful to keep my right hand, my bloody hand, in the pocket of my jeans. I didn't dare meet her eyes, but I could feel her shaking her head behind me as I left.

I prayed there wouldn't be a cop patrolling the platform. There wasn't. The platform was empty except for a middle-aged man in a wrinkled business suit kicking a candy machine at the other end.

"Fucking goddamned machine!" Enraged, he punctuated each word with a kick. "Whore! Bitch! Cunt!"

Behind him, advertisements for Broadway shows and rye bread smiled down on his drunken anger, happy dancers and a gentle grandmother perversely proud of her child's energy. The hot air of an approaching train pushed into the station. There were no cops aboard. The businessman didn't even bother looking up. As the subway pulled away, he was still kicking the candy machine.

The train rattled and rocked through the tunnel, the darkness outside casting back my reflection in the grimy window. The roar was deafening. I squinted and tried to see myself in the window. I looked like anybody else, except for my hair, which I quickly smoothed down with my good hand.

There were only two other people in my car, two black kids wearing jeans, Converse sneakers, and hooded sweatshirts underneath down jackets. Their red, stoned-out eyes wandered to my face and flitted away, down to the floor. They were both standing, hanging on to straps. They didn't want to deal with me anymore than I wanted to deal with them. We respectfully ignored each other, absorbing space with our eyes.

Each time the train stopped I held my breath and waited to see a cop and run. Only once did I have cause to worry. At the Sixty-sixth Street stop, two young cops were lounging at the back of the station, having a chat. I turned away, stepped across the aisle, and sat with my back to them. A bag lady got on, mumbling to herself, and shuffled to the corner seat. Her Bloomingdale's shopping bag, worn and creased, bristled with junk: bits and pieces of cloth, a shoe, an old brush missing its plastic handle.

The doors hissed shut and with a lurch the train started away, gathering speed and hurtling itself into the next stretch of tunnel.

The bag lady cackled and slapped her knees, laughing uproariously. I smiled, reflexively, then caught a glimpse of myself in the opposite window, and the smile disappeared. I felt light-headed and frightened. I leaned back against the vibrating glass behind me. My legs started shaking, then my lips. I gritted my teeth and clamped hard on my muscles, but everything continued shaking, uncontrollably. *You're not a survivor.* The thought crept into my head, and with it a kind of pleasure, the peaceful easy feeling of surrender.

Sitting up straight, I opened my eyes. The two black kids were staring at me but looked away. The bag lady, her face so wrinkled and toothless it looked like it was collapsing, had pulled a paperback from her shopping bag and was now reading it, upside down, wagging her head and clucking in amusement. Was she nuts, or just protecting herself?

The train jerked to a stop, brakes squealing. I was off and halfway up the steps to Broadway before it pulled away, a hiss of closing doors, then the accelerating hum of electricity. As I came up out of the subway into a fresh, stinging wind off the Hudson, my toe hit something on the top step. Looking down, I saw a hypodermic needle, gleaming, like the bloody scissors.

At that time I lived in a one-room apartment on the corner of Seventy-third Street and Central Park West, the front room, third floor, of an old brownstone that smelled like dust and mothballs. My landlady's apartment was on the first floor. Whenever I entered the building, the door to her apartment, at the back of the hallway, would silently open a crack, and her ferret eyes would silently watch me climb the stairs. A nurse lived in the apartment across from mine. Below me, on the second floor, two musicians occupied the front apartment. I never saw anyone in the back apartment. I know someone lived there, though, because sometimes, on my way past the door, I'd stop and eavesdrop, and often I'd hear a human rustling noise inside, the soft slap of what sounded like slippers.

I didn't sleep much that night.

After taking a bath, washing away the blood and cleaning my cut, which wasn't as bad as I had thought, I sat on my bed, smoked a joint, and watched the light in the window change from black to gray. The peeling radiator under the window hissed and clanged, as if there were someone trapped in there, slamming a wrench against the pipes. All I had in my room, aside from the bed, was a wooden table and a straight-backed chair, and a small bookcase against the wall, exactly twenty-one lead soldiers marching across the top. The dented lead and scratched paint gave them odd expressions, saddened by the loss of a pink cheek or one of their round black eyes. I also had a hotplate, and of course a TV, a portable Sony. I kept my room clean, except for the cobwebs high in the corners, the ones I could never reach.

The joint was a mistake. I had thought it would calm me, but it didn't. The walls of my room wouldn't hold still, and when I lay down and closed my eyes, the room jumped into my head, four walls palpitating like a heart, pumping blood. Outside, I could hear early-morning traffic rumble along Central Park West. A faint buzzing drone, the city awakening, vibrated in the windowpanes, as well as a higher, shriller whine I couldn't shake out of my ears, my own blood racing through my body.

I heard the nurse leaving for work, a jingle of keys, her crepe-soled shoes noiseless on the creaking stairs. She always left at five. Once or twice, we had passed in the hallway. I was usually just getting home. She'd press herself against the wall and slide by as if I might try to strangle her.

Someone was playing a radio. The music drifted through the walls.

"Funkytown, funkytown, funkytown."

7

At first, when I awoke the next day, I felt all right. Then, like a fever, memory swamped me. I remembered the kids, and the woman, screaming and pointing her bloody hand at me. I barely made it to the bathroom. I didn't have much in me to vomit, but what I had came up, leaving me shuddering, kneeling at the toilet bowl. It was a relief, almost, to throw up. When I finally stood, I felt weak, yet cleansed, purged of some part of the nightmare. I took another shower, brushed my teeth vigorously. The gash in my hand was already healing. It only hurt if I tried to stretch out my hand flat.

I squinted out through the window at the brownstone across the street. A blue blur of pigeons flapped on the stone ledges. In one of the apartments, a man and a woman were shouting soundlessly at each other. Below, on the sidewalk, a few people strolled along, dragging shadows. An old woman wearing a red overcoat stumbled at the end of a leash after her low, fat dachshund. Two small boys darted between the parked cars, aiming their fingers and shooting imaginary bullets. Next came the mailman. After that, nothing but a cat, slinking through the garbage cans.

I dressed quickly and left the apartment. I could hear my landlady's door opening behind me as I came down the stairs.

"Good morning, Mrs. Woolf," I called.

Her door snapped shut. There wasn't much I could say to that, so I continued down the creaking stairs and out the heavy double doors onto Seventy-third Street. Breathing was easier in the fresh air. I hobbled a bit on my weak ankle. Otherwise, I felt better. As I crossed the street and walked into Central Park, I told myself to forget the woman last night, the bleeding stubs of her fingers reaching for my face. I told myself she was all right and that nothing I could have done would have helped her. I told myself she was insane with fear when she thought I was the one who had attacked her.

The funny thing was, I felt guilty, as if I *had* hurt her, as if it *were* my fault that she lay there bleeding. I knew the way it felt to squeeze those scissors closed on her fingers; I could feel that easy parting of skin and then the harder, brittle crack of bone before the two blades met. And no matter how hard I tried not to remember, I kept seeing her, screaming at me, as the albino raced away through the darkness with her mink coat fluttering behind him, that grin on his face.

Slim young men in tight jeans lined the pathways of the park, eyeing me as I moved self-consciously past them. I'd seen that look before, a hundred times, but I never got used to it. Joggers in bulky sweat suits, towels tucked around their necks, panted by. A yellow Frisbee wobbled and glided through the blue air. I was halfway across one of the meadows, brown grass frozen hard and waiting for snow, when I noticed a family up ahead of me. The man and woman were in their mid-thirties, and they had a girl, about seven, and a boy, maybe five. They were all holding hands, in descending order, by height, the father, the mother, the daughter, the son. The man wore rumpled corduroys and old Frye boots and a heavy white turtleneck. His hair, long enough to cover his ears, was turning gray. His wife had on a long wool skirt and high leather boots that reached her knees. Switching places, they sauntered along in front of me, swinging the girl between them while their son hopped around in jealousy, demanding his turn. I sympathized with the kid. Watching this little family, I felt a moment's envy, a strong desire to be that man, enjoying the afternoon with my wife and children. How easily they all moved together, how little they seemed to need, or even notice, the rest of the city.

I walked all the way to Columbus Circle, then east along the foot of Central Park until I got to the Plaza.

The old hotel was quiet. There were a few limousines pulled up to the entrance, and a short line of waiting cabs trailed to the corner. On the other side of the fountain, I could see a young woman slouched in the Paris ticket booth. It looked like she was filing her nails, but I couldn't be sure.

I sat down on the short wall ringing Central Park, near the horses and carriages. Their drivers were huddled together, talking and smoking cigarettes, every once in a while glancing hopefully at the Plaza. The singer wasn't anywhere around. If I hadn't followed her in the first place, I thought, none of this would have happened. I wouldn't have seen that woman in the U.N. Plaza, and I wouldn't be sitting here now, the stone wall cold under my ass, wondering what to do. Though it hardly seemed fair to blame her.

What I should do, I told myself, is go to the police. I knew the truth. The kids must have jumped the woman from behind, knocking her out before she saw their faces. When she woke up, I was there, holding the scissors. I was the only one who could explain to her, explain to the police, what had really happened. But I could already hear the questions. What were you doing out following people at three in the morning? What were you doing following people *at all?* Why are your fingerprints all over the scissors? Why are your hands covered with the woman's blood? Why did she identify you? *Why did you run?*

That was the clincher. And what was the truth, anyway? That a bunch of kids did it? Who would believe me? No one, absolutely no one. I could see my landlady, Mrs. Woolf, at court. She'd tell them how strange I was. She probably had a log of my comings and goings. Out all night. A loner. No friends. The nurse might show up, too, to tell them how I'd menaced her in the hallway. Alex, Sandy—they'd all testify to my strangeness. Even Harvey the newsdealer would have to confess his true feelings about me. Not natural. Not normal.

I watched a group of women turn the corner from Fifth

Avenue and cross over to the Plaza. They were laughing together, already a little drunk, I thought. When they reached the imposing doorman, one of them bowed, and the rest laughed even louder. Fresh from a reunion, I decided. College friends seeing each other for the first time in years. Maybe. They were still giggling as they trooped awkwardly through the revolving doors and into the hotel. The doorman stamped his feet against the cold, or in anger.

Then, in the wake of the women, a middle-aged man appeared, pausing for a moment at the top of the steps while he adjusted his scarf and switched his briefcase to his other hand. He was wearing a long overcoat with a fur collar, and leather gloves. After a snappy glance around the square—the Paris, the fountain, the trees—he descended the steps, waving away the doorman and striding toward my perch. He passed right in front of me. A stockbroker, I guessed. Or an attorney. Should I follow him? It would give me something to do until work, and I thought it might take my mind off the bleeding woman. He suddenly stopped, pulled back his glove with one finger, and looked at his watch. He seemed to deliberate, then made up his mind, changed direction and started south on Fifth Avenue.

I stayed half a block behind him, forcing myself to concentrate on his youthful walk, his trim and powerful body. He carried himself well for a man of fifty, which is what I decided he must be. He probably exercised a lot. I could see him on a suburban tennis court, splendid in whites, measured and imperturbable as he volleyed in the sunshine. Winters, I suspected, he took his family to Aspen for a few weeks of skiing. Most people, you discover when you follow them, move unevenly, slowing down, speeding up without any apparent logic. This man, my stockbroker, strode along Fifth Avenue at an unvarying pace, stopping only once, to stare thoughtfully into the window of Rizzoli's. He lived a disciplined life, that much was clear. But he wasn't particularly interesting, and I was about to let him go when he turned into the

Yale Club, disappearing through the front door of the gray stone building. The lights were on behind the high windows. I could see a few old men inside, dozing in deep armchairs.

I walked over to Harvey's newsstand. I had to talk to somebody.

Harvey glared at me from his dark cave. "Why don't you shave? Why can't you take care of yourself?"

"I like my beard," I said.

"How come everyone wants to look like Fidel Castro?"

But I didn't answer him, because that's when I noticed the headline. I'd been standing right next to it, a modest fourth-column headline on the front page of the *Times*, a copy of which Harvey had hung for display outside the newsstand, surrounded by tits and naked weight-lifters.

AMBASSADOR'S WIFE EIGHTH VICTIM
Maria di Costini, 52, wife of the Italian ambassador to the United Nations, was mugged at approximately 3:15 this morning by the so-called Finger Mugger, the eighth victim in a series of brutal attacks that have plagued pre-Christmas New York, including the murder, last week, of Mrs. Ronald Greenway, the well-known Park Avenue socialite. Signora di Costini, like all the Finger Mugger's victims, had the fingers of her left hand severed and was badly beaten. Her attacker fled with a near-priceless heirloom, the Tuscany Diamond, a work of Renaissance jewelers which Signora di Costini inherited from her grandfather, the late Prince Bilini of Tuscany.

I skimmed over the next paragraph. Apparently she had been returning alone from a party when her car broke down less than a block from her U.N. Plaza apartment. She couldn't find a cab, so she decided to walk. As I'd suspected, it was her fur coat I had seen flapping behind the albino. They had also taken her earrings, a pearl necklace, and her purse.

Signora di Costini is the first victim to actually see the feared Finger Mugger. She has told police that he is a bearded young man in his early twenties, Caucasian, of medium build and height.

Then I read a sentence that made my face go numb.

He was wearing a satin black jacket with Mickey Mouse embossed on the back.

I was still wearing the jacket. I tore it off and folded it in my arms, hiding Mickey Mouse.

"You gonna look all day or what?" It was Harvey. Thank God he never read his own newspapers. "I got better things to do than provide free reading for the city of New York. Pay or take a walk."

I took a walk.

I was sure that everyone could see Mickey Mouse, no matter how many times I looked down to check that he stayed hidden. The damn jacket burned in my hands, called out for all the world to see my guilt. I had to get rid of it. That was the first thing. Then I could make a plan. I needed a plan. But first I had to get rid of the jacket.

I looked around, focusing finally, and saw that I was across Sixth Avenue from the Hilton. A police car idled at the corner.

I turned left and started toward Fifth Avenue. I needed a plan. I couldn't think straight, I could only walk, like a drunk, first one foot, then the next. I kept my head down, so no one could get a good look at my face. The pavement slid beneath my feet, a concrete escalator. People passed, all legs.

Signora di Costini thought I was the one who had attacked her. The police believed her. They had the weapon, and my fingerprints were on it. They also had my description. Maybe the man leaning down from his window had also seen me. In any case, they didn't know who I was, but they knew what I looked like. They knew nothing about the kids. I'd read about the Finger Mugger in the papers, and like everyone else had assumed he was a single man, another deranged freak stalking the city. Now they thought they knew who he was: me.

I collided with a girl on the corner of Fifth Avenue and had to catch her before she fell. She stared at me, startled.

"Sorry," I mumbled.

Steady on her feet again, she gained confidence and smiled. "That's all right. It wasn't your fualt. Oh, look."

She stooped and picked up my jacket. Mickey Mouse unfurled with a grin.

"You dropped this," she said, straightening.

"Thanks." My hands were shaking as I took the jacket and started to fold it away.

"Aren't you cold?"

"What?"

The girl watched me curiously. "Aren't you cold? Without your jacket?"

I'd forgotten. I was only wearing a shirt.

"No," I said, telling the truth. And then, to reassure her: "It's a warm day."

I took a step away. She was staring at me. I gave her a friendly wave.

"I'm all right," she said, as if I'd asked her. "It wasn't your fault."

I walked another block before I saw what I needed. A mailbox. Making sure no one was watching, I quickly rammed the jacket in through the swinging blue door. The zipper caught. I ripped it loose, stuffing the jacket down, and hurried on toward Madison.

The girl had given me an idea. I had to find the singer.

8

I heard her voice before I actually saw her, that clear, almost masculine voice carrying half a block through the din of traffic, the constant low level buzz of the city—her voice carried through it, above it, and led me the rest of the way to her.

She was standing on the same corner as yesterday, Thirty-ninth and Sixth, wearing the same clothes, playing her guitar and singing. About thirty people had stopped to listen. She was that good. Coins clinked into the guitar case open at her feet. She didn't acknowledge the money, nor thank anyone with her eyes, the way I'd seen other street singers do. She just stood there proud and straight, singing. This is my job, her stubborn chin said. This is what I do. I'm good at it and I deserve whatever I get paid. No pity, thank you.

An old lady in a fake fur looked at me suspiciously. All I had on was my shirt. I was freezing. The old lady moved away, glancing back at me, afraid.

For the first time I could really see the singer's face. Her eyes, blank to the world, hid what she felt, large, dark eyes surprised by everything and revealing nothing. She looked at her audience the way she sang, proudly, defying us to feel sorry for her. Her wool cap was pulled low over her short hair. She swayed slightly while she sang, completely absorbed in her performance, yet, at the same time, self-conscious about standing out in front of these people, pained by their staring eyes, which pinned her like a butterfly for display to the wall behind her—a bank, I saw, looking up.

She sang two more songs before packing up her guitar. As the crowd thinned, I stepped back into the doorway of a tobacconist, not sure how to approach her. The figures of human beings, bent against the cold, striding sightless, passed between us, so that she seemed a still, tranquil island surrounded by whirling eddies. It took her a full minute, moving in slow motion, to finish packing her guitar and pocket the money. I almost went up and asked if I could help. I thought that might be a good introduction. I watched her finish packing and slowly straighten, her free hand going to her back again.

The door to the tobacconist opened. A comforting warmth rushed out with the customer, a small, plump man who looked a little like my father. He smiled. I stood back to let him pass. He stared at me with concern, not horror, or fear, and almost said something. I could see him checking himself in his mind, swallowing the sentence. Nodding, he turned and walked down Thirty-ninth Street, a brightly wrapped package under his arm. The rich, moist scent of fresh tobacco hung in the doorway as the pneumatic door settled shut.

I looked back at the corner. The singer was already halfway across Sixth.

I followed her to Third Avenue, trying to think of an opening. She turned south, her body swaying on the sidewalk like a buoy. I was so cold my teeth had started to chatter. I could feel goosebumps on my face. Yet I still hesitated. It was as if, by following the girl, I saw myself as a leering, demented rapist. I was too embarrassed to stop her. Then she glanced back, over her shoulder, her eyes meeting mine. It lasted a fraction of a second. For that stretched moment we looked right into each other. Her eyes, mask removed, were endless, and knew everything. She snapped the mask back down and increased her pace.

I caught up with her and touched her on the shoulder, as lightly as I could. "Excuse me."

She kept walking. Her eyes gazed straight ahead.

"Excuse me. I've got to talk to you."

She threw me one wild look and continued walking, her guitar case bumping her leg.

"I'm not going to hurt you," I said. "All I want to do is ask you a question. Who were those kids yesterday? The albino?"

This frightened her even more and she tried to walk

faster. Her guitar weighed her down. I felt sorry for her. She was terrified of me. She was terrified of everyone. Watching her try to hurry was like watching a wounded bird try to fly. But she was my only chance.

"The albino was hassling you, right? Who is he? You know him. Just tell me who he is and I'll leave you alone."

She had to stop because she was out of breath. She stood there, one hand on her stomach, her eyes closed while her heart slowed down. Up close, her skin was healthy, clear and ruddy. She had a long, thin nose, and her mouth, even clamped tight in apprehension, looked soft. She opened her eyes, facing mine, but the mask was still there.

"I need your help," I said. "Please. Who are those kids?"

"What kids?" Her voice sounded like her singing, only lower, and less sure.

"The albino."

She acted as if she didn't know what the word meant. "Albino?"

"Yesterday, on Thirtieth Street. They came along and hassled you. I saw them. You were scared of them. Remember?"

"People don't scare me," she said. "Now leave me alone."

She started to walk away.

"Wait." I grabbed her elbow. "Please."

"Why was you following me?" she demanded.

"Because I need your help."

"Yesterday?"

"Yesterday. Yesterday I just happened to hear you sing. And I just happened to see those kids. Now I need to know who they are." It didn't sound very convincing.

"You're lying." She said it sadly. "Yesterday you was following me. I saw you."

I couldn't deny it and I couldn't explain it.

"Are you crazy?" she asked.

Maybe I was.

She shook her head. "I don't know no albino. I don't know no kids. All right?"

"But I saw you with them."

She was walking away.

"Please, wait! You're the only one who can help me!"

I heard the self-pity in my voice, the cringing, whining fear, and it disgusted me. But she was walking away with the only information that could lead me to those kids.

I had to jog to reach her.

This time she whirled on me, standing her ground, angrily defending herself. "Get away from me! Leave me alone! Do you hear? *Leave me alone!*"

Her shouts carried between the tall buildings. There weren't many people on the street, but those that were stopped and stared, waiting for the next development.

The girl backed away from me, glaring. *"Leave me alone!"*

Only when she was a good ten yards farther down the block did she allow herself to take her eyes off mine. She abruptly swiveled on her heels and hurried downtown, her anxious figure and unwieldy guitar case merging with the people who stood at the next corner, waiting for the light to change.

I let her go. She was too scared to tell me anything.

Winter nights come early in New York. It was already getting dark, the sky above the buildings streaked with grays and yellows that looked like trails of smoke.

I started back to my apartment. At least it would be warm there. I thought about climbing the dim stairs past Mrs. Woolf's watchful gaze. I thought about the empty apartment itself, those four walls waiting for me, and suddenly it was the last place in the world I wanted to go, it mocked me even more than my parent's house in Springfield. I had no life, only a room to live in. And for what? So that I could be an actor on the great stages of New York? That was a joke, and not just because I hadn't worked in three months. What if I never went back to my apartment? Would that be so bad? I think I actually considered going over to Port Authority and getting on a bus. I imagined Florida, the Keys, freedom and a long, lazy daydream in the sun. I didn't go, but I considered it. I guess I still had the good sense to realize Port Authority might be watched. And I was cold.

I thought about the girl, the singer. She was scared of me, and maybe the kids as well, just as I was scared by the cops. Everybody I knew was scared. Alex. Sandy. Harvey the newsdealer. We were all scared. And running. That's what New York is about—running. To someplace, or from someplace. Or both. We weren't *here*. Nobody was *here*. We were all looking for happiness, as if it were a place somewhere, a peaceful garden where we could all sit and speak quietly instead of screaming, like the woman last night, screaming and pointing her bloody fingers, or Sandy, screaming and throwing coins to the floor, or the singer, screaming at me and running. They melded into one person, the whole city, an outraged screaming giant.

When I turned from Central Park West onto Seventy-third Street, I almost ran into the police cars. They didn't have their roof lights or sirens on, and so I didn't see them until I was only a few houses away. They had parked in the street in front of my building. Two cops and a plain-clothesman were just climbing the steps to the front door.

I backed away, ducking down behind the parked cars and scuttling back onto Central Park West, then ran north to Eighty-sixth Street. I set a good pace for myself, fast and steady, but not so fast that I'd draw anyone's atten-tion, and kept it up all the way across the park. I jammed my hands into my pockets for warmth. I was shivering in my shirt. But I couldn't stop moving, I didn't dare stop, until I had put some more distance between myself and my apartment.

I slinked down Fifth Avenue, the purple gloom of the park on my right, the handsome apartment buildings on my left. I passed the Metropolitan. The monumental mu-seum looked like Nazi headquarters in an old movie. A banner was draped above the main entrance: MATISSE. A white bird spread its awkward wings behind the blue let-tering. By the time I reached the Plaza, my feet hurt and my legs were beginning to feel weak.

The Plaza glowed, and I stopped for a moment to stare. Was it really only last night that I had first seen the girl singing here? Maybe she's right, I thought again. Maybe I am crazy. I certainly felt as if I were losing my mind. I'd never been hunted before. I clutched my elbows and tried to squeeze some warmth into my sides, but it did no good. The wind cut right through me and made my eyes water, so that the Christmas lights vanishing to a point down Fifth Avenue seemed to shimmer and pop in little explosions.

I checked my wallet. I only had seven bucks. Fanning through the wrinkled bills, it occurred to me that I was also carrying my own death warrant, a bank identification card and my social security card. If the cops knew where I lived, then they had somehow learned who I was, my name, everything. If I were stopped and questioned, I figured, it would be better to have no identification than my own. I could always say I'd lost my wallet or left it at home. Pulling out the cards, I tore them up and scattered them behind the waist-high wall surrounding Central Park.

As I moved deeper into the city, heading toward Times Square, I wondered how the cops had found out where I lived. How had they identified me? I ran the picture of them climbing my front steps over and over again, trying to discover something, a nagging detail I couldn't quite grasp. The plainclothesman walking on stiff legs, a middle-aged man led by a beer belly. The two cops in uniform, both about my age, their guns drawn, cautiously stepping toward the door. I played the film again. Yes, they each held a gun, dull steel in their hands, evil barrels raised and ready. They thought they might have to shoot me. Naturally enough. I was the notorious Finger Mugger, wasn't I? I wouldn't have to pull their guns from their holsters. They had done it for me.

9

"You in trouble, man?"

Henry squinted at me and cracked a wide smile. "Huh. I do believe you in trouble."

Clicking his tongue, Henry rolled back on the heels of his patent leather shoes and looked me over, up and down.

I said again that I needed a coat. I had no choice but to trust him. Henry didn't seem to hear me. He was absorbed in his own mysterious thoughts, probably trying to figure out how he could turn this trick to his advantage.

"Henry, get me a coat, okay?"

"What kinda coat?" He stalled, with elaborate grace.

"Any kind. I don't give a shit. Something to keep me from dying of pneumonia."

He chuckled and searched the ceiling. His eyes looked like prehistoric eggs, smooth and shiny. "You got no money?"

"No. I mean I've got a little, but I need it. *Please*, Henry."

"You want me to get you a coat, free of charge? Is that it?" His eyes wandered to the Hallmark cards next to us. He idly revolved the rack.

"Yes," I said.

"Look at this." He pointed to one of the birthday cards. "Pretty funny, huh?"

"Henry, I'll pay you later, I swear."

He let his eyes rest on mine, curious. "That right?"

He considered for another painful minute, tracing the picture on the birthday card.

"Yeah," he finally said. "I do that."

"Thanks, Henry."

"But someday you pay me, you know?"

"Oh, I will, I will. Soon as I get things straightened out."

"Not money." He smiled graciously. "Whatever. Sometime Henry need what you got, know what I mean? Then we be even. Okay?"

He told me to wait there and he'd be back in half an hour. I watched him saunter out into the night, prince of the drugstore, his white hat rakishly atilt.

I bought a cheap razor, some shaving cream, and went next door into a bar I'd noticed on my way to find Henry. It was dark and filled with dark faces, a huddled mass silently listening to the Eagles on the pulsing jukebox and watching a basketball game on television. I sat down at the bar, ordered a whiskey, chugged it neat, then walked to the back of the bar and into a narrow, smelly hallway.

The bathroom floor was speckled with dots of blood. I ran hot water in the dirty sink, and shaved off my beard and mustache. It hurt, since I didn't have scissors to trim the hair first, but after a while I looked more or less clean-shaven, and had only nicked myself twice. My face felt raw, strangely light and exposed. I chucked the razor and the shaving cream out the small window above the toilet. Keeping my face shielded as best I could, I passed back through the dark bar. Nobody seemed to notice me.

I returned to the drugstore and waited for Henry by the empty phone booths, praying that he'd return, and that he'd be alone. He did, and was, except for the green down jacket he carried over his left arm and which he handed me like a present, shyly. I nearly hugged him.

"Merry Christmas," he said, delighted with himself.

"Henry, you're a saint."

I pulled on the soft parka. It fit.

"You look better with a beard." Henry smiled a knowing smile, leaning closer to whisper, his thin fingers dancing on my chest. "You ain't got no chin, boy."

He stood back and appraised me. I shook his hand.

"Thanks, Henry."

"No problem, man. No problem." He escorted me to the door, glancing up and down the street before letting me out. "Someday you help me, right?"

I hoped it was true. At that moment, I would have died for Henry. I guess that's how pimps work.

A thought occurred to me. "Henry, you don't know anything about a gang of kids, do you? Fourteen-year-olds? Run around jumping people?"

"Lots of kids like that in this city."

"The leader's an albino, white hair, pink eyes?"

Henry's eyes were so moist he looked like he was crying.

"Go on now," he said, nudging me down the sidewalk. "Go on."

Times Square exploded in blues and reds and greens, neon signs and billboards and theater marquees flashing and blinking like a gargantuan pinball machine. Somewhat disguised, warm for the first time since that afternoon, I deluded myself into thinking that things might straighten out, that I might soon be able to resume my normal life, which in the last few hours had come to seem more attractive. I still needed a plan, but I wouldn't acknowledge that. I walked down Broadway like a man escaped from prison, so infatuated by my relative security, warm and beardless, that I forgot I was hunted.

I also needed rest and some food, so I stopped in a smelly coffee shop below Times Square, a narrow room with a formica counter running down one side and three bright lights in misted globes hanging from the high ceiling. Framed posters of Greece decorated the wall across from the counter, sunny islands lazing in blue water. I found it hard to believe that such places existed.

So did the two Greeks behind the counter, I'm sure. They were both young men, in their early thirties. Trim dark mustaches shadowed their upper lips. One of them stood above the sizzling grill, poking at a greasy hamburger and singing along with the radio, Greek music that sounded like someone being tortured. The other guy sat on a stool reading a Greek newspaper spread open on the counter. The only other person in the place was a thin man wearing a suit that was too tight for him. He practically ripped it apart reaching for the sugar. He sipped his coffee and waited for his hamburger.

I sat down on one of the wobbly stools. The Greek looked up from his newspaper, twiddling a toothpick between his teeth. I was hungry, I hadn't eaten anything all day, but the sight of the hamburger on the grill killed my appetite. It looked alive. I ordered coffee and soup.

The round electric clock above the door, crooked on its nail, said 4:30. At least another twenty minutes of daylight left. Better to stay in here until then. Anyway, I was hungry. Or had been. I watched the Greek ladle soup into a bowl. He was talking in Greek to his partner at the grill, and slopped some of the soup onto the floor. Swearing, he held the bowl out before him and placed it in front of me, then poured me a cup of coffee and returned to his newspaper, picking his teeth with a fresh toothpick.

"Petros, do something about the radio, will you?" The thin man had spoken, a hoarse, nasal hiss. "Play something American, for Chrissake."

Without moving his eyes from the newspaper, the Greek reached behind him and turned the radio dial. Martial music.

"That's more like it," the thin man said, taking his hamburger from the other Greek. "Now I can eat in peace."

The cook grunted, wiped his hands on his grease-smeared apron, and lit a cigarette. I got the feeling they went through this every night. I imagined how we might look to someone peering in through the window, trying to decide whether or not to come in and get a bite to eat: four motionless men at the counter, four sets of eyes looking in four different directions, as if we weren't even in the same room. Not very inviting, I decided, trying to swallow the soup. It tasted old. I scraped at the tough bits of rice in the bottom of my bowl and wished that I had never left Springfield. It wasn't true. I was only an atheist praying in panic as the airplane plummeted.

Think. That was my mind, speaking from a long ways off: *think.* On the shelf above the grill, the radio switched from marching music to news, a purring English voice announcing the day's events as if they were items on a menu. I *can't* think, I told myself. What's there to think about? I can't clear myself without finding the kids, and I can't find the kids without the singer's help. And she won't even talk to me.

"Hey, Petros, where can I get a crib?"

The thin man asked the question, but without looking up, addressing his hamburger. "Petros?"

The Greek reading the newspaper raised indifferent eyes. "What?"

"My girl's kid fell outa his crib. It's busted."

The Greek considered his toothpick. "Kid's probably too big."

"I wanna nice one," the thin man mused. "Nothing too cheap."

Sighing, the Greek went back to his newspaper.

"Any idea where I can get a crib?" the thin man asked the other Greek, now idly scraping the grill clean. "Hey, Yanni."

The radio hummed. *"First precinct detective Jim Malone announced this afternoon that the police have a suspect based on the description given by Maria di Costini, wife of the Italian ambassador to the United Nations, the Finger Mugger's latest victim."*

"Must be a nice crib somewhere in this pisshole city," the thin man complained.

"The suspect, Gregory Hartz, is a twenty-six-year-old bearded Caucasian male with brown hair and blue eyes. When last seen he was wearing a black jacket with a decal of Mickey Mouse on the back."

I heard the door opening behind me but didn't turn to look.

"It was because of this distinctive jacket that Hartz was identified by his employer, Alexander Hagen, the owner of an East Side nightclub."

I could just see Alex leaping into action. *Fucking jungle, man. I know crazy when I see crazy. Hartz is crazy.* And Sandy? She must have barricaded her apartment in case I came by for a visit. I felt nausea returning, climbing up my throat. The cops really did know everything about me. Not only my name, and where I lived, but where I worked and what I wore. How long before someone recognized me? I glanced at the two Greeks, the thin man eating his hamburger. They weren't paying any attention to me. I had to get out of there. Two dollars appeared in my thick fingers. My last two dollars. I'd spent the rest on the razor and shaving cream. I laid the bills on the counter and turned on my stool to go.

Two cops were standing behind me, tired eyes moving along the list of goods and prices above the grill.

My legs melted. If I tried to stand I'd simply collapse to the dirty floor. One of the cops, a cool, gray youth sporting a handlebar mustache and thick sideburns, let his eyes flicker down to mine. He looked, instinctively I suppose, for guilt. I felt my mouth tighten into a grin.

He nodded, then looked at the Greeks. "Coffee. To go. Regular."

The other cop pushed back the peak of his blue cap and scratched his forehead. "Same here, Yanni. And give us a few of them donuts."

As I slowly put weight on my legs, trusting them not to give me away, I heard the thin man address the cops. "You wouldn't know where I could get a good crib, would you?"

I walked weakly to the door and left. I had to find the girl again, the singer. She was my only chance.

10

I was lucky. I found her over on Sixth, in front of the bank. She obviously had favorite corners, and this was one of them.

She was singing to a sparse crowd, five or six people hugging themselves in the cold. A few clapped when she finished, but there wasn't much enthusiasm tonight, more curiosity than anything else. Watching her, I almost forgot my own troubles, and once again wondered how she managed to survive. She looked like a gypsy in her long coat and blue knit cap. Above her, an electric sign on the bank blinked the time and temperature.

I hid, making sure she couldn't see me, behind a parked delivery van across the street, glad for my down jacket. God bless Henry. Of all the people in the city, he was the only one who had helped me so far. He did it for himself, making a small investment against future needs, I knew that, but at least he thought he might need me someday.

I watched the girl sing another song. Her audience had dwindled to a solitary man. When she was finished, she methodically packed away her guitar and pocketed her money. Quitting time. She started walking downtown with her touching, awkward gait. I waited until she was well ahead of me, then left the protection of the van and followed her. If she wouldn't help me voluntarily, I'd get her to help me involuntarily. She knew the albino and his rat pack, I was sure of it. I'd follow her until she led me to them. Such as it was, that was my plan. I couldn't think of anything else, and I had to do something.

I followed her into the Garment District, trying not to lose sight of her in the darkness. It wasn't easy. She moved like a shadow. The warehouses and streets were deserted, the opposite of yesterday's frenzy. A Burger King paper bag rustled across my feet and hit a lamp post. Time was slowing down for me. The girl seemed to crawl. What if she didn't really know the albino? What if I was wrong? I pushed the idea out of my head. I had to be right. If she couldn't help me find those kids, no one could.

I realized she was heading straight for the alley where I'd lost her the day before. I didn't want to lose her this time, so I cut to my right, along Thirty-fourth Street, ran through the alley in the middle of the block, and came out on Thirty-third Street. Directly across from me was the alley, dark except for a single bulb above the loading platform at the far end. The street was empty, the buildings on either side of the alley silent and dark. I crossed the street, stepped into the alley, and peeked back around the corner. A long truck rumbled by on Third Avenue.

I looked into the alley. I couldn't see much, the shadows were too thick. I needed a hiding place. I remembered the dumpsters, two of them pushed against the right wall. Staring hard, I made out what I thought were their darker shapes among the shadows.

When I leaned around the corner again, I saw the girl crossing Thirty-third Street diagonally toward me. I waited until I was sure she was coming my way before stepping as quietly as possible deeper into the alley. My foot hit a bottle. It clanked and rolled against a garbage can. My hands waving before me like a blind man's, I groped for the dumpsters. There weren't any dumpsters. They were gone. Wildly, I felt about me in the darkness. Nothing. Just air, black air.

Behind me, I heard the girl's footsteps on the broken glass at the entrance to the alley. I didn't have time to look. I pressed myself against the brick wall of the warehouse, arms spread, facing the loading platform, and waited. I didn't even dare turn and look at her. I stood as still as possible, not breathing. Her footsteps came closer. She couldn't have been more than five yards away. But she didn't see me. She passed by and came into view on the other side, a stolid shadow carrying another, smaller shadow in her right hand, her guitar.

I relaxed a bit, setting my weight back on my heels and releasing the wall. I could feel bits of sharp brick imbedded in my cheek.

She stopped just short of the loading platform. Glancing around, her eyes came to rest on me. I didn't move, I didn't breathe. Suddenly she stooped, as fast and gracefully as she could, and struggled with something. I heard the hollow ring of metal reverberate in the still alley, the clang and drag of heavy iron. She straightened, looked around one more time, then sank down as if the earth had opened up around her, pulling the guitar case after her. I heard the same clanging, dragging sound as before, metal tugged into place, and then silence, or what passes for silence in the city.

A high wind whined through telephone wires above the alley. Distant trucks coughed and surged, drivers shifting gears. Closer, the perennial siren wailed, *woop-woop-woop*, a demented nightingale singing its song.

I moved cautiously toward the spot where the girl had vanished. In the dim light of the loading platform, I saw a grate in the alley floor. Where had she gone? Into the sewers? There must be something down there, I thought. She had descended unperturbed, like anyone else returning home from a long day's work. So this was where she came to hide for the night. I tried to imagine what might be down there that she could use as a house, then decided it was more likely a passageway to an abandoned building, a storage shed maybe, some out-of-the-way place where she could live. I didn't want to go down there, wherever it was. No air. No light. Trapped. But what choice did I have?

That was it, then. The final fact: I had no choice. I couldn't go to the bus station, or get out on a train, or fly away—the cops would still be watching for me there, watching very carefully. I wouldn't stand a chance hitch-hiking, and I couldn't steal a car; I didn't even have enough money for the bridge or tunnel tolls. I stood there, staring at the grate by my feet, listening to the telephone wires click high above my head, not quite able to get it through my head that Manhattan really was an island, and that the only place left for me to go was down. It's hard, when you're used to choices, to realize you don't have any.

I looked back up the dark alley toward Thirty-third Street and saw a police car passing by, slowly, a narrow beam of searchlight probing among the empty buildings. That decided me. I had to go down. I don't remember exactly what I thought as I stooped and lifted the heavy grate. I remember the way the fingerholes formed a circle along the outer edge. I remember the toes of my sneakers, and the shimmering pebbles of broken glass. But I don't remember what I thought. Maybe I didn't think anything. Maybe I'd stopped thinking. I was following my plan now, and my plan said stick with the girl, my plan said don't let her out of your sight until she's led you to the kids.

Holding my breath, as if I were dunking underwater, I found the smooth rungs of a metal ladder with my toes and lowered myself into the ground.

Steadying myself with my left hand, I tugged at the grate, pulling it to my chest, then felt my way farther down the ladder, until my head was just below the surface. The half-moon of light above me grew thinner as I yanked the grate the rest of the way over the hole. It took all my strength, and I wondered how the girl ever did it, carrying her guitar case. The grate settled into place with a solid, ringing finality. Except for the fingerholes, a small circle of lights, I could see nothing but darkness. I rested a few seconds, listening. Somewhere nearby, below me, water dripped. Beyond that, the girl's footsteps echoed, like footsteps in a museum.

I almost gave up then, I almost pushed the grate open and climbed back out into the fresh air. A dank, stagnant stench filled my nose, and even as my eyes adjusted to the blackness around me I could see little but dancing dots. More than anything else, it was like losing consciousness, and I had to grab tighter to the ladder to keep from falling. The girl's footsteps receded, softer. If I waited any longer, I'd lose her.

Testing with my toes, I lowered myself down the ladder, one rung at a time. When I'd gone down about ten feet, I came to a metal platform. Without letting go of the ladder, I turned around and faced forward, into the spinning darkness, where I could still hear the girl's footsteps.

I was staring into a tunnel the size of a two-lane highway tunnel. The ceiling opened out from the shaft that held the ladder, and beneath the platform more empty darkness gaped at me, a deep well at the bottom of which I could barely hear the quiet trickle of water. A railed walkway stretched from the platform into the tunnel. It seemed to turn a corner, for there was an edge of light there, a thin white crack in the darkness that vaguely illuminated the walkway. The girl's footsteps sounded from that direction, or their echoes did, reaching me like the faint thump of a distant heart. I glanced back up the shaft. The holes in the grate were sparkling stars.

Tentatively, I moved away from the ladder and started along the walkway, one hand on the railing, the other trailing the damp wall of the tunnel. Taking small steps, I shuffled after the girl, sure that any moment now I was going to step off into nothingness. The walkway continued, however, and brought me to the bend, making a right-angle turn into another tunnel that was lit by a single bare bulb.

My own footsteps rang loudly on the metal walkway, reverberating in the long, man-made tunnel and drowning out the girl's footsteps. I'd take ten steps, wait for my echoes to fade, and listen for hers before going on. In this fashion I reached the next bend, which turned abruptly, just like the first one, and revealed another long section of tunnel, the railed walkway perched along the left side, a dim bulb lighting the way.

Nervously I proceeded, and nervously I realized I was losing the girl. She was getting too far ahead. I didn't want to make too much noise or she'd hear me, yet I didn't want to get too far behind, either. I tried jogging, thankful for my quiet sneakers, but even the slightest sound, the creak of the walkway and the hushed thud each time I brought my weight down, echoed loudly. Anyway, my left ankle still hurt, and after a few minutes of jogging I was hobbling. I slowed down and settled for a long stride, however lopsided. It was the best I could do.

The stench grew stronger, a nauseating reek of sewage. I clamped my mouth shut and breathed through my nose, happier to smell the stink than swallow it. Up ahead, the girl's footsteps had stopped. No more echoes drifted back, even though I stood still and waited through a count of sixty. Nothing but the distant, dripping water and my own breathing. I decided to forget silence and catch up with her, performing a kind of hop, skip, and jump along the walkway. I made the next stretch of tunnel, pausing only when I'd reached the turn and found myself staring

into yet another tunnel, the long tapering funnel of darkness spiraling toward a single bare lightbulb. I felt I was
moving in circles, and at the same time subtly descending,
lower and lower into the basement of the city, the bowels,
quite accurately, of the world above. The girl must have
found a secret home beneath the city where she slept protected from the cold. She was even more a mole than I.
The skyscrapers sent down roots of wires and pipes, and
among them she had burrowed for shelter.

Halfway along the next section of tunnel I came to another metal ladder. It descended out of sight. I strained
but couldn't hear the girl's footsteps. I waited a long time
at the top of that ladder, making calculations, trying to let
the silence tell me something. Finally it just seemed too
simple that she would continue straight along the walkway. Perhaps, I thought, lowering myself hand over hand
down the ladder into pure darkness, perhaps I'm about to
fall into her lair.

The ladder ended at a concrete floor. No lights. I took a
step and my feet slipped out from under me. The floor
seemed to tilt, sliding me down in the darkness full force.
I couldn't stop. The ground was too slick, though I
clawed with my fingers and tried to dig in my heels. I shot
out into the black air and hung there for a second, then
landed on my ass, hard, a sharp pain at the base of my
spine. My teeth crunched together. I slid another ten
yards before I managed to slow myself down and stop.

I was sitting in a stream of oily, putrid liquid that
dripped off my hands as slowly as honey, the stench so
bad I gagged. Sewage. The ground was level, the stream
no more than a foot deep. Yet when I tried to stand, my
feet slipped out from under me and I landed on my ass
again, the ground too greasy with slime and sewage to
give my feet a hold, no matter how carefully I planted
them and tried to stand. One step and I was down. The
place was completely dark. I couldn't see a thing. Rolling
over onto my knees, I crawled my way back to the chute.
This seemed to take half an hour, my knees sliding back,
my hands squirting out in front of me. When I got there, I

realized there was no way I'd be able to climb back up. The incline of the slick chute was too steep. I tried it, though, desperate in my panic, trapped by earth crumbling around me, filling my mouth, burying me—that's all I could think about, and it made my motions stupid and spastic, wasting energy, cutting up my hands and knees. Finally, out of breath and exhausted, I slipped back into the stream, twisted around into a sitting position, and sat there being calm. I concentrated on my breathing. I pretended I was breath, shit-breath, nothing more. The less I was the less there was to fear. Nothing could happen to nothing. Zen and the art of sewer survival. I was back in the womb, floating in bile, blood-shit that fed me. I wasn't even born yet.

I got onto my hands and knees. Slowly, a few inches at a time, I crawled forward. The sewer had to go somewhere, out into the Hudson, the sea, fresh air and seagulls. Little clots of a soft sticky substance clung to my arms, and I could feel other things, hard and fleshy, like small broken limbs, brushing against my thighs. My back throbbed. The girl! In my panic, I'd forgotten the girl. I stopped crawling and let out a yell. It traveled down the tunnel ahead of me, a ball rolling and bouncing and disappearing. Nobody answered. I'd lost her.

I crawled some more, splay-kneed. Once or twice my hands lost the floor and I went down face first, tasting shit, my chin smacking concrete. I don't know how long this went on. Maybe an hour. Maybe two. I crawled and crawled, and just when I was about to panic again, my shoulder bumped something hard. I searched with one hand. It was another ladder, bolted to the wall and rising up a dark shaft. I laughed. Already flushed, triumphant at my escape, I grabbed hold of the rungs.

My fingers were too slippery. There was nothing to wipe them off with except my hair, which had remained relatively dry, so I ran my fingers back through my hair about ten times and then tried again. They held their grip, enough so that I could do a chin-up on the lowest rung and then quickly grab for the next one, pulling myself like this until I was more or less standing. The hard part was getting my feet to stay on the rungs. They kept slipping away from the smooth metal. Eventually I learned how to swing my weight out with my ass, my arms straight, my feet held in place by tension, and climb like a monkey with stiff legs. If I lost my grip I knew I'd fall back on my head and probably break my skull. There would be no way to soften or stop my fall. So even though my arms soon felt like they were on fire and my fingers became so numb they only kept their grip from memory, I jerked and twitched my way upward.

The ladder was less than ten feet high. It might as well have been a mountain. By the time I reached the top and had dragged myself onto the metal platform, I wasn't a human being anymore. I was a lump of shit.

I sat there breathing hard and waiting for the fire to go out in my arms. There was so little blood in my hands that they raised of their own accord from my knees. I wanted to cry, but I couldn't, and in an odd moment of forgetful calm I wondered when I had last cried, how long it had been. I couldn't remember. I was numb, like my hands, my calm a kind of mindlessness that kept me sitting on the platform in a trance, my legs dangling over the edge. I peered down into the darkness with tranquil curiosity, as if I expected a fish to bite.

A high squeaking sound behind me brought me to life. I turned and looked. Two red eyes glinted at me.

I whispered. "Hello?"

The eyes blinked, once, and then a sluggish plump rat the size of a small dog uncurled from the black shadows and started toward me. I screamed, swiveling around and kicking the thing. My toe hit soft flesh, oozy as mud, and for a second it seemed to be clinging to me, sharp flexible claws tightening around my foot. Screaming louder, swearing, I snapped my leg and sent the rat sailing out over the edge and splashing down into the sewer.

I quickly stood and looked around. The platform was circular, as wide as the spread of my arms and surrounded by a railing. Feeling with my fingers, I found a break in the railing, opposite the ladder. There was a door imbedded in the wall.

11

The door swung out, away from me, a thick, metal-framed door that didn't want to move. I had to lean against it with my shoulder and give it a hard push. Reluctant the first inch or two, it suddenly gave and slammed open the rest of the way, pitching me out into sunlight and summer heat, the warm, blinding glare of a beach at noon.

I remember worrying again that I was losing my mind, that my crawl through the sewers, added to the last two days, had truly cracked my reason. I thought all this while I stood there weaving, weak and dizzy, my right hand still on the crusty doorknob and my eyes squinted closed in the bright sunlight. I was almost scared to open my eyes, scared to see what insanity looked like: a peaceful white beach, blue sky and a puff of cloud, children with small pails and shovels playing in the rippling surf, maybe even a slow, miniature trawler crossing the horizon, trailing a wispy, motionless kite-string of smoke. It was as if I really had been sleeping in darkness, dreaming nightmares of sewers and rats, a cold city filled with bleeding women and police sirens. Awake at last, I would have to scrape the sleep from my eyes and blink a few more times before I'd be able to see that I was a child on the beach on Cape Cod.

But when I finally pried my eyes open, I saw a gray concrete wall, not a beach. The wall curved over my head and became a ceiling, also gray concrete. Hanging from the ceiling was a brilliant bare light bulb.

I was standing in a tunnel. Darkness one way, more darkness, and a distant light, the other way. Stretched along the length of the wall were pipes, four of them, all about two feet in diameter, disappearing into the darkness in both directions. The tunnel itself was the size of those tunnels that connect subway stops, those white-tiled passageways reeking of piss and stale air. Maybe ten feet high from floor to ceiling and no more than twelve feet wide, it was empty, except for me, and the pipes.

I lowered my head and stared at my muddy feet. They were standing on a concrete floor. The light made a shadow of my head. I couldn't think straight, though I was collecting pieces of information that should have helped. Then I realized that the summer heat was still there, already drying the sheen of black shit that covered my body. It warmed my bruised bones, healing, soothing.

I touched the pipes. They were hot, and kept the temperature of the tunnel at an even eighty-five, I guessed. Warm enough to relax, warm enough to curl up and go to sleep. I resisted the temptation. I had to get out of there. I stared down the tunnel one way, then the other. Which way to go? It didn't seem to make much difference, so I started to my right, into darkness, shuffling along with the warm pipes on my left.

Another light glimmered before me, another bare bulb suspended from the ceiling, casting a bright, flat light over the pipes. I made it, and saw that beyond the next stretch of darkness waited yet another light, another island. Encouraged, I moved more forcefully, steering myself along the tunnel from light to light.

The shit on my body slowly dried into a stiff crust, an extra layer of dead skin that cracked and peeled at the joints. I felt like some primeval beast rising from a long slumber, bog-creature, underground animal, my own mute reptilian ancestor lumbering through the tunnel, looking for an exit, the world that would no longer know me. My feet squished in my wet, black sneakers. Sweat, from walking, from the heat, dribbled into my eyes, a sting of salt I didn't dare wipe away with my filthy, encrusted hands. I just blinked a lot and walked as steadily as I could.

I'm sure I walked for hours. Unlike the dark sewers, the

tunnel wasn't so far removed from time. It had light, and light marked a beginning and an end. It took me about five minutes to get from one light to the next. I passed thirty-six lights before I stopped counting. The arithmetic was tricky, but I managed it. One hundred and eighty minutes. Three hours. Then the tunnel ended.

Until that moment I had resisted panic, the scrabbling, screaming panic I'd felt back in the sewer, but when I reached that dead-end wall I felt it again, a claustrophobia so intense I thought the ceiling was getting lower and the walls pinching together, closing around me until the tunnel was the size of a telephone booth and I was trapped inside, unable to move, unable to breath. I didn't scream, though. I choked on the panic but I didn't scream. I closed my eyes instead. There, I re-created the beach I'd originally imagined, the open space of sand and waves and curling clouds and moist, salty air. I stayed on the beach until my heart beat normally and the snake in my throat retreated. Then I returned to the tunnel.

The dead-end, I realized, poking among the pipes, wasn't quite a dead-end. There was a hole, like a small doorway, in the left-hand wall, through which the pipes made a nice, neat turn. Squatting, I eased my way under the pipes and into the hole. Another tunnel, a little narrower but otherwise no different, stretched away in a straight line, following the pipes. Light bulbs dangled at regular intervals. I climbed in and started walking.

Even silence isn't silent, if you listen long enough. There was a vague hissing inside the pipes, an occasional metallic *clink*. I found it strangely comforting, a sign of life. After all, I reminded myself, men had built the tunnel, for whatever reason men like me had walked along this very section, laying pipes. They still came down here, presumably. Someone had to change the light bulbs. This cheered me, so that even when I turned the next corner and saw that the tunnel split into two, branching left and right, I didn't hesitate. I just kept to the left and limped along the tunnel until it became three tunnels, an intersection of right angles.

I could retreat, continue straight, turn left or right. I was in a maze. But man-made. With exits and entrances. Sooner or later I'd reach one. It did occur to me that I could wander around from one dead-end tunnel to another until I lost strength and collapsed. It did occur to me that I could lie wherever I fell and slowly die of starvation and thirst before anyone happened along and found me. That was the panic again, trying to squeeze back up my throat. I gritted my jaw shut tight. If I opened my mouth, the snake would fly out, all of my entrails unwinding onto the floor and slithering away and leaving me dead.

I walked and I walked. I passed a bronze plaque screwed onto the wall. *The Yale Club*, it said, in precise, arrogant lettering. I considered stopping for a drink, a chat with the boys, but decided I'd better keep going or I'd be late for the race. I had a shiny white boat waiting for me in the harbor, tied to a mooring off the shimmering white beach where children were playing with their pails and shovels. I could almost hear the small waves slapping dully against the hull, the *clink* of rigging high on the mast, my boat rocking with the breeze.

I looked up, pausing for a rest. The *clink* was right next to me, in the pipes. The tunnel surrounded me. I was hallucinating bronze signs on the wall, cool drinks in the Yale Club, that formidable stone building I had passed earlier today, the deep leather chairs and varnished paintings within, where gentlemen read the *Wall Street Journal* and napped after lunch. I could even hear their voices, reaching me somehow through the windows, a low, murmuring conspiracy of voices that sounded blissful and removed. I shook my head. The Yale Club wasn't there, of course. But the voices were, light, airy voices filtering up the tunnel and filling my ears like a scream.

I couldn't move. That was the truth. I couldn't move. My legs wouldn't work. I leaned against the warm, padded pipes and listened to the voices that refused to leave with my hallucinations and wondered how long it would take me to clear my confused head. Until then, I couldn't move. Ears control balance. I was off balance, hearing things.

Not only wouldn't the voices go away, they grew louder, and distinct words floated free from the buzz. *"Ah no, man ... gimme that ... shit."* I clapped my hands over my ears. The voices vanished. I listened carefully. Nothing but the beat of blood in my ears. I removed my hands. Voices drifted to me, from outside, one clear word this time—*"mama"*—and then general mirth, bubbling, childlike hilarity.

I peered ahead into the tunnel. It reached for another thirty or forty feet to a puddle of darkness. The next light, a dim gleam, was around a corner. I could see the pipes making their leisurely turn. The voices came from that direction. Human beings. People. Not dreams, not hallucinations, but real people, substantial, talking humanoids. My fellow creatures. My saviors. Workers, I thought, shuffling forward. Workers down to check the pipes or replace the light bulbs. With each painful step I took, limping toward the corner, I left behind the memory of the sewer, the cloying darkness, the stench, the rat with red eyes. I left behind the dead-end tunnel, the maze of tunnels, the fear that I'd never get out of there—I was smiling by the time I reached the corner. If I'd had the strength, I would have laughed. As it was, I made the turn silently, gratefully.

The tunnel lay before me, alternating spots of shadow and light receding in perspective to a last yellow illumination. In the light stood three small figures.

They stood relaxed, their arms folded. I tried to call but my mouth was too dry. I hurried toward them as best I could. They were chuckling, all three of them, until they looked up and saw me approaching. Then their smiles evaporated. A serious, contemplative air settled over their oddly boyish faces. I kept going, into their quiet gaze, working my mouth crazily, trying to speak. Even as I got closer, they remained small. It wasn't the perspective, as I'd thought. It was their size. They *were* small, about five feet tall, and their boyish faces were just that—boy's faces.

I stopped. My mouth, instead of speaking, got even drier. I couldn't swallow, let alone say anything. I stared at the three figures. They didn't move. They remained as before, arms folded, regarding me with puzzled, calculating eyes.

Three boys. Fourteen, fifteen years old. Two with crew cuts, one with long red hair that reached his shoulders. All three wore sneakers and jeans, shirts and ties, and all three had what looked like swords stuck through their belts. Not swords, I saw, peering closer. Ax handles. Long sturdy cords of polished wood, the heads where the ax blade should have been carved to smooth, rounded knots.

No one moved. No one said a word. The pipes hissed softly at my elbow. It didn't much matter what the kids were doing down there, what kind of game they were playing with their mock swords dangling from their belts and their bodies haughtily perched, as if they were leaning on air and the air, compliant, held them. They watched me, I watched them. To move, to break the tableau, would send them into action. I didn't know what they would do but the survivor's voice whispering in my ear told me I didn't want to find out. Better to stand here for eternity, staring into their coolness. I was looking into something awful, the eyes of children grown bored by anything but danger. I could feel that, and I could see the lust for blood flickering behind their lazy appraisal. One of the kids thoughtfully chewed at the inside of his lip. The other two watched me as if I were a small animal they were about to dismember, a terrifying indifference in their dark, placid eyes.

Rolling my tongue around in my mouth, I managed a sentence. "Can you help me?"

At this they actually moved. Not much, but perceptibly, slowly swinging their heads to look at one another and exchange amused smiles. They brought their smiles back to me, false smiles, like their calm. There was no friendliness there. The more they smiled, the more frightened I became. I only had time for a delayed, reluctant acknowledgment: *They belong to the albino's gang.* Then they charged.

They charged silently, still grinning, pulling the ax handles from their belts and swinging them above their heads. The wooden swords made a whining sound in the warm air. Their sneakers padded softly on the concrete floor. The kid with the long red hair looked like a Viking dwarf, his hair flying out behind him. I watched them get closer and closer, unable to move. I was too weak, and my brain had stopped functioning. I saw the whole scene from a distance and I think I giggled. This was the last act of my nightmare, my own avenging angels swooping down to kill me. I couldn't resist, I almost welcomed them. I had followed the singer underground to find a gang of kids. Well, here they were, brandishing their ax handles, ten feet away now.

I didn't want to fight. I'm not a fighter. And I was too tired to run anymore. The desire to surrender that had flooded me the night before, watching police cars careen toward the U.N. Plaza, returned like an old friend. In a way, I was relieved. I gave up, and at the same time knew a kind of peace, a detachment from the silent grinning kids rushing me in slow motion. It took them years to reach me, long enough for me to note it all carefully, the exact arrangement of the tunnel, the pipes, the hanging light bulb, my own blackened hands held out in greeting. *Come, my little saviors.*

The first kid got me in the stomach, swinging his club across my belly with all his might. It knocked the breath out of me and closed my eyes. I didn't see the next club coming. It caught me on the side of the head, a loud crack that sent me spinning off my feet. I slammed into the pipes and half fell, half slid to the ground just as the third club, raised above my head like an executioner's sword, swooshed downward and hit the back of my neck with a dull thump, the force of the blow driving my face into my knees. I heard something in my nose that sounded like splitting wood and tasted warm, salty blood on my lips. I also heard my voice screaming hoarsely, whimpering as I tried to cover my head and tuck myself into a tight, impenetrable ball, like a turtle withdrawing into its shell.

Outside, sticks smashed against my body. Inside, I slept.

12

I almost woke and lost consciousness again several times before finally coming to. I passed through levels of darkness, like a man kicking his way toward the surface through murky, gradually lightening layers of water, each growing warmer with light from the sun. My pain had become a kind of enveloping sickness, nausea, that seemed to increase, like the heat, as I approached the surface. In that sense, I probably didn't want to wake up. I would start to move awkwardly upward, the pain would sting me, unbelievably, unbearably, and I would let myself sink back into the refuge of darkness, back into numb relief. Throughout it all, a weird incantation repeated itself around me, burbling words spoken underwater: *"Gregory's a good boy, Gregory's a good boy."* Over and over again. The only reason I would strain to rise and meet the pain was to escape that somehow horrible refrain.

When I eventually awoke, really awoke, I was aware only of my aching body. It took a while before I was able to focus and look around and see that I was lying naked on a scratchy blanket in a small, dark, stuffy room. It couldn't have been more than ten feet square. The unpainted plywood walls were windowless. A faint light came from beyond an open doorway, a spreading rectangular glow on the red-tiled floor, enough light for me to see a stack of old newspapers in the corner, a Coca-Cola bottle filled with clear liquid next to my blanket. I had no idea where I was, and the room offered no clues, except a trace of cooking in the stale air. I remember thinking that I was back above ground, in a house somewhere. Someone must have found me in the tunnel and brought me here. But who? I wondered. The kids?

When you first wake up from a beating like that, it's hard to think about anything except your pain. My body felt thick and raw, as if my skin had been turned inside out. I touched my nose. It was lumpy, twisted to one side and swollen. Broken. I breathed. Both nostrils were clear. I sat up, slowly, making little deals with the pain, inch by inch. I reached for the Coca-Cola bottle by my blanket and sniffed. It seemed all right. I tipped it back and tested the liquid with my tongue. Water. Cool clean water. I drank it, the whole bottle. Everytime I swallowed, my nose exploded.

I leaned back against the plywood wall and was just arranging my bruised body as comfortably as possible, which wasn't very comfortable, when a shadow danced across the floor and I looked up to see a face in the doorway, a man's face, smooth as the moon's, peering in at me on a thin neck stretched curiously from behind the wall. He had dirty white skin and dark, startled eyes, and his matted hair stuck straight back from his low forehead, as if a wind were blowing. I caught a glimpse of his clothes, a red sweater full of holes, suspenders. Then, before I had a chance to say anything, before I could even move, he was gone, quiet footsteps hurrying away.

I struggled to my hands and knees, climbing the plywood wall with my hands, using it for support until I was upright. My head pounded, and I wobbled, dizzy. I should have tried to escape the minute I woke, I thought. Now it was too late—an old woman stood in the doorway, watching me.

She was dressed in layers of different-colored shirts, and there were at least three frayed skirts wrapped around her short, stout body. She smiled, or rather the wrinkles in her red face parted and revealed rotten teeth. At the same time, the effort closed the wrinkles around her eyes, and she rocked back on the heels of her black slippers, leather cracked into a network of wrinkles matching her face. Her ankles were swollen, grotesque. Short bursts of wheezing grunts escaped her mouth. Laughter, I realized.

Why wouldn't this nightmare end? I thought I'd seen

the last act, back in the tunnel, facing the charging kids. I crouched low, ready to defend myself, though I knew there wasn't much that I could do, even against this cackling dwarf. I was still dizzy. My hands hung down at my side as if they were made of iron. The kids hadn't left me anything, not even the will to survive.

Catching her breath, the woman lowered her head. Her mouth disappeared and her eyes came back, swimming in wrinkles. She took three short steps toward me and held out a bundle of clothes and a pair of smooth-soled sneakers. That close, I could smell her, damp and pungent, like the underside of a rock.

She gestured with the clothing: old, faded jeans, a shirt. I took the bundle and for a second our hands touched. Her clawlike fingers were rough, calloused. Then we were staring at each other again, five feet of air between us. I kept myself at a distance, my back to the wall, embarrassed by my nakedness.

She giggled, her eyes briefly vanishing, black teeth opening in a grin: "You stink."

I almost said she didn't exactly smell like perfume, but I let it pass. "Who are you?" I asked instead, my voice cracking.

Her brow furrowed, her mouth collapsed. She sighed, a melancholy heave of her ugly shriveled body. "Love is love. He never come back. But he was a good man. Educated."

I was in a nuthouse. Why hadn't I guessed? Someone had found me in the tunnel, decided quite rightly that I was out of my mind to be down there, and had carted me off to Bellevue. This old woman was crazy. Just like me— the Finger Mugger. The windows, wherever they were, would have bars.

I tried again. "What's your name?"

She turned, mumbling to herself, and started toward the door.

"Wait!"

She didn't stop. I watched her shadow lengthen across the floor of the next room and disappear.

I looked down at the foul-smelling clothes in my hands, dazed, I think, because I just stood there for a while, staring at the shirt she'd left me, a worn Oxford that had once been yellow, so thin and patched it felt like it might dissolve in my hands. It was missing most of its buttons, and the cuff of its left sleeve. Those clothes had never been washed. They lay there like dead matter, a bad joke, except I had to put them on.

I tried not to think about where they'd already been, what bodies they'd touched. The jeans almost fit, a little long but about right in the waist. The sneakers were at least a size too small. They pinched my toes. I combed my hair back as best I could and explored my sore nose, wondering if it would heal straight or bulge like that forever. My tendency was still to revert to my pain. It was almost welcome, because at least it consumed me. My whole body still ached. Simply bending over to tie my shoelaces was enough to make me forget everything except the pounding behind my eyes, the burning spots on my back where the kids had hit me.

Finally I was dressed, if you can call it that, and ready to make my next move. It hurt to walk. My legs were stiff. I hobbled over to the stack of newspapers in the corner. A *New York Times* lay on top, dated January 31, 1968. The yellowing pages flaked and crumbled when I picked them up. A headline, big for the staid *Times,* announced the Tet Offensive in Vietnam, and there were photographs of GIs firing their M-16s into the jungle, photographs of small bare-legged Vietnamese children. Fourteen years ago. I was twelve years old. I fumbled through the rest of the papers. They were all dated either 1968 or 1969.

I looked around the room again, more carefully this time, determined to get my bearings, and noticed what looked like two large picture frames on the opposite wall, the one wall in the place that wasn't made of bits and pieces of plywood. This wall, I realized, was made of dark tiles, and embellished by a zig-zagging Aztec pattern of smaller, lighter tiles that vanished in either direction behind the plywood walls. I limped across the room. There was glass inside the frames, hidden by dust and soot. Wiping away the grime, I saw two poster-size drawings. Each was identified at the bottom in slanting white script. One was of Bristol, England, in the summer, a bird-cage pier of white wooden girders, packs of long-skirted women wearing wide low hats and bulky men puffing on pipes as they stared out to sea. The other was a picture of Piccadilly Circus, crammed with horses and carriages.

Now I was really confused, and starting to feel panic again, the panic I'd felt in the tunnels. It was all that I could do to shuffle to the doorway, press back flat against the wall, and listen. I thought I heard voices, the muted babble of a crowd, garbled, muffled. I tried to make some sense of the voices, but I couldn't; it was like listening to a radio late at night. Everything blurred and merged. I remembered the old lady, and the guy who had stuck his head into the room. Whoever they were, they weren't the kids. They were both out there, I figured, and from the sound of it they had company. The company could be the kids, but why would the kids bother to leave me a bottle of water, why would they bother to send in some deranged woman to give me clothes?

I made myself lean over and look through the doorway. Another room greeted me. It was empty, about the same size as mine, and like mine it was hot and stuffy. No fresh air had been in there for a long time. Again, there were no windows, only unpainted walls of plywood and odd bits of lumber. The light came from a chipped and dented desk lamp sitting on the floor. Next to it was a thin mattress, speckled with yellow stains. A rocking chair that had seen better times filled one corner, held intact by packing wire. The other corner had been carpeted with a neatly laid square of newspapers.

Across the room waited another open doorway. Through it, I could hear the voices, louder now, but when I got there, all I could see, at first, was a hazy blue light. As my eyes adjusted, I realized I was staring out into a huge hall of some kind. The blue light came from swan-shaped lamps spaced regularly around the tile walls, and a chandelier hanging from the high ceiling. The walls were decorated with the same zig-zagging pattern of tiles I'd seen back in my room, and there also seemed to be a fountain in the middle of the floor, two statues, dancing boys, bowing to each other across a scalloped shell. Glancing to my right, I saw an ornate yellow subway car, motionless on dark tracks. I wasn't in a ballroom, or a nuthouse. I was in a subway station. I was still underground.

I didn't know which to try and absorb first, the station itself, with its elaborate chandelier and fancy fountain, or the stilted blue figures I now saw crowding the station floor. There were fifty, maybe sixty of them. Men or women, I couldn't tell, but they weren't the kids. They were barely human, the kind of sick, dirty shapes you usually see huddled in doorways or stretched open-mouthed across sidewalks in the Bowery on Sunday morning, reeking of rotted teeth and death-breath. The blue light of the chandelier scarred their faces, digging deep gouges beneath their already dazed eyes. They sat among piles of junk—packing boxes, pots and pans, bottles, broken chairs, more stained mattresses, more newspapers spread and flattened on the floor. Some were crouched over the cardboard boxes and seemed to be picking through the contents. Others just lay around on those newspapers, talking and smoking cigarettes.

It was as if some poison had dripped down from the streets and bloomed.

13

I spotted the freak who had looked into my room. He was sitting right outside the doorway, hunched above a magazine, his gangly legs sticking out from a pair of paint-splattered khakis. His feet, crossed at the ankles, were stuffed into a pair of decrepit boots, boots kept together at the toes with masking tape. That stiff tangled hair of his rose four inches back from his smooth face. He sensed me staring at him, for he lowered his magazine to his lap and looked up, eyes widening when he saw me.

I took a tentative step out into the blue light. There wasn't much else I could do. The wild-haired man in suspenders shrank back, even more scared of me than I was of him. The magazine on his lap, I saw, was *Money*.

My throat was dry. "Where am I?"

A puzzled smile crossed his frightened face.

"He can't hear you."

I looked down into the misted, searching eyes of a blind man, an old man with thin white hair who sat cross-legged on the floor, one of the cardboard boxes open before him. He was lifting things out—a rusted frying pan, torn and yellowed underpants, a stub of a candle—and sorting them into piles. He wore threadbare wool pants and a brown sweater that seemed to be unraveling. Dirt covered him, it had become part of his skin, yet there was also something distinguished about him, a reserve reflected in his long straight nose and high, arched eyebrows. His white hair was carefully cut and combed.

"Ralph's deaf," he said, his blank eyes moving to the freak at my feet. "He can't speak neither."

The old man's blue-veined hands took a splintered wooden serving spoon from the cardboard box, felt it with his fingers, made a decision, and placed it on a pile of pots and pans. He was staring up at me, not quite at my eyes, but about an inch to the left. I unconsciously moved sideways to align them with mine. They were flat, glazed eyes that seemed to be sizing me up, measuring me, my worth. "Kids really got you, huh? They must of thought you was one of us. They been doing this for weeks. Beating us up, stealing from us. First it was just on the streets. Then they started finding their way into some of the tunnels. That's how come they got you. They're demons. But they ain't found their way down here, not so far, anyways. Too many tunnels. It's safe down here."

"But who are they? Where do they come from?"

He pointed up at the invisible ceiling.

"They must *live* someplace," I said.

"No," he answered slowly, shaking his head. "They don't live nowhere. That's why they act like that."

His deft fingers went on sifting and sorting, each new piece of junk assigned to a pile.

"Will you please tell me where I am?" I gestured at the chandelier, the fountain, then remembered that he couldn't see.

He understood me anyway. "This is the way we found it. Well, almost. We done a few things here and there. McOmbie's a genius."

He nodded toward a thick-chested black man across from him, a legless man sitting on a low wheeled platform. Pale peeling spots dotted his hands. Like the others, he wore dirty, disintegrating clothes: blue shirt, three or four vests, baggy black pants that covered his stumps.

Sad, red-rimmed eyes looked back at me. "You from Boston? You look like you from Boston. I been to Boston once. Near froze my ass off. I remember the library. Slept there, and the park, what's it called? The Common. Yeah, the Common. Too cold for me. They found some guy frozen in the roses. You know that? Looked like a statue, they said. I got the fuck outa there. Been living here since nineteen hundred and thirty-eight." His thick finger pointed at the floor.

I glanced around the dark station. Behind me, the room I'd just left, and the room I'd woken up in beyond that, formed a sagging shack made from mismatched pieces of plywood, slabs of indoor-outdoor carpeting, and strips of formica. There was another shack next to it that looked pretty much the same, and three or four more clinging to the wall on the other side of the station. The air reeked, a dank, musty smell, rancid and cloying. This wasn't a home. This was an underground prison, the lowest place in the city, as far down as you could sink. The bottom. The end.

The irony was that the station had once been a rich man's fantasy. I could still see that, despite the junk, despite the dust and grime. Aside from the blue chandelier, and the fountain, there were three marble benches, facing the sunken track, and the only entrance into the place, a gaping tunnel opposite the yellow subway car, had a delicately wrought glass sign perched on top, *EXIT* in formal red script. Within the tunnel, more swan-shaped lamps cast their blue glow over four ticket windows, four grates of bronze scrollwork.

I looked back at the legless black man, the one they called McOmbie. He had lighted some kind of cooking contraption, a homemade Bunsen burner, and was heating a can of food over it.

"How'd I get here?" I asked him.

"Scissors found you." He bobbed his head, indicating a skinny, grubby boy sitting next to him, a young boy, no more than eleven, who raised deep curious eyes to mine when he heard his name.

"Found you in the tunnels and dragged you here hisself," McOmbie said.

"I know the tunnels better'n anyone," the kid boasted.

He had a bony face, skin so thin it looked translucent. He was busy going through one of those cardboard boxes, his small body lost in big overalls, a checked flannel cowboy shirt covering his narrow shoulders, the colorful plaid faded to a fuzzy purple.

"Thanks," I said to him, and I meant it.

That made him nervous. He bent back to work, burying himself in the cardboard box.

The black man, McOmbie, had started eating whatever was in the can he'd heated. It looked like dog food, but I was starving. I hadn't really eaten since breakfast with Henry.

I squatted down beside him. "Can I have some of that?"

"You g-g-gotta get your own f-f-food." A sallow scarecrow of a man had spoken. His pockmarked face watched me, not very friendly.

"Why should you get something for nothing?" someone else demanded, a big, slope-shouldered man on the other side of the kid. He had a nose like a bell curve, puffy, anxious hands, and the palest face I've ever seen.

His voice was low and gravelly, a hoarse, rasping whisper.

"Let him eat," said the blind man. "He'll pay us back."

The stuttering scarecrow brightened. "You got any money?"

"Naw, I already checked," the gravelly voiced man said. "The kids musta got it. 'Less Scissors took it."

His big hand swept out and caught the boy across the head, hard enough to make Scissors drop what he was holding, a tin cigar case that clattered to the tile floor.

"I told you," the boy wailed. "I ain't found nothing."

"John, leave him alone," the blind man said.

The big man started to swat Scissors again, but this time the boy ducked under his swinging arm and ran away, speeding toward the tunnel entrance.

"Here." McOmbie handed me his can of food. "Have some."

He also gave me a bent tin spoon. I peered into the can. Stew, I told myself. It tasted okay, once I got it in my mouth, but for all I knew I was eating a cat. I had to choke it down.

"It ain't *right*," the scarecrow protested, his gnarled face screwing tighter. "It ain't f-f-*fair*."

"Ezra, shut up." It was the blind man, and he sounded stern, but also tired, as if they went through this often.

"Nothing's f-f-fair anymore. George took my place today. Right in front of the b-b-*bank*. My best spot. I made f-f-fifty bucks there last week. Then he come along and take it from me. Just l-l-like that. I t-t-told him it was m-m-my corner."

"I'll talk to George," the blind man said.

"You beg?" I asked. "You're beggars? Is that it?"

They didn't like the word.

"Some of us," the black man admitted, reluctantly. "Me, I got two jobs. Up above, sure, I work corners, particular streets, mostly Columbus Circle these days. But down below, I fix things. I *make* things. That's my strength, if you understand me. Fixing things."

He gestured around the station, a craftsman's smile lighting his round black face. "That there chandelier. The lights. Showers. Toilets. It taken me thirty years to collect the necessary tools. You see that car?" He pointed to the yellow subway car. "That's mine. That's where I work."

I couldn't really react to what he was telling me, I could only record it, store it away, save it for now, when I can say with some certainty that I was sitting somewhere beneath the city, in an abandoned subway station, eating dinner with dozens of winos and bag ladies and beggars. This was happening while above me, simultaneously, New Yorkers went about their business, completely unaware that under their feet breathed another world, a perverse mirror image of their world, a world these bums and cripples had somehow found and claimed.

The singer, the girl I'd followed down, came out through the tunnel entrance into the station. I stared in amazement. This was where she lived? She was carrying a large metal pitcher, and was walking with great concentration, trying not to spill whatever was inside it. When she saw me looking at her, she hesitated, swaying forward, and a little water slopped over the top of the pitcher. It wasn't that she seemed frightened to see me, or even surprised. She simply waited, as if I'd asked her a question. For a second, we stayed staring at each other like that, balanced and unmoving. Then she remembered where she was, her mask dropped back over her eyes, and she abruptly turned and retreated, no longer caring how much she spilled.

I realized the station was getting quiet. A few people had to be hushed, and the group farthest away was a little slow on the take, but gradually the voices all lowered to a murmur and stopped, so that the only sound in the place was an occasional cough, the scraping of a pot on the tile floor, an isolated, tinny clatter of silverware. Silence enveloped the huge blue station, a waiting silence that seemed directed at me. I grew hot. But they weren't looking at me. Everyone was staring at the blind old man.

He sipped a glass of water and pretended not to hear the silence. His deaf-mute friend Ralph waited, too.

The blind man cleared his throat and ran his small hand

back through his white hair. A slow-burning anger started across his face. He controlled it, fussing noiselessly with a fork, a shoe, a broken lamp.

McOmbie reluctantly started to speak. "Frank—"

"I told you!" the old man exploded. "I told you all! No more! Do you hear me?"

His voice echoed, unanswered. He stared into space, his jaw stuck out stubbornly, his hands clutching the broken lamp in his hands. The station stayed quiet, everyone disappointed, subdued now, deflated by the blind old man's strange refusal. I was just about to ask McOmbie what they had wanted from him when I heard the noise, the soft *whooshing* sound, like a thousand birds beating their wings.

The station grew even quieter, faces raised to the steady, nearing *whoosh-whoosh-whoosh*. The sound was coming from the tunnel. As it got closer, louder, it became more of a whine, a high-pitched buzzing noise that seemed familiar, a whine I'd heard before.

"What is it?" I asked McOmbie.

He looked frightened.

Scissors materialized at the tunnel entrance, sprinting into the station. "They found us! They found us!"

Right behind him, the first kids appeared, ax handles whirling above their heads.

14

They charged, swinging their ax handles, hitting a cluster of bums near the tunnel entrance and smashing into them, wading into them, flailing to left and right, hitting faces, soft bellies, the crack and thud filling the subway station. There was a moment's pause, stunned immobility, before the screaming began, an awful, terrified, escalating wail that soon rose above the sound of ax handles hitting flesh. More and more kids poured from the tunnel, fast and silent in their sneakers. There had to be at least thirty of them.

Like everyone else, I tried to run, but I was too weak, and there was nowhere to go, the kids controlled the entrance. I made for the subway tracks, thinking I might escape that way. Two kids caught me and let me have it with their ax handles. Demons, Frank had called them. He was right. They pushed me and kicked me, driving me into the middle of the station. I saw McOmbie making a break for it on his wheeled platform, his thick, strong arms pumping wildly. Suddenly he skidded to a halt and pivoted 180 degrees, a perfect racing turn, as he tried to slip away from another group of charging kids. But they caught him, too, and sent him spinning back.

I recognized the kids who had first attacked me, the tiny Viking most vicious of the three, barely able to restrain himself from really letting loose and breaking somebody's head. They didn't all wield ax handles. They had pool sticks as well, cut short and deadly, and sawed-off broom handles. A few even had pistols, small black guns, Saturday-night specials, tucked into their belts.

Then the albino appeared in the tunnel entrance. The sight of him, the murmuring rumor of him, was all it took to shut us up. Here he was, finally. The one I'd come to find. Only he'd found me.

He wore tight faded jeans and a gray suit coat that didn't fit him very well. A thin black tie straggled down the front of his shirt. His ax handle, which he was resting on like a cane, had been carefully carved and painted, so that it looked like a totem pole. Over his small shoulders he wore a fur cape, not the coat he'd stolen from the di Costini woman, but a longer, silkier fur that glistened in the blue light. His white hair swirled to his dirty shirt collar. The matching white eyebrows looked like something pasted on his face, an afterthought.

The other kids, his army, seemed drained of life, sucked dry, sucked empty, but the albino seemed never to have been quite human. There was nothing, absolutely nothing childlike about his glaring pink eyes. They were dead eyes, past caring. Eternity lurked behind them. He was the night staring back.

"These are my men." His scratchy voice echoed manfully in the high-domed ceiling above the chandelier. He pronounced each word separately, the same way the echo returned, four weighted stones falling in water: "*These-are-my-men.*"

He waited for the echo to die, or for someone to defy him. "You're trapped." I swear, he grinned. "I got you trapped and now you gonna do what I say."

His ax handle tapped the floor, and he stared down at it for a second, thinking. He's just a kid, I kept telling myself. He's just a kid.

Contradicting me, his voice rang out again. "From now on, when you come down here at night, you're gonna give us half your money. Half, do you hear? We'll collect it in the tunnels. And don't try to hide nothing. We'll be watching you when you work, and we'll search you if we think you're holding out."

He lifted his head high, seeing something he alone could see, an invisible vision across the station. "You oughta be making more money anyway, don't you think? Especially now. It's Christmas, ain't it? Well, people get soft around Christmas. You know that. From now on you're gonna make twice as much. From now on you're gonna work the best corners. And everybody works. All of you. Nobody stays home. Got it? We're gonna cover the whole city!" He stretched his arms, encompassing the world.

Another short silence passed, while he stared us down, defiantly.

"Now line up!"

The other kids lashed out, ax handles and pool sticks hissing through the air, and the screaming resumed, high-pitched and helpless, as the kids herded us toward the tracks, making us form a long line along the length of the subway platform, facing the yellow subway car. I stumbled and almost fell, knocking against the wizened midget who had brought me my clothes. She was trembling and muttering, her curved, knobbly fingers plucking at her face, like a monkey after lice. Beyond her sat McOmbie, the black man, quiet on his wheeled platform. I looked for the singer, but I couldn't find her in the confusion. Except for the albino, none of the kids had spoken yet, and I began to wonder if they had tongues.

The albino patrolled the line, pointing with his stick when he didn't like what he saw, when the arrangement seemed too disorderly, and then a few of his subordinates would rush over and slam their ax handles around until he was satisfied. Behind us, three more kids dragged a large cardboard box into the station. I thought they were going to pull out guns and start shooting us. Instead, they reached in and came up with armloads of red Santa Claus outfits—fake beards, bells to ring, the whole works. I still don't know where they got all that stuff. They must have been preparing for weeks.

"Whadya do, up above?"

It was the albino. He'd stopped in front of me.

"I beg," I said quickly.

Up close, his face was more clearly a kid's face, pale and soft under the dirt and trails of sweat. He had a small nose, unhealthy skin, and full pouting lips arranged in a sneer. He seemed to need that sneer; it propped him up, supported him, making him feel taller, taller and more powerful. A jagged welt about an inch long crossed his chin, marring the beginnings of a fuzzy adolescent beard.

His washed-out eyes, flat, impenetrable, stared at me, calculating. I couldn't help worrying that he might know who I was, what I'd seen him do to the di Costini woman, and that if he did he'd kill me. Could he see that in my eyes? He saw something he didn't like, because he hesitated before moving on, gazing at me suspiciously, as if he were trying to remember where we'd met.

He shifted his attention to the old lady. "What about you?"

She had no idea what to say, she didn't understand what he was asking her.

"Whadya *do?* Up above?"

"She collects things," McOmbie said quietly.

The albino almost slapped him.

"What kind of things?" he asked the woman.

"Nice things," she spoke up, understanding. "Pretty things."

"Tomorrow you're blind, witch-face. Got it? Tomorrow you're blind."

"Blind? Blind?" She blinked, as if she really were blind.

The albino raised his painted sword and pointed at the large cardboard boxes in the middle of the station, the Santa Claus outfits growing in piles on the floor. "Some of you gonna ring those bells and tell those fucking assholes up there it's *Christmas!*" More kids were pushing in another cardboard box, from which they started removing dozens of white-tipped canes and dark glasses. "The rest of you gonna be *blind* and make those rich fuckers up there feel *bad*, 'cause it's Christmas and you can't see shit."

The albino stepped on to Scissors and his father, the big man, John.

"You." He prodded Scissors. "What're you looking at?"

"Nothing," Scissors muttered.

"You're already blind then, right? That's good. Poor little blind kid. And you." He nudged John. "What do you do?"

I thought John was going to faint.

"He can't leave the tunnels." McOmbie's voice, amazingly calm again, called up from the floor, where he sat waiting a few yards farther along the line.

"What?" The albino's angry eyes swiveled down to the black man. "What'd you say?"

"I said he can't leave the tunnels." McOmbie's black face rose to meet the albino.

For the first time, the albino had been challenged. Challenged simply by McOmbie's steady, unfrightened voice. And he knew it.

"Stay outa this, shorty." He turned back to John. "Tomorrow you put on one of them Santa Claus suits and you get up there and beg your stupid fucking head off. Got it?"

"He can't," McOmbie said reasonably, a scientist solving a problem.

The albino whirled on him. "I said shut up!"

"He ain't left the tunnels for over ten years," the black man persisted.

I've never seen a face change so quickly from confidence to uncertainty, and the albino fought against it all the way. "I said shut your fucking trap!"

"I'm just trying to tell you that he wouldn't be no use to you," McOmbie said.

"You gotta learn to listen!" The albino was already moving, three long strides to McOmbie.

He grabbed the little black man by the back of the neck and started running him across the platform, wheeling him toward the tracks, gaining speed and then letting him go. McOmbie couldn't stop himself. He'd gathered too much speed. He shot out over the edge of the platform, like a man on a flying carpet, but then his carpet dropped from underneath him, clattering onto the subway tracks and leaving his legless body alone in the air, hurtling forward and smashing into the cement wall on the other side of the track. He screamed, and fell, a sickening soft thud, into the dark canal, disappearing from view, his one scream hanging in the stale air.

I could hear the wheels of his platform down on the track, ticking around and around, still spinning.

15

I've always known I'm not brave, but until that moment when I stood by uselessly and watched them do that to McOmbie, until then I hadn't realized I was a coward. I didn't even know what it meant, *coward.* For me it had always been an imaginary word, or a word for an unimaginable situation. War. Movies. Books. But never my life. In fact, if anything, I'd always thought coward was a politician's word, a bit of propaganda to urge others on to fight and die. I can't get it out of my mind, even now, that I didn't do anything. I reason with myself that it happened too fast. I also ask myself, equally reasonably, what I could have done. But I don't think courage is a practical consideration, as Scissors proved.

He darted from the line and charged the albino, leaping onto his back and locking his arm across his throat, trying to choke him, squeezing hard. Blood flooded the albino's face, his head popped, about to burst. Staggering, he tried to shake Scissors off, but Scissors wrapped his legs around the albino's chest, his wiry little body tenaciously clinging as the albino lurched and started to fall.

Just as fast as Scissors had attacked, though, the Viking and some of the other kids reached the struggling pair and ripped Scissors from their leader's back. Scissors sailed through the blue air and landed on his back, a quick *smack*, the breath knocked out of him, a moan as pain hit him. The albino had already recovered, one hand massaging his throat. He jumped to Scissor's side, drew back his foot, a swinging pendulum, and brought it kicking forward as hard as he could into Scissor's face, hard enough to lift Scissors from the floor and crash him back down again, a small heap, collapsed on the tiles.

The albino straightened the fur cape on his shoulders, surveying the station, our faces. How could a kid be so evil? Though I knew what he'd done to di Costini, seeing him in action was a different matter. It left nothing to the imagination, nothing the imagination could repress. I looked back at Scissors. He was just coming round, groggy, shattered, not sure what had happened, his face dark with blood. John picked him up, carried him over to the nearest shack, and leaned him against the wall.

"Is he dead?" The albino was talking to some kids down on the tracks, who were investigating McOmbie.

"Naw," one of them called. "He ain't dead." They did speak, after all.

"Put him in there." The albino nodded toward the yellow subway car, the open sliding door and the tools I could now see inside scattered across a low worktable: wrenches, screwdrivers, chisels. I thought I even saw a drill press.

The kids handed McOmbie up to more kids, then his low wheeled cart. It took two of them to carry him. Missing his legs, he was the size of a child, but he seemed to be heavy. They had to struggle to get a good grip, almost dropping him. He lay unconscious in their arms, his head lolling to one side, mouth open and eyes closed, his arms draping to the floor and dragging as the kids quickstepped their way into the subway car, depositing him there, along with his platform.

"Okay?" the albino asked us, rhetorically. "Satisfied now? Believe me?"

I believed him. I believed he'd do anything. That's what set him apart, that's what made him unique. He made things happen. He did things. He didn't float around in a daze, waiting for something to happen, or following orders. It was almost admirable. How could I ever compete with such ruthlessness? I didn't think I could. If he knew what I knew about him, I thought again, he'd kill me. Simply, carelessly, without hesitation.

He gestured to the other end of the station, where the Viking was already hurrying to take charge of a group of kids who had lugged over the Santa Claus outfits and now stood waiting in a silent semicircle. I realized I was standing in front of a pile of canes and sunglasses. The albino, sauntering, sent some people to join the Viking, others to take their places behind me. In the blue light filtering down from the dusty chandelier, he looked like a priest saying Mass.

"Go on! Move!" His ax handle was as effective as an electric prodder.

John was one of the first to be sent to the Viking, and he must have thought he was going to torture him, for he approached the kids cringing, spit lacing his half-open lips, those huge pale hands floundering at his sides, grasping at the air, trying to pull something down. Two of the kids roughly grabbed him and shoved him the rest of the way. Next came Ralph, the deaf-mute, leading the old man Frank up to my line. He jerked his round dark eyes in little stabbing motions from face to face. Frank, bewildered, gazed in the direction of the albino. He was lucky he couldn't see.

"All right, put on them clothes." The albino pointed to the Viking's group. "The rest of you get canes and glasses." His ax handle poked toward the pile near my feet. "You're gonna be blind. You gotta learn to talk blind, walk blind. Otherwise it won't work. And the rest of you gotta act jolly. Got it, assholes? Jolly. Ring your stupid fucking bells and act like you like everybody. Ho-ho-ho!"

Once again, a series of echoes rippled beneath the ceiling, falling back down to the albino and dying. He let the silence stretch until it had the strained tension of a ticking bomb.

"Pass out equipment!" he shouted.

This was what the other kids, especially the Viking, had been waiting for. They whirled into force, shoving the lines forward. Since I was at the head of my line, I had to step up first. A freckled kid in a leather jacket gave me a white-tipped cane and a pair of dark glasses. Across the way, I saw John, so terrified and confused he didn't know what to do, get bashed on the shoulder. Kids tossed him a Santa Claus outfit, a beard and red cap. They had practiced this. Somewhere, like troops preparing for an invasion, they had practiced every move.

"Faster!" the albino barked. "Faster!"

Brutal ushers, the kids kept the lines moving at a fast clip, a kind of shuffling trot.

"Put them on! Put them on!"

Through the dark lenses of my glasses, everything looking even bluer, underwater. I briefly considered using my cane as a weapon, but quickly gave it up. There wasn't any point. They'd snap it like a twig, like a thin leg.

"Come on, do what I told you," the albino yelled, de-

lighted with the spectacle, his hands on his hips. "Ho-ho-
ho! Come on!"

The station seethed with dozens of misshapen Santa
Clauses. Hesitantly, they started chanting, "Ho-ho-ho."

"Louder!"

"*Ho-ho-ho.*"

"Ring your bells!"

I searched before me with my cane, mumbling impre-
cations, while around me the rest of the newly blind did
the same, holding their white-tipped canes like divining
rods, thirty pairs of dark glasses hiding their eyes, black
mirrors catching and multiplying the fringe of glass above
us, the blue chandelier. Not only wouldn't my nightmare
end, it kept getting worse, and this was the worst of all,
this grotesque charade.

They set up obstacle courses, making us pretend we
were on a city street, that one kid was a telephone pole,
another a truck. We had to act as if we couldn't see them,
and they tried to trick us by suddenly starting to charge,
or raising their clubs. There was no end to their cruelty.
Watching the albino supervise, I thought of him carefully
placing Signora di Costini's fingers between sharp blades
and squeezing down hard until he heard the bone crunch,
the fingers pop and separate. He had done that, and yet he
was only fifteen years old, sixteen at the most. He *was* a
kid—that's the part I had the hardest time understanding.
A kid with a mother somewhere, and a father, unless
they'd died. He was born somewhere. No kid is born evil.

The other thing I didn't understand was why he bothered with these underground wretches. What could they
make for him compared to what he plundered daily from
the rich up above? Nothing, peanuts. Nickels and dimes.
His intent pleasure, however, as he appraised us, lost in
the details of his operation, gave me the answer. He didn't
know we were real. We were an idea, a game played inside
his head. We were his revenge for something done to him
by the world, the city overhead that had driven him down
to seek satisfaction among the outcast. I'd thought a few
times that I was crazy. Next to the albino, I was a paragon

of mental health. He was insane. Gone, over the edge, beyond anything I had ever known.

Pain blasted through my legs. I turned to see one of the kids swing his pool stick against my other shin. By the time they were through with me, I wouldn't be able to walk. His eyes never changed expression. He looked at me as if he'd just pulled a lever.

"Over there." He pointed.

Hobbling, almost crying with pain, I moved as ordered, left at the telephone booth, right at the chestnut stand.

16

When they grew tired of their game, the albino dismissed us. Cocky general, disdaining labor, he strolled to the station entrance, where he turned and watched the rest of the kids nudge and prod everyone into the tunnel, into the shacks, back to the newspaper beds scattered about the dim, cluttered floor. Rehearsal was over. I took off my dark glasses. John, still in his Santa Claus outfit, stooped and lifted Scissors, carrying him away into the crowd. The boy was conscious, but barely.

The moaning and crying didn't stop, nor did the kids. They roved the station, looking for someone to punish. A group of them saw me and started toward me, ready to move me on to wherever I was supposed to go. I felt my swollen knees buckle and something like acid spill in my stomach. I looked around for some place to flee. I was standing right in front of the yellow subway car. The sliding door was open. Not knowing what else to do, I quickly stepped inside, trying, at the same time, to act as if I belonged there, walking through the door with the natural familiarity of a man crossing the threshold into his own home.

The subway car was a long, narrow room lit by two electric lamps, regular light, not very bright, picking out

stacks of lumber and tar paper and cardboard boxes overflowing onto the floor: nails, screws, nuts, bolts. Piles of
wires and motors and broken radios lay strewn across the
old subway seats. Some of the seats had been removed,
leaving space for a worktable, a plywood door set down
flat on cinderblocks, about a foot from the ground, and
littered with McOmbie's tools, including—I was right—a
drill press. To my left, two wooden chests rested against
the rear wall, a window partially covered by red-and-
white café curtains. Withered advertisements circled the
top of the car: a woman, her hair in a bun, smiling happily, whatever she was selling obscured now beneath the
dirt; a Singer sewing machine; a wooden roller-coaster,
Coney Island's first.

The only other thing in the room was a sloppy pyramid
of rags sloping toward the opposite wall. No McOmbie.
Yet I'd seen them carry him in. I stepped farther into the
subway car, out of sight of the open doorway.

"McOmbie?"

The pyramid of rags moved, and from its depths poked
a scratched and bleeding black hand. I hurried over,
avoiding the cardboard boxes. There was McOmbie,
lying on his back, half buried in rags. This was his bed, I
realized. I stooped down next to him. Except for a red
scratch across his cheek and chin, and the swollen purple
bruises, he looked all right. I wondered if either of his
arms was broken.

He tried to speak, his tongue moistening his lips.

"What?" I leaned even closer.

"Help me up."

I had to reach in there and scoop him up with my
hands, and for a second I hesitated, staring at the stumps
of his legs, not wanting to touch them. Then I slid my
hands under his arms and helped him swivel up into a sitting position, his back resting against the wall. Close, he
stank, like all the others.

"*Move it!*" I heard the albino shout out in the station.
"*Move it, move it!*"

McOmbie took a deep breath and again licked his lips.

"I'm sorry," I said, apologizing for myself as well as the kids.

He shook his big head. Seeing him, battered and slumped, his hands raw where they had tried to stop his plunge from the subway platform, I felt a hot rage begin to prickle through my body, starting in my feet, rising up my legs like water filling a glass, spreading into my gut, my chest, my arms, pushing up into my head and building pressure, pushing harder and harder until I thought the top of my head would crack open and my rage would shoot into the air, splashing onto the floor, red as the blood, the gash, on McOmbie's unwrinkled black face. He closed his eyes for a minute. "Know why them lights is blue?"

He meant the lights in the station.

"Zircon," he said. He pronounced it zire-*cone*. "Makes this blue light, see? Ain't it nice? Something special, I believe. Left it that way on purpose."

His eyes left mine and wandered to the workbench, his tools. "I coulda changed it, sure." He faced me. "But I like blue."

He couldn't concentrate on the kids, he couldn't accept that they really existed. He had withdrawn into his own world of mechanical problems, which he could solve.

"Let me show you something." He bowed forward and started tugging at a loose floorboard, raising it just enough to get his hand in and pull out a carefully wrapped package, neatly folded newspaper held snug by twine.

He handed it to me. "Go on. Look at it."

Underneath the newspaper was an old leather Bible, scrolled with gold vines and flowers. A gold clasp kept it closed, a clasp with heavy hinges, a clasp that hooked, hole to pole, over more inlaid gold. Across the front, etched in still more gold, was the name *J. P. Morgan.*

"I found that in an old car back in the tunnels," McOmbie said. "Its got gold velvet seats, and chandeliers, like the ones out there." He gestured toward the station.

He picked at one of the rags beneath him, an old tie, blue with red sailboats, then brought his sad face back up to me. I sensed more than heard someone behind me. I was getting better at that kind of thing, my antennae sensitive, alert.

The albino stood in the doorway, staring at us silently, his right hand draped over the hilt of his ax handle, which was stuck into his belt like a sword in its sheath. Without a motion to betray himself, McOmbie let the Bible slip quietly into the pile of rags around him. It disappeared among the old ties and torn shirts.

I stood, my knees cracking. "Just leaving."

I started for the door, but the albino wouldn't move, he blocked the way. A detail of three kids, including the Viking, waited behind him in the subway station.

The albino looked from me to the low worktable, then at the stacks of lumber and tar paper, finally finding McOmbie among the rags. Pushing me to one side, he walked into the middle of the room, idly glancing down into the cardboard boxes. McOmbie watched him warily. So did I. The kid moved as if coiled. He never relaxed.

He spotted the wooden chests beneath the back window. "What's in there?"

"Nothing," McOmbie muttered.

"Nothing?" the albino gazed at McOmbie. "I think I'll just take a look-see. Okay with you?"

The first trunk opened easily, the top lifting back, held in place by large brass hinges. The albino reached down to see what was inside, and as he did so the sleeve of his jacket slid up his arm. Purple pinpricks dotted the fleshy white skin, needle tracks, hundreds of them. They looked like little bruises. The kid was a junkie. He straightened, pulling out a handful of tattered *Mechanix Illustrated*. He chucked them onto the floor and reached down for more, making sure there was nothing hidden underneath them.

The second trunk had a padlock.

"Open it," he said to McOmbie.

"There ain't nothing in there."

"*Open it.*"

I thought McOmbie was going to get beaten again. Sweat moistened his forehead. He was afraid. More than losing his life, he feared what would happen when the albino opened that chest. I watched McOmbie's face as he tried to make a decision. He looked at the kid, he looked at me, imploring me to do something. Then, as if suddenly realizing where that would get both of us, he slowly undid a safety pin that kept the flap of his shirt pocket secure, his fingers coming out with a key. He handed the key to the albino, who snatched it roughly.

The three kids behind me had crowded in closer so they could see what the albino pulled from the chest. He had to try twice, finally getting the key into the padlock. McOmbie sat exhausted on his pile of rags, staring numbly while the kid undid the padlock and threw back the chest top.

Inside, like carefully wrapped eggs, lay small packages of folded newspaper, each tied with a string and placed on top of one another so that the chest was evenly filled. The albino took one of the top packages and ripped off the string and newspaper until he got down to what looked like a collection of dead worms—rusty nails, I saw, when he raised them higher, toward the light of the nearest lamp. About four inches long, they had square heads and three-sided shafts. The Viking flung them onto the floor and took out another package. This one he opened even more brutally, discovering, when he was done, that he held a torn and faded cardboard sign with FOR GENTLE-MEN written across it.

"What is all this shit?" He was talking to McOmbie.

The black man's gloomy eyes flickered to the long-haired kid. "I told you. Nothing. Just some stuff I found. Old stuff. It ain't worth much."

Suspicious, the albino let the sign flutter to the floor. Working quickly, methodically, he began tearing open the rest of the packages, flinging their contents away as soon as he'd seen them: old mechanical parts; a tortoiseshell comb missing most of its teeth; a lady's pair of lace-up boots, too small to fit anything but a child today. I looked at McOmbie, who sat unmoving, impassive. These artifacts were things he must have found hidden underground, in the tunnels somewhere, like the Bible.

The albino kept digging until he had emptied the chest

of everything except a single package that was about a foot square and wrapped even more carefully than the rest, the flaps creased and folded, the string tied twice. McOmbie didn't say anything, but the sweat on his forehead had spread. His whole face was glistening. In three violent moves, the albino tore away the newspaper, an excited kid opening his biggest Christmas present, a spoiled kid already ignoring the litter at his feet. He paused, amazed. Then, respectful for the first time, he lifted a gleaming necklace from the last layer of newspaper. He forgot, briefly, that he was a conquering general, he forgot the terrible game he was playing. His pale eyes lit up and a delighted grin cracked his stern pink face.

"Wow," he breathed. "Look at this."

I couldn't really blame him. It was a beautiful thing, the necklace, three V-shaped strands of interwoven silver and diamonds, green gems, emeralds, lining the top of each strand. It tinkled delicately as he held it before him. If it was real, it was worth a fortune.

The albino glanced triumphantly at McOmbie. "Nothing, huh?" He laughed. "Nothing my ass. Where'd you get this?"

He chewed his fingernails, I realized, looking at the albino's small hands, the gnawed, stubby fingers holding the necklace.

"Where'd you get this?" he asked McOmbie again.

"Found it," the black man said, so softly I could barely hear him.

"Where?"

McOmbie shrugged.

"*Where?*"

"In the station."

"You got any more?"

"No."

"Don't lie, nigger." Still holding the necklace in one hand, the albino took a threatening step toward McOmbie. "Don't lie to me."

"I ain't lying."

The albino stared at McOmbie, trying to decide if he were telling the truth. Then he noticed me, remembered me. "What the fuck you still doing here? Get back where you belong before I break your face."

He'd do it, no doubt—I'd learned that much about him. He'd happily break my face.

He returned his attention to the necklace, gloating over his find. Without looking at me, he called, "Get him outa here."

Two ax handles dug their way into my back.

I didn't know where else to go, so I hobbled across the station back to the shack I'd woken up in, and there, in the outer room, found the old blind man Frank and his deaf-mute friend Ralph. The old man was frowning, sitting on his mattress like some kind of statue, the Thinker, only blind, and instead of supporting a thoughtful chin with a closed fist, he kept his hands folded before him, his thumbs working the loose mottled flesh on the back of each hand. The harsh light from the lamp pushed a small shadow away from him and lay it thin and flat on the floor.

Ralph gave me a curious stare, cocking his head, and then started rocking furiously back and forth in the rocking chair, scribbling wiggly lines of gibberish in an old spiral notebook. Around us, invisible in the underground maze, pipes choked and gurgled, suddenly clanking loudly and rapidly, calling for help, a frenzy of noise. I leaned against the wall. My knees weren't working right.

I cleared my throat. "Is there a main entrance, up above, to the tunnels?"

Frank's blind eyes were fixed straight ahead, his frail hands rested on his knees. He was abstracted, somewhere else, and said nothing.

"Do you know how the kids got down here?" I asked.

He moved, his eyes wandering to Ralph, then meeting mine. Exchanging a look with a blind man shouldn't be possible, but we did it.

"I forget things," he said. "I can't do it no more." He shook his head, slowly. "I forget things. You know what that means?" His eyes seemed to open up, black holes, and suck me deeper and deeper into his head, his despair. "I used to tell stories. People liked that. Came around and listened. But I can't do it no more. I can't do nothing."

I remembered the scene before the kids attacked, the silent demand made of Frank, and wondered if that's what they had wanted—a story.

He looked at Ralph. "I ain't much better than him now."

He felt defeated, that was clear. Not just by the kids, either. Something like shame crept across his face. His fingers absently picked at his knees. Ralph turned a page in his notebook and continued with his idiotic scribblings, writing nonsense, his pale, flaccid face scrunched up in concentration. They were both helpless. All those people were helpless. That's why they were down there. They were losers, and what really frightened me was that I almost believed I deserved their company, just as, in another, equally frightening way, I thought I deserved to be punished for a crime I never committed.

"What's the name of the girl who sings?" I asked Frank.

"Delia," he finally answered, coming out of his trance.

"Where is she? How do I find her?"

He hesitated, then told me. "You got to go out through the entrance, into the main tunnel, and then there's a hole in the wall, on the right, where some of them pipes go. Follow that to the end. She's there."

17

The station had thinned out. About fifteen kids sat around the fountain, their faces blue in the aquarium glow cast by the lights on the walls. The chandelier was dark. Hell had settled for a brief nap.

Two more kids guarded the entrance to the main tunnel. I knew that if I tried to cross the station they'd stop me, probably rough me up again and then send me right back. I looked at the yellow subway car, motionless on the tracks. Remembering what the kids had done to McOmbie, my anger returned, enough to get my adrenalin pumping. Bluff your way through, I told myself. I didn't know if it would work, but at this point I think I'd become a little suicidal, without realizing it. And I needed to keep moving. I hoped, just to have something to hope, that the girl would know more than Frank about where the kids came from, where they kept their plunder. So I moved out into the station and as casually as possible started toward the tunnel. I had my blind man's cane with me.

The two kids guarding the entrance stepped forward to deal with me, blocking the entrance, their ax handles ready. One of them had dull, widely spaced eyes, gray-blue, that looked without seeing, too busy searching for danger to make contact. He was wearing torn and wrinkled corduroys, sneakers without socks, a sweat shirt that looked as if it had been dragged through mud, and an overcoat that reached his ankles. The other one, who only came up to my stomach, slouched anxiously in a tweed jacket, the sleeves way too short, his gawky, fourteen-year-old hands kneading the end of his ax handle.

"I have to go to the bathroom," I said, trying to sound stern, grown-up. "Okay?"

They weren't too sure.

"You want me to shit all over the floor?" I raised my voice. "I can't go anywhere. You've got the place locked up."

I knew that if I didn't act now, move while they were confused, I'd blow it. Yet I was scared to turn my back on them.

"I'll be right back," I said.

I eased my way between them and started into the tunnel, waiting for the ax handles to hit me. I could hear the kids talking behind me, in low voices, but they didn't come after me, and I didn't give them time to change their minds. Passing the old ticket windows, the bronze scroll-work, tarnished birds and fleurs-de-lis, even more elaborate than I'd first thought, I came to the pipes Frank had mentioned. They ran overhead, perpendicular to the tunnel, and disappeared into a hole on my right. The hole had been knocked out with something heavy, like a sledgehammer. I poured myself through, as Frank had instructed, and into another, smaller tunnel, one of those tunnels with pipes along one side—steam pipes, I've since learned, carrying heat to radiators all over New York.

There were no blue lights in there, only a few dim bulbs hanging from the ceiling. Hurrying, I walked along the tunnel, my sneakers squeaking, my shadow accompanying me on the gritty wall, leaping, shrinking, as wild with panic as I would be if I allowed myself. The tunnel made its turn, pipes on my left, steam leaking out from some of the joints. I could hear water dripping somewhere, and then a guttural clanging sound, as if a god were clearing his throat at the other end of the pipes.

I passed a small, dead-end tunnel, three toilets bolted to the floor, pipes leading, undoubtedly, to the sewers. Each toilet had been closeted for privacy by blankets draped over a crude framework of clothesline. They got their water for washing from one of the wadded pipes, a wired-together spigot dropping steaming water, when it was tipped, into big tin tubs. McOmbie's handiwork.

I was surprised there weren't any kids in the tunnel. I got all the way to a row of lean-tos without getting caught. The lean-tos sloped against the wall opposite the steam pipes. They were made out of bits of sheetboard and plywood and old signs, tacked together and fitted with blankets for doors. Inside, I saw beds of newspaper and a few lumpy, stained mattresses. Piles of rags. Old pots. A crucifix on one wall. I had to squeeze between some of the lean-tos and the steam pipes. The people inside stopped talking as I passed, a few furtive eyes glancing out from behind blankets.

I kept going, not wanting them to call out or make any noise, my eyes fixed on the next turn in the tunnel. I was just about to pass the last lean-to when I felt myself yanked inside by strong, grasping hands.

The single room was about ten feet long and five feet

wide, and hardly high enough to stand up straight in. A kerosene lamp, the glass almost black, gave off a vague, sputtering light that made John's face look like a battle-field, a destroyed landscape of deep ugly bomb holes. He held me close, his sour breath hot on my face. His eyes were wild, crazy with anxiety, spinning in his head, and his hands squeezed my arms so tight they stung. I re-membered to whisper, despite the fact that a gerbil in a wheelcage would have had a hard time keeping pace with my heart. "You scared me."

He released me, his gravelly voice rumbling in the small lean-to. "Sorry."

He took a step back, his hands hanging uselessly.

I looked around the lean-to. Even with that little light I could see that the place was a junkyard, a shapeless con-fusion of pots and pans and old clothes. Scissors lay stretched out on a bed of newspapers near the back wall. He was so still I hadn't noticed him.

"He's asleep," John whispered. "The boy's asleep."

We both stepped over and looked down at Scissors. His eyes were closed, his face swollen and puffy, his lips twice their normal size. He breathed slowly, rasping, shallow heaves of his bony chest. Pink wounds tattooed his arms and legs.

"You should put something on those cuts," I said.

"I already did. Whiskey."

We were both whispering, John's voice hoarse and sad. "That punk bastard really got him. He tried, though. Scissors wasn't scared. He's a good little fighter. He's just small, that's all. He's just small."

I didn't know what to say, I didn't know how to com-fort him. I wasn't very good at that kind of thing.

"You want some?" John asked, leaning toward me and pulling a bottle out of his pocket. He unscrewed the cap, took a swig, and passed me the bottle. "Whiskey."

I hesitated before drinking. The stuff was probably poison. Not that poisoning myself would make much dif-ference at this point. I stared down at the bottle, trying to read the label, if there *was* a label, then up at John, who was waiting next to me, huge and lumbering, his eyes just visible in the smoky kerosene light. They kept shifting to the motionless figure asleep on the newspapers. I *need* a whiskey, I thought, and immediately brought the bottle to my lips and took a long, deep chug. Fire spread pleasantly through my chest, into my gut. I shivered visibly, and John chuckled, a low, friendly laugh.

"Go on," he whispered. "Take another."

I did, letting the heat burn away some of my anxiety. So men become drunks. I understood that, and that what I shared with John was his fear. Conspiratorially, we passed the bottle back and forth a few times before he screwed the cap back on and slipped it into his pocket.

"It weren't his fault," John said, gazing at Scissors. He was ruminating, considering. "The kid tried but he's just too *small.*"

"Let him sleep," I offered.

John nodded, taking my advice seriously. I stared at his scraggly beard, his pinched, nervous hands, his large, somehow pathetic head.

"I've got to go," I mumbled. Part of me wanted to ask for another shot of whiskey.

He came to himself, almost apologetic. "He's a good kid. He's strong."

Self-pity suddenly overtook me. I had to get away from John. He made me feel too much like him. John seemed to understand, that was the worst part. He put his heavy hand on my arm and gently guided me out of his lean-to, pulling back the blanket and stepping with me into the tunnel. The pipes hissed, leaking steam.

"He's strong but he's too *small,*" he whispered.

18

I remember that the tunnel vibrated, a deep rumbling hum, as if there were an engine behind those walls, a huge heart I kept circling and circling but could never reach. Finally it ended, and I found myself facing another one of those ramshackle lean-tos, only this one was larger than the others and set aside in its own courtyard. A plaid blanket covered the doorway, a faint glow coming from a light beyond. Suddenly a shadow moved across the inside of the blanket, one way, then the other, then was gone. Farther down the tunnel, someone cleared his throat, loudly, grossly, and spat. I stood rooted to the darkness while I stared at the lean-to and wondered why I was so nervous. It irritated me, a kind of shy reluctance that kept me from acting, from simply stepping to the girl's door and asking her, again, for help. Maybe it was the memory of her fear of me. I didn't think she'd want to see me, and I wanted to see her more than I admitted to myself.

Before I could move, the blanket drew back and her dark figure filled the doorway. She must have sensed me out there. Seeing who it was, she abruptly disappeared back into her lean-to, the blanket swaying closed behind her.

I stepped up to the shack. "Delia?"

She didn't answer. I drew aside the blanket, the flame of a kerosene lamp fluttering wildly in the draft that followed me into the lean-to. At first I didn't see her. As the flame steadied and settled, it illuminated a heavy velour armchair, torn in places and missing a leg. Her guitar leaned against it, one of the strings only half wired, dangling like a loose spring over the frets. Her bed was a mattress on the floor, a thick patchwork quilt made of old clothes. Next to it I saw a neat pile of clothes, and a Coke bottle, like mine, of water. She had covered her walls with photographs clipped from magazines: pastoral scenes, pigeons on a roof, beautiful young women advertising bras and perfumes. Shadows fanned over the plywood walls, making the girls in the advertisements grimace and twitch.

Staring harder at her bed, her stitched-together rag quilt, I realized she was sitting in the farthest corner, in darkness, a small, bowed shape that didn't move. "Delia?"

She slowly raised her head. "What do you want?"

She was acting tough, as she had before, and it almost intimidated me. But then I remembered her striding along the street daring people to bother her, and the aloof pride with which she sang, and decided to push back a little. She isn't tough, I told myself. She's just scared.

"I need your help, that's all. I didn't mean to scare you."

"You didn't scare me."

She stood, picked up her guitar, sat down in the armchair, and went to work winding the loose string tightly around one of the guitar pegs. On her feet were the kind of sweater socks you get as a kid, the ones with soft leather soles. Hers were red, threadbare and dirty, the leather almost worn away, a design of what had once been white squares circling her narrow ankles and disappearing under the cuffs of her baggy army fatigues.

"Why won't you talk to me?"

A full twenty seconds passed before she said, "I don't know you."

"How can you expect to know me when you won't even talk to me?"

I had scored a point. Her eyes, like a camera shutter, opened wider. "Go away. Leave me alone. I already told you, I don't know nothing about the kids."

"All I need to know is where they come from, where they live. That's all."

She tightened the new string and started tuning her guitar. "I only saw them a few times before now."

"Where?"

"Different parts of the city. You was following me. You should know."

I ignored that. "You have no idea where they live?"

"They live on the streets."

I didn't know then what I know now, that at least ten thousand homeless kids roam the streets of New York. Ten thousand kids without a place to live, without a home of any kind. Ten thousand kids wandering around as if they didn't exist, ten thousand kids who can't tell the difference between what's happening to them and what they think about it. There were a lot of things I didn't know then.

Delia plucked a bass string, screwed it tighter. "I thought you was one of them, at first."

"Me?"

She nodded. The truth, I thought, was that everything aboveground scared her. But I didn't say that.

"What about the albino?" I asked. "I saw you talking to him. Remember?"

"I don't know him," Delia said flatly.

Then she was silent, avoiding my eyes, concentrating on her guitar. Outside her shack, the steam pipes hissed and rattled. I stared at the magazine pages tacked to the wall. Idyllic barns. Half-naked debutantes. I inhaled deeply, fighting panic, a familiar heaviness pushing on my chest. I was having trouble breathing.

She left the armchair and shuffled over to the Coke bottle, pouring herself a glass of water and sitting down on the edge of her mattress. Lines that hadn't been there yesterday now ran around her face like creases of pain, little dark crow's-feet spreading from her eyes, wider, defeated lines dropping down from her nostrils to her disappointed mouth. She looked like a woman who's finally had to face something she thought she could escape. She held the glass of water on her knee, not drinking, staring down at it as if it might reveal something to her. It was hard for me to understand what she was doing in those tunnels. She was, beneath the fatigue, beneath the sheen of sweat and dirt, an attractive woman. She tried to take care of herself. She took care of her room. Her ankles weren't swollen beyond recognition, her arms weren't covered with scabs, she didn't seem to be a drunk, she wasn't crazy. And she had that pride, that aloofness that gave her grace.

"Where did you come from?" I asked. "Before here."

"Chicago." Her voice climbed a notch. "I ain't ashamed to say this is home. I hated Chicago. I hated the slaughter-houses. The air smelled like blood." She looked at me. "My mother and father used to hit me. They hit each other. It ain't right, what they did. I tried being a waitress, but the guy who owned the place wanted to sleep with me, so I left. I came here. I couldn't find no job, all I can do is sing." She took a deep breath. "It's not so bad. Better than the shelters. I got my freedom, at least. And it's warm."

This little speech seemed to exhaust her. It also embar-rassed her. She blushed, then leaned back against the wall and massaged her neck, loosening the muscles, eyes closed. The clanking steam pipes sounded like deranged crickets.

"But you don't have your freedom now. Not with those kids here."

She laughed, and it had an ugly, strained ring to it, hol-low and sad. She glanced around the pictures on the wall, the quivering kerosene lamp.

"You could leave."

She took a swallow from her glass of water. "I'm tired."

"You could leave tomorrow, when they let us out. What's stopping you?"

"I'm tired," she said again, and she really sounded it.

I was getting tired myself. Tired of being afraid, tired of running. I'd been running for days. All my life, it felt like. I looked down at my hands and saw the grime caked there, the black fingernails. Filth covered me. She couldn't save me, I realized. No one could save me. I was stranded underground, trapped deep among the sewers, the refuse, the shit and mangled abortions and used rub-bers and washed-away vomit of an entire city. I suddenly wanted some more of John's whiskey. A lot more. Enough to send me under, into oblivion. "This places stinks, you know that?"

"No one asked you to come," she said.

"I didn't have much choice." I told her what had hap-pened. She didn't seem particularly surprised.

The warm light from the kerosene lamp and the dry warmth cast by the steam pipes were making me sleepy. I didn't really want to go, but I couldn't think of anything more to say. She didn't know anything about the kids, or if she did she still wasn't telling. I suspected that in fact she didn't know much about them, because though she continued to keep herself distant, not quite trusting me and ready to defend herself, she had also relaxed enough to stop treating me as if I were the enemy.

She finished her water and carefully placed the empty glass on the floor.

"I gotta sleep." Small veins pulsed in her bruised eyelids. "You can stay if you want, but I gotta sleep. There's a coat there behind you. You can use it for a pillow."

She lay flat on the mattress, her hands folded on her stomach. I couldn't figure out what she wanted me to do. Did she mean it? I stared at her, lying on her mattress, composed as a dead person, and then decided I'd take her at her word, I'd sleep on her floor, anything was better than going back along the tunnels to the station. Anyway, there was something soothing about her.

My body still aching from the beating the kids had given me, I crawled the few feet to the smoky kerosene lamp and blew it out. Darkness enfolded me, complete except for an edge of light around the plaid blanket hanging in the doorway. Delia didn't say anything, so I crawled back to my spot beside her on the floor, groping for the coat. I found it, a big heavy overcoat from the feel of it, and lay down, arranging the coat beneath my head.

I couldn't see anything, just the thin lines of light coming from the tunnel, and the faces parading before me in the half-dark, John with his confused eyes, bleeding Scissors, blind Frank and the deaf-mute Ralph, legless McOmbie, the crazy old woman who had brought me my clothes, stuttering Ezra, the grinning albino, his redheaded friend the Viking raising a club to strike—they all passed before me, like the sheep I should have been counting, an endless rotation drifting around and around my head. I tried to think of something else, anything else.

But what? My normal life? My stupid job, my empty
apartment? I pictured the toy soldiers on top of my bookcase, those little emblems of childhood. They didn't reassure me.

As I lay there, more aware of my own breathing than
anything else, a stab of fear, barely repressed until then,
finally arced across my heart. I gasped and opened my
eyes, only to find more buzzing darkness. It was true, I
thought. I really was trapped. I'd been buried alive.

19

I must have slept, because the next thing I knew there was
a foot in my face and something hard poking the back of
my neck and a kid's sweet voice crooning, "Rise and
shine, cocksucker."

Somehow, once asleep, I'd crawled onto Delia's bed,
seeking creature comfort. We awoke with our arms
around each other. Opening my eyes, I found myself
looking directly at her. The kids had left, but I could hear
them out in the tunnel, kicking everyone else awake. Delia
stared back at me, and then she actually smiled. I had a
flash to that di Costini woman, the way she'd smiled,
sleepily, from the pavement, before really coming round
and feeling her pain. I could smell Delia's sleep on my
face.

She sat up, hugging herself.

"Come on, hurry!" One of the kids had pulled back the
blanket in her doorway.

I stood and helped Delia up, my muscles sore and stiff.
I couldn't quite stand straight. We didn't have to dress, of
course, except that Delia had to change her slippers for
boots. She pulled on her overcoat and picked up her guitar. I remembered to take my white-tipped cane and blind
man's dark glasses.

"Wait." Delia pointed to the overcoat on the floor near

her mattress, the one I'd curled up with last night. "Better take that. You'll need it."

It was a ratty tweed overcoat, way too big for me, with a purple scarf inside one of the sleeves, which I wrapped around my neck. I put the overcoat on, then followed her out into the tunnel, where the kids were waiting for us. They shoved us along into the stream of moaning, bewildered shapes already headed toward the subway station, a gathering, stinking surf rushing past the shabby lean-tos and newspaper beds and spilling out onto the tile floor of the station, crashing against the others, a crowd packed into a human rectangle and facing the albino, who had climbed up onto the fountain and was now waiting for the rest of us, a dopey smile on his pink, ashen face. His long white hair glowed in the blue light. His small hand rested on the hilt of his painted ax handle, McOmbie's necklace gleamed at his neck, the diamonds or whatever they were mirroring the dangling glass orbs of the chandelier above our heads.

"Today's the big day, my friends. Today you go up and work harder than you ever worked before. Today you work *for* something. You got a purpose now." He raised his arms above his head, as if purpose were a tent he could physically describe. "Someday you'll thank me for this." Lowering his arms, he stared benignly into our faces. "Now some of you might wanna fool me." He smiled. "That'd be a mistake. I been checking, see, and I know what you can make. I expect that much, and more."

It was only then that I noticed Ezra, the stutterer, standing next to the albino's pulpit, looking up at him, awe spread across his dirty face.

"All right," the albino went on. "Now get your asses in gear and *make money*. And remember, there ain't no point in running away, no point at all. We'd getcha anyway, right? So just do your job, and everything'll be okay. Like I said, you'll all thank me someday, you'll thank me for helping you out and giving you a little fucking *pride* in whatcha doing. Believe me."

He swirled his fur cape around his shoulder and flung out his last order. "*Get moving!*"

With that, the kids standing in a ring around us un-coiled, driving us into the tunnel entrance. I tried to grab hold of Delia and keep her with me, but she was pulled away by the tide of moving bodies. She slipped farther away, ten feet in front of me, as we were forced one by one through the hole in the right-hand wall and into the steam tunnel leading back toward her shack.

"Delia!"

I couldn't catch up with her, there wasn't enough room, I was hemmed in by shoulders. The best I could do was try to keep her in sight, but after jostling along the steam tunnel for twenty yards we were divided into two groups and squeezed into separate tunnels, and she disappeared, swallowed by the darkness of one tunnel while I found myself pushed into the other. A kid got me in the ass, kicking me forward. There was no way I could get back to her. I could barely stay on my feet.

I bumped into Santa Clauses, I reeled off blind men flashing their canes like switchblades. It was impossible to get my bearings. We were shoved from tunnel to tunnel. I couldn't tell, after a few minutes, which one I was in. They all looked the same. The same shivering walls, the same shrinking shadows, the same muted shuffling. Kids prodded us along, guiding us from one tunnel to the next, up slippery metal steps and along creaking, grated walk-ways, then into more tunnels, tracing the winding, rising path of the wadded steam pipes. I tried to memorize something, anything, that might lead me out later, but I felt like Hansel without his bread crumbs.

I did see one kid act a little more kindly than the rest, helping an old woman when she stumbled and fell, taking her hand and helping her back to her feet. That shone out from the thick churning darkness like a miracle. For the rest, it was the same orderly violence, the kids lashing out with their ax handles, the rest of us tripping and stumbling.

Slowly we climbed, surrounded by the metallic clang-ing, the soft, nearby hiss of escaping steam. I hadn't real-ized how far down I'd been, how far I had to climb to reach fresh air. Instead of being reassuring, the thought of surfacing reinforced my claustrophobia, miles and tons of concrete and metal pressed down on my head, holding me under.

"Get your goddamned hands off me!"

It was John. I recognized his voice, but I couldn't see him, I couldn't pick him out from all the other Santa Clauses. I hurried along, looking up into each bearded face, meeting nothing but fear, grabbing a new Santa Claus by the shoulder and spinning him around only to find myself staring into different eyes, wide with terror and obedience.

I heard John's gravelly voice again, up ahead, and jogged forward. He was lumbering along near the head of the line, unmistakable once I saw him, towering over the others. He clutched his begging cup as if it were something he could squeeze and kill.

"John."

He whirled around, ready to defend himself. When he saw who it was, I thought for a second he was going to hug me. Then we were bumped forward by the surging mass behind us, pushed forward with the rest.

"How's Scissors?" I shouted.

He shrugged, ridiculous in his Santa Claus outfit, which was too small for him.

"Where is he?"

John jerked his thumb back in the direction of the subway station, leaning closer and whispering loudly: "I hid him. He's too sick to go up."

I thought of Delia and felt guilty. Maybe I should have hidden her, too, forced her to stay down. But she didn't want me to be responsible for her. She'd made that clear. I thought of her though, swept away among the protesting bodies, her small figure growing even smaller before vanishing. I wished I had done something, I wished I'd had the power to do something.

John grew more and more apprehensive as we continued along the tunnel. I remembered what McOmbie had said about him, that he hadn't left the tunnels for ten years. The huge man's size seemed to diminish, shrivel

like a punctured balloon, until he was just a flapping red
Santa Claus costume, his eyes sinking deeper into his
head, his grip on his begging cup getting tighter and
tighter, the blood draining from his fingers.

He sniffed the air—fresh air I couldn't smell? I strained
to see anything ahead but more tunnel, rising, link by
link, toward the streets. Excitement began to creep up and
down my legs, my arms. I wanted to run until I fell out
into the cool air of the real world. I had no idea what
I'd do when I got there. That didn't seem important.
The main thing was getting out, seeing the bright blue
sky. The dark, glaring skyscrapers that had once seemed
so threatening now, in my imagination, stretched above
me like the welcoming branches of a thousand friendly
trees.

I looked at John. He was shaking, and his skin was purple, like someone who had taken too much acid. His eyes
revolved wildly as he glanced frantically around him at
the kids. No exit. Just a straight tunnel, and a sudden
change in the air even I could detect: cooler.

We turned a corner and there, screwed to the wall, was
a brass plaque: *The Yale Club.* So I hadn't imagined it. I
stopped to stare. Up above, old men rustled their newspapers. Relaxed in their leather chairs, they sipped good
whiskey and chatted about stocks and sailboats. One of
the kids whacked me with his ax handle, driving me on. I
caught up with John just as he turned the next corner. A
hundred feet ahead was daylight. At the same time, a hard
blast of cold, wet air hit me, fresh air filled with a trace of
childhood early mornings. John, his trembling out of control, couldn't walk. He fell to his knees.

I tried to haul him up. "Come on."

Three of the kids, sensing a problem, started toward us.

"John, *come on.*" I heaved with all my strength, but he
wouldn't budge, his heavy frame had no strength of its
own. His skin was cold. Little bumps of fear crawled up
and down his arms. There was a moment there when,
once again, I tried to understand what it would be like not
to have seen daylight for ten years. I quickly gave up on

that. I was torn between my own need to charge out into the fresh air and John's need for help.

We were blocking the passageway. The line piled behind us.

"John."

It was too late. The three kids had reached us. Looking up, I saw the Viking hurrying over from the tunnel entrance, where he must have been waiting. His eyes were furious. Time was being lost. Schedules delayed. The albino wouldn't be pleased. Order could crumble.

John had started whimpering, then crying, his big stupid face paralyzed and wet with tears, his gaping mouth clutching for breath. The three kids poked at him as if he were a wounded turtle they'd just found.

"Move, you fuckhead!" The Viking had reached us, his ax handle lashing at John's face, opening a slash across his forehead. "Push him out!"

The other kids kicked and hit at him. I picked up his begging cup, stuffed it in my pocket, hurried over to him and lifted him with a strength I didn't know I had. I somehow got him to his feet and pushed him forward. My own feet slipped and I nearly went down. Holding on to him and heaving against him, I forced him to the tunnel entrance, where his moans turned into shrieks, screams of pain, as if the daylight were stabbing him. Taking him by the arms, I pulled him out into the dawn.

20

It was snowing. Whiteness, damp and clean-smelling, blurred the world, flakes swirling and falling. Early morning light, a distant, rising sun just visible through the haze, cast an oblique red streak across some nearby brick buildings. That's all I could see. After the darkness of the tunnels, this pale white blinded me.

John had covered his eyes with both hands and just

stood there swaying and whimpering while everyone else swarmed out of the tunnel into the snow. I grabbed him and yanked him after me, away from the tunnel into the chaos of snowflakes. He was shaking still, his tears freezing on his phony white beard, which had slipped down and dangled, like a lopsided grin, from his cheek. Gradually he stopped crying, venturing a few peeks from behind his cupped hands. We stumbled into some trashcans, and then reached the brick wall, feeling our way along until we came to a corner. The snow made the city silent, almost peaceful, and I remembered the pleasure of walking to school in the morning through freshly fallen snow, the secret thrill of leaving my own single track of footprints behind me, the squeaking crunch of my boots.

"John, listen." We stopped. "It's not much brighter out here than it is down there. Okay? So take your hands off your goddamn face. What're you scared of?"

I reached up and gently as possible pulled his hands away from his eyes. They were closed tight, his face ready for more blows, the world to clobber him.

"John, open your eyes."

Slowly, one at a time, he did, darting terrified glances into the snow. He couldn't speak. He just stood there, hunched, contorted, blinking as flakes accumulated on his eyelashes.

"John?"

He looked at me.

"Okay?"

Reaching into his red outfit, he fumbled around and came out with his whiskey bottle, which he uncorked, hands trembling. He took three long swallows, shuddered, and offered me a swig. I was tempted.

"That shit'll kill you."

He took a few more frantic pulls on the bottle and slipped it back inside his coat.

"Don't get drunk, John. I'm going to need you."

We were standing at the dead-end of a street I'd never seen before. What seemed to be warehouses and office buildings, squat, big-windowed stone and brick buildings built in the 1930s, stretched vaguely away from us in the snow. The only car around was a 1957 Chevrolet, all the wheels missing, the windows smashed, resting at the curb. Snow was piling up on the roof. I didn't know if we were on the East Side or the West Side, uptown or downtown.

I was cold, freezing in fact, and didn't know it yet. The snow, the exhilarating dry smell of snow, made me smile. Yes, I think I actually smiled. I took the air in, all the way in, deeper than I'd ever breathed in my life, filling my lungs. I was alive, all right. This was real snow, and this was a real street. There was a calm to be had there beneath the invisible skyscrapers. I lifted my face into the snow and stuck out my tongue, catching the soft melting flakes and tasting them, each one of them. Snow slid down my collar, cold on my neck. I leaned down and scooped up a handful of snow and rubbed it on my face.

John stood swaying in the snow, mute, terrified. I took him by the elbow and steered him onto the street, past the Chevrolet. "John, you and me are going to save our asses."

He shuffled beside me, drunk, I suddenly realized. He must have been drinking all night, trying to steel himself for this ordeal. He lurched and whimpered, kicking at the snow on the ground as if it were an army of ants trying to crawl up his legs.

"Where we going?" he finally muttered.

"To tell the cops."

He stopped. "Cops?"

"Yeah, cops."

"You crazy? *Cops?*"

"Come on, keep walking. We've got to find a phone booth."

"Cops?" he wondered aloud, dreamily.

We struggled on through the snow, a drunk Santa Claus and a blind man. My thought was to get the cops down into the tunnels. That's all I could figure to do. Maybe they'd find out something about the kids that would make them realize I wasn't the Finger Mugger.

When we reached the next corner, I had to stare hard to read the street sign, the swirling snow was so thick. Tenth and Eighteenth Street. I could hear the snow falling, a steady *shhhh*, so quiet it could have been inside my head. Then a truck appeared out of the snow, the whiteness forming itself into a high blue cab, flapping windshield wipers, finally a whole truck, crawling north. Next came a rattling Checker, speeding the other way, recklessly, sliding around on the fresh, slippery snow.

Guiding John uptown, I saw lights glimmering high in the office windows, and soon we were passing small stores, some of which were opening, sleepy people moving around inside, getting ready for the day. The snow grew whiter as the sun rose higher, whiter and brighter. More cars, mostly cabs, moved up and down Tenth Avenue, their tires swishing through the snow and turning it into mud. I had a quick memory of high school, the smell of snow, the sound of a pencil sharpener, a parking lot with fresh tracks, and then I was back on Tenth Avenue, turning east on Twenty-fifth Street and maintaining an even stride until John and I had reached Eighth.

A phone booth rose before us, like a perfect model of a phone booth. The doors flapped and slammed open. No phone book. The chain dangled empty-handed. John started to wander in small circles, a dog beating a nest for himself, only this dog was drunk, and getting drunker— he'd pulled out his rotgut and was taking another pull.

"John, cut it out. I'm going to need your help." I corked the bottle and slipped it back into his Santa Claus outfit. Tears were frozen on his cheeks. "Straighten your beard, for godsake." I looked up and down the sidewalk. "You don't have a dime, I don't suppose?"

He stared at me as if I'd just asked him for a Rolls-Royce. "Okay, we've got to get a dime, John. How the hell are we going to get a dime?"

He scratched his head, a low moan starting from his chapped lips. I took him over to the phone booth.

"Now stand here," I said. "Okay? Just stand here and look like Santa Claus. Where's your cup?" I remembered it was in my pocket and took it out. "Here. Now, anytime somebody goes by, just . . . where's your bell, for christsake?"

He blearily removed it from his coat.

"Okay, somebody goes by, ring this and say something cheerful. Like 'Merry Christmas.' John? You listening to me? We need a dime."

He nodded dumbly. I doubted he'd be able to do much more than stand there.

Putting my dark glasses back on and flexing my white-tipped cane, I tried to convince myself I could do this. I'd seen plenty of blind men before, plenty of beggars, and God knows the kids had gone out of their way to teach me the trade. I started walking toward the corner, my cane tapping the sidewalk in front of me, my head raised in a poised, listening attitude. Through the dark glasses, the snow looked malevolent. The streets were filling as people went to work, and I could see hurrying, hunched figures approaching me on Twenty-sixth Street and down Eighth Avenue from the subway stop, dark figures rising from the ground, just as I had done. An old lady passed, then a burly man in a black overcoat. Two secretaries, talking about their boyfriends, hurried by. At least a dozen people had walked through me before I worked up the courage to say anything.

"Please, a little money for a poor man." It came out high-pitched, pathetic all right.

Three more people, stragglers from the subway crowd, passed without pausing. "Please?" I called after them, tapping my cane.

They stared at John, who was now leaning against the phone booth, but didn't stop. John had dropped his bell and cup and covered his eyes again.

It occurred to me, as I stood there watching a single, tall figure grow closer through the murky snow, that my glasses and cane did serve one useful purpose: they disguised me.

"Please, won't you help a poor man enjoy his Christmas?" I croaked, blindly stepping out in front of the thin figure—a man, about my age, long-haired and wearing a blue wool seaman's cap. His hands were shoved deep into his P-coat pockets, and he looked up at me surprised. He'd been walking along in a daydream.

"Please, a dime? Just a dime for coffee? It's so cold."

"Coffee my ass." He squinted knowingly. "Thunderbird's more like it. Cough syrup maybe."

He started to walk away, hesitated, pulled one hand from his coat, and plopped a cold coin into my open palm. "What the fuck."

"Thank you," I mumbled. "Thank you."

But he was off and away, his hands plunged deep again, his shoulders hunched, back into his walking reverie.

I fumbled around trying to get the dime into its slot, my hands uncoordinated in the cold, and finally managed to dial the operator. She told me the address of the nearest police station.

21

John dragged along at my side as we headed north through the snow. His eyes were small and puffy and red. Snot had frozen in a smeared mess under his nose.

"We can't go to no *cops.*"

"I can't." I glanced at him, holding my breath. "But you can."

"Me?"

"Yeah."

"I can't go to no cops!"

I thought he was going to start wailing again. There were more people on the sidewalk now, and a few of them stopped and stared back over their shoulders at us as we passed. I put out my cane, tapping it before me and moving my head with the stiff, attentive awareness of the sightless.

John had drawn a deep breath and resumed his hoarse

moan. "I can't talk to no cops! You gotta be outa your mind! No." He shook his bearded head.

"You have to. You have to tell them what's going on in the tunnels, so they can do something about it. We sure can't do anything."

"They'll just clean us out." John was getting lucid in his panic, and I noticed, with hope, that he'd forgotten, for a moment anyway, that he was out on the streets. "They'll come down and clear out the tunnels. They done it before. They come down and make us leave."

"So what? They can't keep you from going back down. Anyway, what's the point of staying down there with those kids? Think what they've already done. They won't stop. It's just going to get worse."

He didn't know what to say. His face grew even uglier with the effort of thinking. "How come I gotta talk to them? What about you?"

"I can't."

"Why not?"

"I just can't, that's all. They're looking for me. If I go in there I'll never come out again."

He screwed his face up for another yell.

"John, if you don't shut up we're going to get arrested before we even get there."

An old woman unlocking her pawnshop watched us walk by, her mouth a small hole. Her breath puffed out in clouds, vaporizing in the snow.

As the sun rose higher the snow began to get thicker, softer, a sure sign that it would soon stop. The streets had been slashed to slush by cars and buses. It was still early—seven-thirty, I guessed. Eighth Avenue looked tranquil in that fine, white mist. John had settled into a limping, reluctant shuffle, his watery eyes peering ahead in apprehension. I thought how strange it was that the place I now felt free from, the tunnels, he longed to return to. I guess they really were home for him.

We passed a newsstand on one corner, and I had the dubious pleasure of seeing my name in the headlines again, this time because the Finger Mugger had struck yet another victim, an old man on the Upper East Side. There was a full-scale search going on for me now. The FBI had been called in. I was one of the most wanted men in America. That's what I read, hurriedly, trying, at the same time, to keep John from wandering away. There was a photograph of the old man, sprawled on a sidewalk at night. The kids had been busy working overtime. While some had kept us trapped in the tunnels, the albino must have led the rest on a raid. I also learned the date. December 24th. Christmas Eve.

Walking along next to John, I wondered what my parents were thinking. This had to be a law-abiding parent's worst fear come true. Our son the insane killer. What would clients say coming into my father's dealership? What would my mother's friends say when they ran into her in the Safeway? How's Gregory? It was cruel, what they must be suffering now. Maybe they couldn't even go out of the house, maybe they were surrounded by reporters and TV crews, all trying to get their one little scoop, a moment of pathos from a weeping mother or a distraught father.

I tapped my cane before me as John and I approached the next corner, Thirty-seventh Street, and turned east, crossing Eighth Avenue and heading into a darker canyon sprouting striped awnings and antique furniture stores, huge gloomy rooms filled with pianos and tables, clocks and armchairs, my vague reflection, too dim through the early light and falling snow to really see, gliding next to John's across the store windows.

The police station was a three-story brick building on Thirty-seventh Street, wedged between two, much taller office buildings that disappeared into the snow. A few police cruisers idled outside at the curb, exhaust clouding the air. Cops, hunched against the cold, came and went through the glass door at the top of the wide, shallow steps. Seeing them, I shrank back against the wall, trying to hide, terrified once again by the guns waggling on their hips. John, too, stepped back.

"I hate cops," he mumbled.

"They won't do anything to you. All you've got to do is go in there and tell them. That's all. Nothing'll happen."

John's desperate face was beginning to crumble, cave in on itself, like sand, and for the first time I really worried that he wouldn't be able to do it. His knobbly, veined nose quivered in the cold air. Tears streaked the dirt on his cheeks, staining his fake beard.

"You do it," he said. "I ain't going in there."

"I told you, I can't. They'd arrest me."

"What about me!"

I had to convince him to help me. "John, you know the kid, the albino, who kicked Scissors? You know what he does when he's not down in the tunnels hassling you? He goes around cutting people's fingers off."

John flinched. "Cutting off fingers?"

"Up here on the streets. He jumps people and takes their money and he cuts off their fingers so he can get their rings. I saw him do it."

"You saw him?"

I nodded.

"Jesus Christ, that's disgusting."

"He killed someone, too. And the cops think I did it, John. That's why I can't go in there. The cops think I'm the one they want. They don't know about the kids. So will you do it?"

"You want me to talk to cops dressed like a goddamn Santa Claus?"

"You can take the outfit off," I said. "John? Do you hear me?"

I pulled him into the alley behind us. It was dark, crowded with loud trash cans. John knocked the top off one and it sounded like a gunshot, quickly muffled by the snow.

"Okay, take it off," I told him, trying to sound as much like Frank as I could—what I imagined he would sound like, a mixture of stern authority and calm sadness, a resignation that John could share and that would give him purpose. "We'll hide the stuff here. Now come on." I started unbuttoning the red jacket.

"I can't do it," he whispered.

"Yes, you can." It was like undressing a child. He just stood there while I unbuttoned and yanked at the Santa Claus clothes. "Don't worry. I keep telling you. They won't do anything to you. Believe me. Just tell them the truth. Tell them the kids have come down, and tell them what they're doing."

"Cops won't help us," John said.

"They might."

Underneath the red jacket and baggy red trousers he was wearing his usual heavy turtleneck sweater and too short flannel pants, torn in places, mended in more, and, like the sweater, clotted with mucus, old food, booze. His stink rose from him, a nauseating reek of stale air and damp decay.

John fumbled in his pants pockets and brought out his fifth. I let him take a few swallows. "That's enough. You can have the rest later."

I freed the bottle from his hand and put it with the Santa Claus outfit in my arms.

He kept licking his lips. "One more?" he pleaded.

"Later." Resting his stack of clothes inside an empty cardboard box, I edged him out of the alley and onto the sidewalk.

We were only twenty or thirty yards from the station. I could see a cop inside one of the parked cruisers lighting a cigarette, the brief flare of a match that lit up his features, thick, ruddy slabs for cheeks, eyes narrow against the light under the peak of his blue cap. Then he shook out the match and vanished behind the fogged-up window.

"Go on, John."

He was leaning forward and staring at the street.

"I'll be right here. Okay? Now go on."

"I can't."

"You can. You've got nothing to be scared of. All right?" I nudged him forward.

He teetered on the curb.

"Go on. Now."

Watching him waver at the edge of the street, his long

thin hair waving in the wind, his hands working again, clutching at the snowflakes, I knew that if he did do it he'd be acting against his own nature, taking steps he'd spent years avoiding underground, moldering like some fleshy vegetable. If he crossed that street, if he took that first step, he'd be doing something heroic, something absolutely beyond his capability. I wanted to cheer him on, but right behind the cheer came guilt. I was just another officer sending another soldier off to get massacred. *Forward, my good man. Head high. Do your duty.* I told myself that they wouldn't hurt him, knowing full well that they might easily arrest him and throw him in jail for the rest of the winter, as they did so many of the bums they scraped off the streets of New York.

Looking back at me one last time, John reached into his pocket, looking for his booze, and came up instead with his courage, for he suddenly spread his empty hands before him and stepped off the curb into the brown slush of Thirty-seventh Street, heading toward the station. But he never got there. His courage failed him halfway across, leaving him stranded in the middle of the street, helpless, swaying.

"Go on, John!"

It was no use. He came shuffling back to the alley, his face of broken veins looming through the snow. I leaned against the brick wall while John jumped for his bottle of whiskey and took a quick sip. His hands were trembling as badly as my legs.

"Give me some of that," I said.

He handed me the bottle and I tipped the awful biting stuff down my throat. I felt like a flame swallower. My insides ignited.

"It's so simple, John," I said, trying to keep calm. "All you've got to do is go in there and tell them."

I gave him back his whiskey. He took another swig and wiped his mouth with the back of his hand, then looked at me and shook his head, miserable and apologetic.

"*What's wrong with you?*" I shouted, up close to his clouded eyes. "What the fuck's wrong with you that you

can't do a simple job like go in there and get the cops to
come help us? Huh? You *brain*-damaged or something?
You big stupid freak, what the fuck's wrong with you?" I
was jabbing at his chest with my fingers, screaming into
his baffled eyes. "You dumb fucking ox! You idiot!" I
started shoving at him, hitting his shoulders with the
heels of my hands, driving him back in small circles. Soon
we were crashing among the garbage cans. "Now what're
we going to do? Huh? Any ideas?" He could have killed
me but he didn't resist. *"How the hell are we going to get
rid of those kids?"*

I let my hands fall to my sides and stood there panting.
What the hell was wrong with *me?* Anger? Frustration?
The booze? John cringed, half crouched, waiting for me
to hit him again. I almost did. Just the sight of him, his
fear, infuriated me, made me want to hurt him. I was unraveling.

"Shit." I turned and stared out at the street, cars slush-
ing by through the snow.

"I'm sorry," John whined behind me. "I'm sorry."

I was the one who should be sorry. Another cruiser
pulled up to the police station across the street. I watched
the blue doors open and two cops emerge. I had to find
someone who wasn't as scared of them as John. I considered going into the station myself, but I knew I couldn't
take the chance of being recognized. Then I remembered
Delia. She might be scared, but I was willing to bet that
she was also too proud to admit it.

"Come on, John," I said. "Put your suit back on. We've
got to get out of here."

22

We walked over to Sixth Avenue, then up toward Thirty-ninth Street, where I hoped to find Delia singing at her favorite spot. I wasn't bothering with my blind-man routine. John shuffled beside me, sniffling into his sleeve, a lumbering Santa Claus on his way to a funeral. He still couldn't really bring himself to look around at the world, at daylight, and kept his eyes on the ground, as if he were searching for something he'd lost, house keys or a wallet. Hands crammed into his armpits for warmth, moaning to himself, he limped along, jumping away from people, terrified. Snow whirled at my face as wind scooped it up from the sidewalk and scattered it like flour. I was thankful for the snow, the snow and the cold, because it kept people from having to deal with us. They were too preoccupied inside their overcoats, trudging to work, half asleep. We moved among them, invisible, ghosts or memories they'd rather not see anyway.

A small park rose up out of the snow, a few bare trees and a solemn statue striding through the snowflakes. Sixth Avenue was already blazing with bright store windows and Christmas decorations, a party to which we weren't invited. My eyes wet from the cold, I stared at manikins wearing better clothes than this real person next to me, whimpering John, would ever know. In another store window, a toy train ran around and around a miniature landscape of thatched chalets and cozy villages, puffing smoke, while behind it a dozen mechanical bearded dwarfs worked merrily at their benches, making presents for no one, bright, sparkling castles and dolls.

John stopped, pressing himself against the wall of an office building, face first.

"Come on." I tugged at his arm. "Keep moving."

He shook his head, rolled his head back and forth.
"John."

Again, passersby were starting to stare.

"John, dammit, come on."

He moaned something into the wall.

"What?"

"I gotta go back down."

"You can't. Don't you understand anything? They'll
kick the shit out of you if you go back now."

He was big, and heavy. I couldn't budge him.

"Fuck it. You stay here if you want to. I'm going."

"No, no, no." He was crying. "Don't leave me."

I left him standing there, rocking against the wall. I
hadn't gone ten yards when he caught up with me. Irritated, I realized I didn't want him around, that his fear
only brought back the meanness I'd felt in the alley. I
wanted to run away and leave him behind. I didn't,
though, because I felt sorry for him, and because I knew
he'd fall apart if I left him alone.

When we reached Thirty-ninth Street, I moved toward
the blinking time and temperature of the bank near the
next corner. Delia wasn't there. Instead, I saw Ezra, pretending to be blind, coins clinking into his outstretched
cup.

"God b-b-bless you," he was stuttering, a beggar's
smile parting like a wound. "A p-p-penny for the
p-p-poor. P-p-pity the blind, God b-b-bless you."

I looked around for Delia, hoping she'd moved farther
down the block, but I couldn't see her, and when I listened I didn't hear her voice, raised above the traffic, as I
knew it could be. I approached Ezra, forgetting about
John for a minute. Ezra saw me and nervously took a step
back, then tried to recover by resuming his blind-man's
stance, expressionless behind his dark glasses.

"M-m-merry Christmas," he intoned, thanking a plump
man in a camel hair coat who had surreptitiously let a few
coins slide into Ezra's cup before hurrying on to catch the
light. "God b-b-bless you," Ezra called after him.

I sidled up to Ezra. "Where's Delia? Do you know
where she's working today?"

"G-g-g-go away," he whispered, not looking at me. "You g-g-gonna ruin everything."

He rattled the coins around in his cup and smiled into space. "P-p-penny for the poor."

"I need to find her," I said.

"G-g-go away," he hissed out of the side of his mouth.

There was something about Ezra I didn't like. For some reason, I didn't trust him. I got the feeling he knew where Delia had gone. Putting my hand around his scrawny arm, I slowly tightened my grip. I could feel bone through the thin layer of coat and flesh. A brittle bone easy to break. Very easy. Too easy. I was beginning to enjoy torturing these people. It worried me. "Where's Delia?"

"G-G-Grand Central," he sputtered, trying to twist away, saliva freezing on his lips. "It's b-b-better there. W-w-warmer."

"She's in Grand Central?"

He nodded, frightened. "I told her it'd be n-n-nicer there. M-much warmer. B-b-better for a l-l-*lady.*"

Over his shoulder, I saw three of the kids approaching us from the west. Except for their sinister swagger, and the slight bulges under their coats that I knew were ax handles, they looked like three kids on their way to school. One of them, leading the pack, noticed me, and John, and said something to the others. They picked up their pace.

John was trembling again, stock still in fear, awe, anxiety, whatever it was that paralyzed him.

"Listen," I said. "You stay here."

I backed him against the wall.

"Stay here and be Santa Claus. You've got to make some money anyway."

"No!" He was panic-stricken.

"John, just stay here with Ezra and do what he says. Everything'll be all right. I've got to go find Delia. So stay here."

Bewildered, he gazed around the crowded sidewalk, at all the normal people walking in straight lines.

"Stay here," I said again, patting his arm to reassure him.

I turned and moved away. He started to follow me. I waved him back, suddenly self-conscious about my supposed blindness. No one seemed to have noticed. John retreated to the wall, as if the people swirling on the sidewalk were attacking him. I hurried away, not wanting him to change his mind and come after me. When I reached the corner, I glanced back to see what the kids were doing. They had stopped to talk to Ezra, who was waving his hands excitedly, jerkily, a stuttering motion in the settling snow.

23

Hunched, shivering figures hurried in and out of Grand Central. The sooty building itself seemed, through the falling snow, to be shivering, as cold as the rest of us. Yellow cabs pulled up to release their passengers. Another Santa Claus, probably one of the underground people, stood ringing his bell near a newsstand. Christmas carols, scratchy and mechanical, floated into the air, into the snow that had started to thin, flakes spaced farther apart, the sky growing blue behind all that whiteness. I paused and watched the scene as if it were one of those small plastic globes which, when shaken, sends snow flurrying down on even smaller people and houses, a miniature world encased in water.

I noticed one of the kids, hunkered down into his trenchcoat. He was standing outside a luggage store diagonally across the street from me, watching the newsstand, and, I realized, looking again, a blind beggar standing motionless in the snow, his outstretched hand catching the melting flakes and an occasional coin. The kid had his back to me.

I pulled on my dark glasses, tapped my cane tentatively

before me as I waited for the light to change, and then joined the cluster of people crossing to Grand Central. I tried to bury myself in the middle, so the kid wouldn't see me. I got some stares. A few people were even sympathetic, touched, warmed in their Christmas spirit. I tapped my cane and kept my head rigid.

The Christmas carols grew louder, phonier. Blossoming tits poked from magazines on the newsstand, the pink, smiling girls oblivious to the cold. The man to my left, a businessman carrying a leather briefcase, turned to the man next to him and said, "We've got them by the balls. We'll just squeeze tighter and tighter until the fuckers scream. And that'll take care of Cincinnati." They shared a chuckle, moving ahead of me into Grand Central.

The huge, domed lobby was packed with people hurrying to catch their trains. Others poured out of the tunnels that led to the platforms and jostled their way across the ringing marble floor, fighting to keep their Christmas packages in their arms, struggling with heavy suitcases. Loudspeakers announced train arrivals and departures, a woman's drugged voice filtering down into the pandemonium. Through my dark glasses, the glamour dimmed, but not completely. I descended the wide steps, cane tapping before me, eyes swiveling to see Delia.

I decided to work my way around the lobby, systematically. A new Chrysler gleamed in the middle of the floor, roped off by red cords. A gigantic Kodak ad, Michael Landon and his happy family smiling down at me in living color, graced one end of the lobby. Remembering my own role, I stretched my cane before me and tap-tap-tapped my way past a group of children gathered together around a woman with tired, exasperated eyes. I wanted to take the dark glasses off, it was hard to see through them, but I didn't dare. At this point I really did have to play a blind man. Otherwise, I'd be a simple bum, an eye-sore and an offense, and hustled right out by the station guards I could see scattered about the lobby, cops standing with their arms folded and watching for trouble. The sight of them made my mouth go dry. What if one of them came over and asked me what I was doing here? I forced the

possibility out of my mind. Just act pathetic, I told my-
self. No one wants to interfere if you look sad enough.
After all, it was Christmas Eve. The night before
Christmas.

I couldn't see Delia anywhere. I listened for her voice.
Nothing. Just the roar of trampling feet, the loudspeaker
interrupting. I made a complete circle of the lobby without finding her. I did see another blind man, begging,
though I didn't recognize him. And at one point I thought
I saw McOmbie scooting along on his low wheeled platform, but I couldn't be sure, he was lost among the brisk,
scissoring legs. Except for the fact that most of the people
here, travelers and passengers, had complete faces and
more or less nice clothes, I could have been underground
again, in the abandoned subway station, mingling with
beggars. There was no difference.

Another one of the kids stood under the Kodak sign,
eating a hotdog. He wore a trenchcoat, too big on him,
and a narrow black tie. I turned and hid behind a pillar.
The boy watched the crowd move around him as he ate, a
half-satisfied buzzard looking for more. There was a scar
on his left cheek, a knife wound, healed, a swollen welt.
He ate quickly, tearing at his hotdog until it was almost
gone, then sucked the rest into his mouth and wiped his
small, dirty hands on his coat. Mustard stuck to his lips.

I turned and slowly backed away, along the edge of a
display booth, photographs of New York—the Statue of
Liberty, Brooklyn Bridge, Washington Square—tacked to
the four-sided cork stall. I kept the pillar between me and
the kid. When a new group of passengers swarmed by, I
joined them, letting them carry me wherever they were
going, across the loud hall toward one of the platform
tunnels.

"Are you all right?" A woman with a kind face, her
gray hair long and schoolgirlish, smiled at me. "Can I help
you?"

"No, thank you," I mumbled.

"Are you sure?" She kept her smile, concerned. "Are
you trying to catch a train?"

She had a nice, upper-class accent, Vassar and Connect-

icut, yacht clubs and cocktail parties. I suddenly wanted
to cling to her, beg her to take me with her. But she was
already detaching herself, having done her duty, the smile
fading, I realized, into a distant, relieved disgust. "Have a
good Christmas," she said, slipping a dollar into my hand.
Then she was gone, leaving me stranded alone in the
middle of the floor, next to the sparkling new Chrysler,
my arm nudging the red rope.

I felt trapped inside my blindness, as if my dark glasses
were a thick, hermetically sealed window. I was beginning to feel more and more like John. Things bombarded
me. Voices, smells, rattling jewelry, sailors with their
duffel bags, old women arm in arm, refugees from Europe,
my own grandmothers perhaps, lost in an American gran-
deur they couldn't understand. I swayed against the rope.
I had to find Delia. That's all I could think. The words,
like the things and people around me, charged, fled past
me and left me mindlessly trying to remember one, the
echo of a word.

"The two-ten to Baltimore is now loading at Track
Seventeen," the sing-song overhead voice droned. "All
passengers for Baltimore please go to Gate Six."

I lifted my head up to the high, painted dome of the
lobby. It looked like a cathedral ceiling. I wanted to
scream. Why couldn't I board one of those trains and ride
up into the snow hills of New England to one of those little stations with a red peaked roof? I wanted to kill everybody for having what I didn't have: freedom. A couple
passed, laughing, their arms around each other, the young
man leaning down to hear what she was saying. If I'd had
a gun, I would have shot them, happily, gladly. The
thought of their smiling faces suddenly shattered into bits
of bone and spitting blood filled me with an awful, furious
joy. I gritted my teeth and grinned, shooting them. Yet
they continued past, the girl's handbag slapping her thigh,
their heads tilted back in a shared laugh.

I chose an empty gate and walked to it, into one of the
tunnels, past advertisements for musicals and Scotch. Bits
of phlegm stuck to the tile walls. I stood back to let a

group of soldiers pass. They were drunk, singing an obscene song, their uniforms rumpled and their eyes red
from a long night on a train, a long night hurtling through
the dark from some base in the wilderness. Down south, I
thought, watching them go by. Most bases are down
south.

One of the kids stood staring at me, thin and formless,
somber as an usher, his back to the disappearing soldiers.
He'd been following me. I spun around and hurried down
the steps. I could hear him running behind me as I
reached the long, badly lit platform. A silver Amtrak train
hissed and steamed on one track, people spurting out of
the doors and tumbling onto the platform, wrestling with
their suitcases. Porters, black men, scurried around dragging luggage racks. I pushed into the crowd, glancing
back. The kid had reached the bottom of the steps. Poised
on his toes, he craned his gawky neck, looking for me.

"Here, let me help you."

A priest, a young man, blinked at me behind pink-
framed glasses.

"Take my arm," he said.

I couldn't move. The sorrow in his eyes mesmerized
me. It wasn't sorrow, actually, so much as helplessness.
His colorless hair was thin, receding up his white, patchy
forehead, dusted with flakes of dandruff. His breath
smelled of peppermint, and his fingers, when they landed
on my arm, showed bleeding, bitten fingernails. He was
trying to turn me around and lead me back toward the
kid. He carried a beat-up cardboard suitcase, held together with a belt. It didn't seem to weigh much.

"This way." I nodded blindly at another set of steps
rising behind him.

The priest guided me along, as Ralph guided Frank. I
wanted to look back and see if the kid was following us,
but that would have given away my disguise. We bumped
our way through the crowd, fur hats and overcoats,
squealing children. I could hear the priest breathing
through his nose, laboriously, asthmatically. When we
passed a cop he didn't even glance at us. Hurrying tra-

velers, oblivious to my supposed blindness, forced us to the edge of the stairway.

"Take your time," the priest gasped. "Take your time."

I had to get away from his goodness, his selflessness.

"Thank you," I said, reaching the top of the stairs and freeing my arm.

He tried to hold on to me. "I'll take you the rest of the way."

"Good-bye," I said, not knowing what else to say. "Good-bye."

A fat woman carrying a box from a bakery, neatly tied with string, climbed the steps toward us, a little man behind her staggering as he grasped two heavy suitcases. "Slowly, Ida," he called. "Slowly."

"We're late," she shrieked back, not even turning her head. "We're always late."

The priest hadn't moved. His bitten nails moved nervously on my sleeve, and his desolate eyes peered up at me—he was very short, I suddenly realized.

"Good-bye." I was walking away, a few steps backward.

"Wait," he said again, raising his thin arm. "I'll help you."

I turned and walked fast, almost ran, sweat all over me. That damn little priest, his dirty collar, his depressing suitcase. I could feel his eyes, even after I'd taken the first corner of the passageway. People were staring at me. Slowing, I feigned sightlessness, my cane groping before me as I moved with the crowd. I had to get away from all those people. I had to be alone, catch my breath, make sure the kid wasn't following—I looked back. He wasn't. I peered at the tunnel ahead of me, the muted shapes and colors of overcoats and hats. I had to find myself a private place. A bathroom? That sounded good, I had to piss anyway, but I couldn't see one, just the walls running endlessly, and the mocking advertisements. Tunnels. All those tunnels, no matter where I went.

There was a split up ahead, the main tunnel bending to the right, or at least I assumed it was the main tunnel, because that's the one everyone was taking. The other one turned off abruptly to the left, a likely one to lead to bathrooms, I decided. It was the same as the main passageway except there were no advertisements on the walls. I thought at first that the echoes of my footsteps were the footsteps of the thin kid following me, but when I stopped and listened the echoes died.

I came to a set of concrete steps. Looking up, I could see people passing by in another main tunnel. Suitcases and legs. Their voices rang, high and hollow, distant. There was nothing ahead of me in my tunnel except a door with a sign on it: *Personnel Only*. Above the door, someone had scrawled *Thunder Road* in blue chalk. A deadend. As I stood staring, the doorknob turned and the door started to open. At the same time, I heard a voice on the other side, the albino's unmistakable, highpitched voice. ". . . after we get them back tonight, that's when."

24

I didn't look back until I'd reached the top of the steps and the sanctuary of the crowd, people in a hurry bumping against me, apologizing when they saw my dark glasses and cane. I stared down the short, dim flight of stairs, trying to keep people moving between me and the entrance. I only caught flickers, glimpses, of the albino as he climbed the steps. He'd changed into his overcoat. There were three other kids with him, respectfully letting him lead the way. I moved back, so they wouldn't see me, and watched them come out into the main tunnel and turn right. Then I followed them. I thought I might be able to find out where they came from, where they hid when they weren't out pillaging.

The albino looked drawn, wired, his pink skin stretched tightly across his bones, and he walked with a hesitancy I hadn't seen before. No one seemed to notice him. He was just a kid on his way to a train. His overcoat was too small, pinched between his narrow shoulder blades. His white hair fell in a swirl over the tweed collar. Even I found it hard to believe, looking at him, that he led another life, hidden from daylight, words of violent advice hissed into his ears by the night. I could accuse him now, I thought, avoiding a flock of nuns. I could run up and grab him and scream until the police came, then tell them he was the Finger Mugger. And no one would believe me. His white hair bobbed among the innocent travelers. What would any of them think if they knew what really went on when they were asleep? Or did they know, and choose to ignore it, try to forget and leave the streets to criminals and cops, an endless death waltz danced to the sound of sirens?

"Watch out, you—"

I'd collided with a family.

The man caught himself. "I'm sorry. I didn't realize."

His wife and children, two boys, gaped at me. Beyond them, I saw the albino disappearing into the crowd. I didn't want to lose him.

"My fault," I said.

I caught up with the albino and the other three kids as they descended more steps to another tunnel. There were plenty of people around, so I didn't have any problem following them. They walked the length of that tunnel, reached another set of stairs, and started climbing. The passageway had ended, subway turnstiles to one side, candy machines and advertisements to my left. I stopped and waited a second. The crowd was too thin here to protect me. I rested my hand on one of the cold metal turnstiles, greasy from so many other hands, and watched the albino vanish upward. I gave him time to get well ahead of me, then cautiously climbed the steps myself.

I walked into a lobby, past a wall of metal lockers. The green marble floor, scuffed by thousands of shoes, stretched toward a newsstand. People hurried into the various tunnels that lead away from the place like the spokes of a wheel. Through the passageway directly opposite me, I could see the main lobby, the hood of the new Chrysler, a corner of red rope. To my right was a bathroom, a varnished wooden door with MEN stenciled on it in fading gold. A few people stood at the newsstand, flipping through magazines and buying cigarettes. More headlines warned of the Finger Mugger.

A space opened in the middle of the floor, a momentary gap in the crowd, and I saw the albino. He was sitting on a chair, raised high, next to a guy about my age who was also sitting on one of those chairs, getting his shoes polished by an old black man. The other kids stood nearby, idly. The albino was sweating, I saw, his pale face paler than usual, his hands shaking as he leaned toward the man getting his shoes polished. I thought I saw him smile, weakly, but even his smile looked vicious, a thin, intense smile that didn't know how to be happy. He talked excitedly now, fast and nervous. The guy my age said nothing, in fact seemed to ignore the albino, studying instead the progress the black man was making on his shoes. He was wearing a black turtleneck and a long black leather coat, his blond hair swept back like a 1920s movie star's, a small gold ring in his left ear.

My bladder, I realized, was very close to giving up and exploding. I glanced back at the bathroom door, then at the albino. He didn't look like he'd be going anywhere for a while. He practically clung to the sleeve of the blond man's leather coat. Shuffling sideways, hidden by the scurrying travelers, I pushed open the bathroom door and stepped inside.

A single light at the far end of the long room flickered and waned, a feeble strobe sputtering across the dingy cracked mirrors, the row of marble sinks, the yellowed tile walls covered with graffiti. Another swinging door led to the urinals and john stalls. One of the urinals had overflowed, a slippery sludge flooding the floor, so I went into one of the stalls. The john seat had been ripped off, there wasn't any toilet paper.

I peed thankfully, eased moment by moment of my pain, and was just zipping up and getting ready to leave when I heard the outside door open, then the swinging door, and finally the albino's voice, not ten feet away.

"I told you, I got the bucks. Whadya want? Bucks is bucks."

I quickly, quietly climbed up onto the toilet, crouching down and pressing both hands against the wall of the stall to keep my balance. The door to my stall was closed, but it wasn't locked—there was no lock, only shredded screw holes where it had once been.

Another, older voice said, "So you're moving up in the world, eh, Hymie?"

"Don't call me that. It ain't my name."

"Sure it is. Hymie the Hustler. The Soho Sucker."

"Shut up." The albino's voice quavered, not at all in control here. "Just give me the shit. Here's the money."

"I don't know, Hymie. I don't know."

"You said you had the stuff."

"Oh, I got it all right. Don't you worry about that."

"So let me have it," the albino squealed, panic cracking his voice. "Give it to me."

"Don't you think you owe me a little more than that, Hymie?"

"Whadya mean?"

"I mean I been good to you, ain't that right? I think you oughta show some appreciation, know what I mean, Hymie?"

A long pause followed. I leaned forward until my face was against the door and gently nudged it open an inch with the tip of my finger. I could see the albino. He was standing across from me, his face twisted and sweating. Next to him stood the guy with the earring, and beyond him stood someone else, an older man, in his forties, with thick sideburns and long greasy hair. He held a gun in his hand, not pointed at anyone, just resting loosely in his fingers.

"Know what I mean, Hymie?" the blond man drawled again, inspecting his fingers.

"My name ain't Hymie," the albino croaked.

He held out a fistful of bills.

"Lotsa money for a kid. Where'd you get all that money?"

"Gimme the shit. Come on."

The two older men exchanged a look.

"You're really ungrateful, you know that?" the blond one said to the albino. "I gotcha started in business, didn't I? I was the one set you up, remember? You didn't have nothing then. Now look at you. You're doing all right. So why can't you show a little gratitude, that's what I'm asking. You used to be good at it."

"Whadya want?" The albino was desperate.

The blond man smiled. "You know."

The albino turned red and swallowed hard. "I need that shit, man. Just give it to me."

"I will, I will."

There was a real tension in the room now. The albino's eyes flickered to the man with the gun, then back to the other one, who was slowly opening his leather coat, a sadistic, gloating smirk on his face. He started unzipping his tight pants, and I finally realized what he wanted, what it was the albino was supposed to do.

"What's the matter, Hymie? You used to be good at this, remember? The best. You made plenty doing it, anyway." They guy pulled out his prick, a flacid purple tube of flesh. "Remember how I taught you? Huh? Remember how you used to do twenty, thirty a day? What's the matter, Hymie? Forgotton how?"

A fit of shivering had come over the albino. He lowered himself to his knees, facing that drooping prick. I felt sorry for him then, quaking on the floor, and at the same time, remembering the needle tracks puncturing his arms, understood what it was he needed so badly he'd humiliate himself like this to get. A fix. The kid needed junk, and this guy was going to make him blow him for it.

"Come on, Hymie." The man stepped closer, flopping his prick before him, but just before the albino took it in his mouth the man suddenly laughed and cuffed the albino across the head. "Jesus, Hymie, you ain't got no self-respect, you know that?"

The other man laughed. His friend stuffed the prick back into his pants and zippered up. The albino was left kneeling there on the wet floor, his mouth still half open, tears of rage or desperation leaking from his pink eyes.

The blond man leaned down, yanked the bills from the albino's clenched fist, counted the money, turned and started away. "Give it to him."

The door swung closed behind him. The albino was already on his feet, anxiously holding his hands out to the man with sideburns, who silently handed him a small package of tinfoil. Then he, too, turned, dropping the gun into his coat pocket, and went out through the swinging door.

That left me alone in there with the albino. He ripped open the tinfoil, tasted the dope, evidently was satisfied, for he then glanced around the bathroom, looking for a place to shoot-up, and his eyes came to rest on the toilet stalls. I thought, for a second, that our eyes met. I didn't let myself move, though I had cramps in both legs now, stiff from crouching. Water dripped from one of the faucets in the next room. The albino started toward the stalls. I pulled my face away from the door and waited. If he found me, I was determined to put up a fight. After all, he was alone, and even though he probably had a gun I figured I might have a chance because of his need, the way it weakened him.

I could see his sneakers beneath the door, hesitating, then passing by and continuing toward the last stall. He wanted to be as far away as possible, in case someone came into the bathroom. Not that anyone would, I thought. The place stank, quivering in the bad light. Most people would torture both their bladder and their bowels a long time before coming in here. I could hear him opening the stall door to my left, the hurried scraping of a match, a long silence as he heated the heroin to liquid and sucked it into a hypodermic, slowly easing the poison into his vein. With it came what? His own oblivion? No, that's too simple. What came with it, surely, was relief, pure and simple. A dream of confidence, a layer of warm air between himself and the rest of the world.

I was beginning to get a clearer picture of this kid. Homeless, as Delia had said, he had either run away or been left by his parents, somehow ending up on his own, alone, fending for himself on the streets, sleeping in alleys, maybe, or deserted buildings, scavenging for food. Then someone, like the guy with the gold earring, had found him and turned him on to heroin, using it as a weapon to make him sell his mouth to surreptitious queers. Meanwhile, he had discovered other kids like himself, loose on the streets, and had organized them into a gang, and now they took care of themselves, roaming the city in search of victims, undetectable, shadows that killed. Only he still needed heroin. His freedom would never be stronger than that.

What I'd always liked about acting, aside from the thrill of creating an illusion, of being good at that, was that for a moment I could be someone else. I realize now that I understand the pleasure the albino took from his role as executioner. He feared himself, his own life, more than anything else in the world.

I heard him leaving the stall, saw his sneakers pass by, then heard the creak of the swinging door, the more solid thump of the outer door settling closed. Quickly, before I lost him, I jumped down from the toilet seat and started after him. But both legs were asleep and wavered uncontrollably. I got as far as the swinging door and had to wait, stamping my feet to get the circulation going, almost crying out at the sting of returning blood. Finally I was able to walk, if with an awkward limp, and moved through the next room, past the sinks, and out into the crowded lobby, where people continued unconcerned, garbled Christmas carols floating down from the high ceiling above them.

The albino and his three friends were walking away toward the main lobby. I followed them, almost getting caught when they stopped to admire the Chrysler. They leaned across the rope to touch the shiny steel, exchanging excited information like any other kids. It was horrible, what had been done to them, what had happened to them, as horrible as what they were doing to the underground people, as horrible as what they did to the solitary rich people they found strolling the streets at night. They confirmed my worst fear, I realized, hiding behind a German tour group and waiting for the kids to move on. There is no underlying order, nothing but a thin, fragile veneer of civility and faith that we use to protect our feelings from what's really going on, escape from our nakedness, like nice clothes. They left the Chrysler, sauntering through the crowd and up the steps leading to the entrance onto Thirty-ninth Street. I followed them out into daylight.

The snow had stopped, and a high, blue sky greeted me, cloudless and cold. Shoppers packed the street. The kids turned the corner, heading north on Park Avenue, the albino walking with his usual cockiness again, the heroin doing its job. Then I heard Delia's voice, a low, clear song cutting through the babble on the streets, direct as a command, angry, rough, and true. I only caught fragments of verse, the usual words, *heart* and *soul* and *night* and *rain,* yet wrapped around that voice they came alive, spoke as they must once have spoken to tribesmen gathered at the fire.

She was singing halfway down the block. Her eyes gazed blankly into her audience, ten or twelve people persuaded by her voice to stop and listen for a moment before rushing away. The albino approached her, the other three kids lingering behind. He paused, as transfixed as everyone else by her singing, a dreamy expression in his eyes, the softest I'd ever seen them. He didn't go up to her, or say anything, he just stood there, at the edge of the small crowd, and listened. She saw him, a catch in her voice, a moment's fumbling, then went on with the song, finishing it to a burst of applause.

He confidently stepped forward, dropped some money into her open guitar case, gave her a smile. I waited for him to hurt her, but he didn't. He nodded slightly, that's all, lordly in his stupor. Next, he summoned his entourage and walked on toward Fortieth Street, leaving Delia watching him.

25

It was good to see her again. I gave up on my idea of following the albino and stayed instead to talk to her. Better odds. She looked as tired as she had last night, and she moved slowly, tuning her guitar for another song, her fingers fumbling in the cold. Her crowd had dissipated. She'd have to start all over. Ezra had been right, she was here, but he'd been wrong, or lied, about her comfort. This place was no warmer than the corner near the bank on Thirty-eighth Street.

"Hi."

She looked at me, startled, and almost let herself smile with relief when she saw it was me. "What're you doing here?"

"Looking for you. I need your help again. Are you okay?"

"Cold." She shrugged. "And I ain't making much money. They made me give my spot to Ezra."

"They?"

"Him," she said, nodding in the direction the albino had taken.

"Why?"

"It's a better spot."

"I mean why would they give it to Ezra?"

"I don't know." She glanced up and down the empty sidewalk. "I wish they hadn't, though."

"Will you help me?" I asked.

"Do what?"

"Go to the cops."

I watched her inhale, a quick intake. "Cops?"

"All we've got to do is persuade them that the kids are down there, and tell them what they're doing, and maybe they'll go down and do something about it." I kept talking, hurriedly, before she could protest. "I can't talk to them. I told you why. I tried to get John to do it, but he's too scared. So I thought—"

"I'd do it?" she interrupted.

"Well, yeah."

She shook her head, kneading her hands for warmth. "There's no point. They'd never believe me."

"We won't know unless we try."

"Anyway, even if they did believe me, they wouldn't do nothing about it." She looked at me steadily. "Right?"

"You never know, that's all. It's better than nothing, isn't it?"

A few people were strolling down the sidewalk toward us, a young couple in parkas, holding hands, a well-dressed middle-aged woman. Seeing them, Delia started getting ready to sing.

"Come on, you've got to do it," I said. "Please."

"I gotta work is what I got to do."

There it was again, her stubbornness. Her cheeks were red from the cold wind. Her eyes, despite her fatigue, shined fiercely. She should have looked pitiful, standing there in her dirty overcoat clasping her cheap battered guitar, but she didn't. Her pride, I thought—and then, selfishly, I asked, "Are you scared?"

"No, I ain't scared. I'm just not stupid. Now I gotta work, okay?"

"I think you're scared. You're as scared as John."

"Fuck you."

"You won't do it?"

"No."

I hadn't counted on this. I'd convinced myself too well, too easily, that she'd help me, and now I began to feel frustrated again, a frustration quickly becoming panic. "Delia, please, think about it. How else are we going to do anything?"

"We ain't." She strummed the strings of her guitar, playing a few simple chords.

"Look, we don't have to go to a police station." I was begging now. "We can find a cop, any cop. Right here in

Grand Central. We'll pick the one with the most sympathetic eyes. Explain to him what's going on. Ask him for help. It's simple."

She opened her mouth, but instead of answering me, she started to sing, a slow bluesy song. An old man passing by stopped to listen, tapping his toe in appreciation.

"Delia, I need you."

She went right on singing, squaring herself and pitching her voice higher, thin notes evaporating in the bitter air. More people were gathering around her, glad for the diversion, it seemed, attentive and serious as ever. She was cutting me out, disassociating herself, colder than the wind.

For the second time that day, I lost my temper. "Okay, don't do it. Let them kick McOmbie around. What the hell. Who cares, right? I mean, who the fuck cares?"

It was strange, shouting at her, while she sang, ignoring me, only a foot away. People were staring at me.

"Why don't you leave the lady alone, fella?" a tall man in a trenchcoat demanded, aspiring to heroism.

"Why don't you mind you're own fucking business?" I shot back.

He stepped toward me menacingly, a weathered face getting ready for action, two huge fists dangling at his sides. "You looking for trouble?"

I backed away. "Not me."

"Then scram."

Delia was watching us out of the corner of her eye, but she did nothing to interfere, nothing to stop him.

"Scram," he said again, stepping even closer, so that I could see the pores of his skin, the beginnings of a beard, the angry tension under his trenchcoat. "Beat it."

Still Delia sang, and still I waited for her to change her mind. She wouldn't meet my eyes. She sang to the sky, which once more had filled with clouds, thick, heavy clouds drifting ponderously across the tops of the skyscrapers. She *was* scared. Even then, I knew I couldn't blame her.

"Fuck it," I muttered.

I turned and walked away, not really paying any attention to where I was going until I had turned the corner onto Thirty-ninth Street and found myself back by the main entrance into Grand Central, near the busy newsstand and the trumpeting headlines: FINGER MUGGER STRIKES AGAIN! What claim did I have on Delia, what right to feel this pain? She hadn't betrayed me. I barely knew her. Yet that's how I felt, betrayed. It was fear, I think, as much as anything else, that made me feel that way. Without her help, I didn't know what to do, and that left only the kids, and the cops, and the bleak winter city, with nowhere for me to hide except underground.

People moved around me on the sidewalk, leaving trails of clouds behind them, as if they were all smoking pipes. Pigeons flapped from ledge to ledge on the buildings across the street. At the corner, the light changed, red to green, Walk to Don't Walk. Horns shrieked, cabs maneuvering, yellow missles fish-tailing in the slippery slush. One of them came nosing full speed around the corner from Fifth Avenue.

I stared dumbly as a little girl, about seven years old, stepped off the curb and started across the street, right into the grinning grill of the cab. She was wearing red tights, boots, and one of those fake leather coats with a puffy fake fur collar. In one hand, she carried, proudly, a shiny plastic purse, the object of her undoing, for she was too preoccupied pretending to be a grown-up to take care of herself. The cab was already halfway around the corner and bearing down on her.

"Stop her!"

I couldn't get across the street in time, there were cars coming the other way.

"*Stop her!*" I pointed frantically.

My voice, despite the noise of traffic, carried loudly, and a woman across the street, her back to me as she gazed into a store window filled with Christmas temptations, slowly turned and in horror saw what was about to happen.

"*Gloria!*" Her lipsticked mouth contorted, a puddle of blood in the rain. "*My God, stop her!*"

A beefy man in a short green overcoat, waiting for the light to change, sprang out and grabbed the girl, his squat body amazingly fast and assured as he yanked her up by the elbow and pulled her back to safety just as the cab driver slammed on his brakes and went skidding and sliding sideways into a mailbox, missing them both. The thick thud and screech of metal pierced the cold winter air. People hurried eagerly to look. The cab driver opened his door, shaken. The woman was weeping, clutching at the girl, hugging her, moaning unintelligibly, the beefy man standing back respectfully, the little girl stiff and bewildered and a little resentful, her purse still held purposefully in her hand.

Nearby, people were staring at me. Curiously, suspiciously. Two cops came running out of Grand Central, looking around for the source of the trouble, one of them moving toward the group gathered around the girl and her mother, the other one stopping at the newsstand to ask what had happened.

Time to run again. Time to flee before the gaping witnesses pointed to me, directed the cops to the girl's blind savior. Already, a tight pack had started to surround me, not malicious, but puzzled, as if perhaps, on Christmas Eve, they had in fact witnessed a miracle, an act of God performed for them all. One old lady even reached out and touched me, reverently, her pasty face and stupid eyes begging me to tell her it was true.

I managed to slide tentatively through the curious bystanders, mumbling polite excuse me's. It was like wading through water. They caught at me and slowed me down, picking at me. I could see the cop at the newsstand, looking at me now, his head tilted to one side in disbelief as the newsdealer spoke from the depths of his booth.

"Excuse me, excuse me." My white-tipped cane wavered before me, an insect's antennae. "Excuse me."

Clear of the throng, and hidden by them from the cop at the newsstand, I walked east, trying not to run, trying to stay blind. I could hear voices rising like a bubble behind me, excited, murmuring voices that suddenly burst into amazement. The cop must have reached them, and they must have been telling him their story. I didn't look back. Not once, though the need was intense, the same kind of curiosity that draws you to stare at a dead body. I kept going and had finally reached the corner when I heard heavy footsteps approaching me from behind, and then, before I had a chance to prepare myself, a young nervous voice calling, "Wait a minute!"

I stopped. There was no point in running. Slowly I turned, facing the cop, who was watching me curiously, a young man, all right, and as nervous as his voice. His hand shook a little as he pointed at me. "What happened back there?"

The trick, I told myself, was not to overplay it. Yet I had to remember that I was blind. I stared over the cop's right shoulder, my ear tilted toward him. "What do you mean?"

He stepped closer, his curiosity mingling with what I'm sure he considered professional suspicion. "Back there." He jabbed his thumb toward the accident, the crowd gathered on the sidewalk. "People said you saw what happened."

"Me?" I felt the air with my cane. "I can't see anything. What are you talking about?"

"They said you called out."

"About what?"

"The girl."

"The girl?"

He began to lose confidence. "The one who nearly just got herself killed."

Some of the people in the crowd, including the old lady, started to drift in our direction, bored now by the steaming taxi and hysterical mother. I had to get out of there. "I was walking by when I heard someone scream," I said hurriedly. "Then I heard the car crash. That's all I know."

He was writing in a small notebook, carefully printing. "What's your name?"

"Sammy Sloan," I improvised.

"Where do you live?" At this he gave me a quick once-over, doubtful that I lived anywhere.

"Salvation Army."

That seemed to satisfy him.

"Can I go now?" I asked, worried about the nearing crowd, what they'd say to the cop.

I wasn't quite ready for what happened next. The cop tested me, the way the kids had underground, suddenly raising his hand as if to slap me, hard, across the face. I almost flinched, then remembered I was blind, I couldn't see. I gazed at him blankly, unmoving, a statue of a blind man. It took all my concentration, and I don't think I could have done it, in fact, if the kids hadn't already put me through my paces. Ironically, perversely, they had helped me. Also, I'm a pretty good actor.

Closing his notebook, the cop said, "Okay, you can go."

The crowd was almost upon us.

"Thank you," I said obsequiously, backing away.

I turned, my cane leading, tapping on the snowy sidewalk, and as slowly as possible moved around the corner. I glanced back, in case the cop decided to test me further. He wasn't there. I started running, ignoring the stares I got. My feet slid awkwardly on the ice and snow. I couldn't get up much speed.

A hand fell on my shoulder. My heart heaved. I whirled around, expecting the cop. It was Delia. She was out of breath, too, her face flushed from running. She held her guitar case in her right hand.

"I'll do it," she said. "I'll go to the cops."

26

We walked the six blocks in silence. We could have been strangers, that's the way she preferred it. Halfway there, it started to snow again, slow, thick flakes that clung to Delia's eyelashes and collected on top of her blue wool hat. I'd become immune to the cold at this point, immune enough, anyway, to pretend I didn't feel it, that it was simply part of me, like bone or blood. Delia's guitar case bumped against her knee. I kept my dark glasses on, my cane waving before me as we hurried down Sixth Avenue. Snow swirled heavier and faster, turning the streets into a white maelstrom, the tall buildings vanishing above the eighth floor into a silent white sky.

When we got there, I pulled her into the same alley where John and I had stood hours earlier. Each broken bottle and dented trash can wore a sliding cover of snow. Across the street, two more police cruisers, both empty, waited at the curb, while people filed in and out of the station through the glass doors.

"That's it," I said.

She rested her guitar case against the alley wall, behind some garbage cans and out of sight.

Straightening, she gazed across the street. "You want me to tell them the kids come down into the hole, tell them they're hurting us?"

"That's right."

She smiled, a touch of sarcasm in her voice. "And they'll come and save us."

"Maybe. The main thing is, they'll find the *kids.*"

"If they believe me."

"They'll believe you," I said, without much conviction.

We were standing close together, at the entrance to the alley. I didn't let myself think about the fact that the cops might keep her. Looking along the length of the street, I saw a Coca-Cola sign farther down the block, on our side of the street, almost directly opposite the police station: Nat's Café.

"I'll be waiting for you in there," I said, pointing to the sign.

"What about my guitar?"

"It's safe here. No one will see it."

There was fear in her face, but she struggled against it, tucking her head slightly, an unconscious dipping motion, and straightening her shoulders. I suddenly felt terrible sending her in there, even worse than I'd felt sending John.

"Delia."

She looked at me.

"Be careful. Don't push too hard. Don't get in trouble."

"I'll be all right," she said.

My worry was growing. "Maybe you shouldn't do it."

"I'll be all right, like I said." She flashed me a smile.

Then, giving me no more time to think about it, she left the alley and stepped out onto the sidewalk. From behind, she looked smaller, more vulnerable, and I felt another pang of guilt, of anxiety.

"Delia," I called, stepping out after her.

She ignored me, already moving across the street, weaving her way between the sluggish cars, their wheels spinning uselessly on the slick snow. I followed her progress, sideways along the sidewalk on my side of the street, parallel to her, until I reached the coffee shop. Here I stopped, and across from me she stopped, too, staring up the steps at the station, the forbidding glass doors. She nervously patted her hair, like a debutante getting ready to enter a ball, and then started the slow climb. I was holding my breath, I realized. Each step took her higher and farther away.

I turned and looked at the coffee shop behind me. It was just another coffee shop, nearly identical to all the others scattered throughout New York, with a plate-glass window on one side of the door and that Coca-Cola sign above the door. A cheap plastic Christmas wreath showed through the steamed-up glass. It occurred to me, just as I opened the door, that I might find as many cops here as I would in the station, but the place was empty, except for a middle-aged man behind the counter, who was in the process of tying an apron around his sagging paunch, and two older guys, construction workers, sipping coffee and reading newspapers on the two stools at the end of the counter. Nobody even glanced at me as I came in. I kept my cane out of sight. My dark glasses were stuffed into my pocket. I didn't want to draw any attention.

Wiping a circle in the steam, I stared through the window and saw Delia hesitate as she reached the top of the steps. She looked back in my direction, to see if I was watching. Snowflakes fluttered around her. A delivery van pressed between us, blocking her from sight, and when it moved away she had started opening the glass doors, swaying slightly. Then she disappeared inside.

Looking around, I had a strong desire to stay in this coffee shop for the rest of my life, consoled by the murmuring voices of the construction workers, the occasional sound of a newspaper being turned, the sizzle of hamburgers on the grill. The room was warm and smelled of warm coffee. It seemed the coziest, warmest, most welcoming coffee shop in the world, not just another coffee shop, as I'd first thought, but the best coffee shop, the Platonic coffee shop. The construction workers had each rested his hardhat on the stool next to him. Steam rose from the coffee pot behind the counter, next to the paunchy man cooking hamburgers, whistling to himself as he flexed the spatula. He was obviously Greek. Every coffee shop in New York seems to be run by Greeks. It's an ethnic franchise.

I cleared another hole in the steam on the window and peered back out. The steps were bare. The police cruisers had left. Snow continued to fall, more slowly now, fewer and even thicker flakes. This might work, I thought, starting for the counter. Delia might actually be able to do something. I decided to have some coffee while I waited. It wouldn't take her long, but I did have time for coffee. Then I realized I had no money, and at the same time the

Greek behind the counter looked up and saw me.

His face reddened. Dropping his spatula and wiping his hands on his apron, he came at me around the counter. "What're you doing in here? Out. Go on." He waved his hands, trying to shoo me away. "Out. Out."

The two construction workers looked up from their newspapers, curious.

"Out!" the Greek kept shouting, getting closer. "Out! Out!"

"What's wrong with you? What did I do?"

Anger throbbed in his neck, a thick vein. "I don't want people like you in my place! This is a good place! A clean place!"

"What?"

"Out! Out! *Out!*" The Greek had worked himself into a violent rage. I was afraid he'd try to hit me, and shied back, two or three steps toward the door, turning to my left slightly as I did so, raising my shoulder to protect myself.

In the gold-flecked mirror behind the cash register, I saw a disfigured bum, his greasy hair matted in thick clumps, a swollen, misshapen nose, one eye half closed and bruised, scabs on his forehead, a two-day beard bristling from his pores, snow melting on the shoulders of his torn rag of a coat, itself splotched with what looked like puke and cum—a monster. I twitched my head in horror and the head in the mirror moved. It was me.

"I said *out!*" The Greek had grabbed me by the back of the neck and was pushing me to the door, keeping me at arm's length. "Goddamn it, get the hell outa my place!"

With his free hand he yanked open the door. He pushed me out as hard as he could, hard enough to send me slipping and falling onto the sidewalk, scraping my hand as I hit the pavement. The door slammed shut behind me, the Christmas wreath swaying back and forth.

I sat there. Nobody passed me. My cane lay a few feet away. Snowflakes gathered slowly on my arms, my legs, while the snow on the sidewalk soaked through my jeans.

My ass was freezing and I started to shiver, my teeth knocking together. I thought they were going to break and fall out of my mouth like seeds.

Some old command, the remnants of Gregory, struggled through my beggar's mute helplessness: *Get up.* But why? Why bother? I remembered John's whiskey, and wished I had it with me now. I needed a drink. I looked up into the falling snow. In the distance, a patch of blue showed, incongruous against the nearer sloping drift of heavy flakes, millions of them.

Hands were trying to lift me, Delia's hands, her face close enough to kiss. Grunting, she hauled me to my feet, held me steady as I gained my balance.

"Get me into the alley."

She did her best, supporting me with her hands, and we limped our way into the narrow passageway.

"What happened?" I asked her.

"Nothing," she said.

"Nothing?"

She shook her head.

"Did you talk to them?"

"Yeah."

"So what did they say?"

"They said if I didn't get outa there they'd grab me for the winter, that's what they said."

"Did you tell them what's going on?"

"I told them."

"And?"

She shrugged sadly. "I went in and stood there at the desk and told this cop the kids'd come down the hole and beat the shit outa everybody. I told him what they done to Scissors. But he didn't care none. He said to stop wasting his time."

Once again, I thought of going in there myself. I didn't think they'd recognize me. I'd learned that much about myself. My own mother wouldn't recognize me. But there was a good chance they'd throw us in jail this time, lock us up as vagrants. I couldn't take the chance.

My face shrank, the muscles in my throat thickened, and a loud gasp escaped my mouth, a moan that brought

tears. I turned away from Delia and tried to control myself, but the tears wouldn't stop. They forced my eyes
closed and pushed against the back of my throat, choking
me. It was humiliating. There wasn't anything I could do
about it, though. The tears just kept coming, along with
that gagging sound children make when they can't stop.
When Delia took me in her arms and held me, it only got
worse. I was practically wailing. She held the back of my
neck and pressed me to her, her dank smell, the skin smell,
the underground smell.

I don't know how long this went on. A couple of times I
thought it was over, but then I'd start choking again. All
the while Delia held me, and all the while I was aware of
her, the touch of her hands through my overcoat, the bitter, smoky smell of her hair in my face. She kept surprising me, and her holding me now, her comforting me, was
the biggest surprise of all. I tried to tell her that, but only
sobs came out. It was as if years of not crying were forcing
themselves through my pores. I was leaking.

Finally I was able to stop. I pulled away from Delia and
dried my eyes with the palms of my hands. I felt drained.
My scratchy eyes ached, and there was a tight, dry pain in
my throat. It hurt to swallow.

Delia looked away, trying to spare me more embarrass-
ment, or embarrassed herself, I couldn't be sure.

"You ought to just leave the city," she said in a quiet
voice. "You should try and get out."

"I can't. I don't have any money." My voice sounded
muffled in my ears. "Anyway, look at me, *smell* me. They
wouldn't let me on a bus even if I had the money."

"Sure they would." She looked back at me. "You could
get cleaned up somewhere. A public bathroom."

"The cops will be watching all the stations, the airport,
everything."

"They might not notice you." An involuntary smile
flickered quickly across her face. "You do look pretty different."

"I don't have any money," I said again, petulantly, it
seemed to me.

"Can't you get some?"

"No. I got rid of my bank card. Not much in my account anyway."

"How about friends? Don't you know someone who could lend it to you?"

"No," I said, thinking, suddenly, of Sandy.

"You sure?"

"Well, there is one person, a girl I worked with. But she thinks I'm the Finger Mugger, for godsake. She thinks I'm a killer."

"Did she know you pretty good?"

What did she mean by that? I looked at her more closely, trying to read her face. She waited for an answer.

"Well, sort of. We were close for a while." But we weren't, I thought. We weren't, not really.

"Then she'll know you ain't no killer," Delia said.

I wondered. I knew she might be home. Work wouldn't start for hours. So maybe I could find her, maybe I could talk her into giving me some money, maybe I could risk trying to slip out of the city on a bus or a train. At least I wouldn't be alone. The Christmas crowd would hide me. Maybe I could make it. A lot of maybes. But I was ready to try almost anything now.

27

Everywhere we turned there were cops. Usually in cruisers, idling at curbs, inching their slow lethal way through traffic, and sometimes on foot, in pairs, wandering along the sidewalks, writing out tickets. And when we didn't see cops, we saw the kids. They lurked on corners, checking their territory. They gazed out at the passing world from warm doorways. Cops and kids. They patrolled the city, and we had to avoid them all. The rest—the swirling snow, the tourists in for one last look at the Christmas trees on Park Avenue and a final browse through the stores on Fifth Avenue, the weak, hopeful Christmas carols—had nothing to do with us. We passed among them, sure. We could have reached out and touched all those people. But we were as separate from them as time from space, two lines that can never meet no matter how far they travel side by side.

We'd reached the Upper East Side before I stopped feeling sorry for myself. I wasn't going to lie down and die. That's what they wanted me to do, I thought, staring at the ladies in their fur coats and the men in their warm overcoats. They avoided us, of course, casting their eyes in any direction but ours and steering clear of us, crossing the street if they had to rather than meet us in their path. They wanted me to die, and Delia, not because they hated us, but because we weren't quite invisible enough. They still had to smell us, glimpse us from the corners of their averted eyes. They hated us because we were ruining their Christmas.

Sandy lived in a narrow townhouse on East Sixty-eighth Street, between Park and Lexington, a four-story building that had been converted into apartments years ago and was now under rent control. That's why Sandy could afford to live there. Her apartment, on the third floor, looked out over an air shaft and the back windows of another building. Standing on Sixty-eighth Street, there was no way to know if she was home. I stared up into the falling snow, Delia beside me, an art gallery behind us, imitation Impressionists in the window, pink beaches, umbrellas, shadows.

"That's where she lives?" Delia asked.

"Yeah."

She gazed across the street in admiration. "It's a beautiful place."

From her point of view, I realized, it was: a strong, solid nineteenth-century building, brass bars on the front door, healthy plants showing behind the windows. She'd probably never lived in a building like that, nothing even close.

I beat my arms, hopped from foot to foot, no longer able to ignore the cold. "What if she isn't there?"

"Let's find out." Delia switched her guitar case to her other hand and got ready to cross the street.

"Wait a minute."

"What?" She hesitated, glancing back at me.

"I don't know. It makes me nervous, that's all."

"Seeing her?"

"I guess."

"There ain't nothing else you can do."

"I know."

Sandy was up there, if I was lucky, and if I was luckier still she'd help me. Yet I didn't move, I stood paralyzed by the idea of her face when she saw me. I was a bum now, a reject, a derelict, the scum of the earth.

"Come on," Delia said, reaching and tugging at my arm.

I was looking both ways, resolved to cross the street and walk up to the door and ring the buzzer under Sandy's name, when I saw her. She was on the other side of the street, heading toward the door herself, wearing a long scarf wrapped up high around her neck and carrying a Christmas shopping bag, a department store's logo emblazoned among wreaths and angels. She looked delicate, in the snow, trying not to slip on the ice, her head leaning to one side, her eyes on the sidewalk before her.

"That's her," I said.

Delia followed my gaze. "Did she see you?"

"No."

I let her get all the way to the door and start searching for her keys, a raised knee supporting the shopping bag, before crossing the street. She didn't hear us as we came up behind her, our feet quiet in the snow.

"Sandy."

She turned, gasped, started to scream, then changed her mind, a puzzled contradiction working its way across her face. I must have looked more pathetic than frightening. My throat had turned into a heating duct. If I spoke again, nothing would come out except dry air. She stood there, her weight on one foot, the shopping bag pressed protectively to her breasts. Her hair looked different—shorter, I thought. I begged her with my eyes not to panic. I begged her with my eyes to trust me, to believe that I wasn't the psychopathic killer I'd been made out to be.

Her eyes flickered to Delia, to me. She was too scared to move, too scared to scream, and I didn't want to move in case I scared her even more. Her own gaze passed back from confusion to horror and then on to a kind of mixed pity, a moment's concern.

She licked her lips and swallowed. "Gregory?"

I stepped closer. "I'm not going to hurt you, Sandy. I didn't do any of that stuff. You must know that. You have to know that."

She couldn't help but cringe. "What happened to you?"

"It doesn't matter. I just need a little help. Then I'll go away." I felt like I'd done nothing the last three days but walk around asking for people's help. The word was getting to have an irritating ring to it.

"Who's she?" Sandy asked, indicating Delia.

"This is Delia. Delia, Sandy."

They exchanged nods, Sandy cautious, unsure of herself, Delia more curious than anything else, looking hard at Sandy's clothes, the Afghan coat that kept her warm, the new mittens, the shiny leather boots. Neither of us was a very pretty sight. I'm surprised Sandy could stand to look at us directly. She did, though, trying to compose herself.

"Sandy, can we come in for a minute?"

"Come in?" she asked, startled.

"Look, it's me, old fucked-up Gregory, remember? I've never hurt anybody in my life. I'm not going to hurt you. Okay? You've got to believe me, Sandy. There's no one else I can turn to."

"All right, all right." She turned and fumbled with her key, finally getting it in the lock and pushing open the front door.

We stepped into a small vestibule, black-and-white tiles on the floor, unopened magazines and junk mail piled on a small table against the wall. Another glass door led to the stairway. Sandy opened this with steadier fingers, though she was still scared, I could see, worried, I think now, that I really was going to do something awful to her when we got to her room. Every time she looked at me, fear filled her eyes. I also think now she would have screamed had she thought it would have done her any good. But I could have killed her before a scream was out. If I'd been a killer.

She led the way up the creaking wooden steps, passed the closed doorways of other apartments. I remembered climbing those stairs with her the time we'd slept together. Nothing had changed, and that only made everything stranger, more unsettling, as if I were a ghost visiting my former life, no longer part of it, but not free of it yet, either. When she unbolted the door to her apartment and we stepped inside, first Sandy, then me, finally Delia, the sensation only increased, for there was the small bed against the far wall, under the map of Ireland, and there was her bookcase of paperbacks, the cramped kitchen where she had made us coffee and eggs.

She set her shopping bag down on the floor, nervously brushing snow from her head. "What do you want, Gregory?"

It was so warm and pleasant in that room that both Delia and I stared around it in awe. Snow drifted by the windows, obscuring the building across the air shaft and gracing the room with a soft, white light. Plants thrived on the windowsill. Sandy only had two chairs, two canvas-and-metal armchairs, and her coffee table was an old trunk, but to us it all looked close to elegant. I wanted to take a hot bath and then sit in one of those chairs forever, watching the snow through the window.

"Gregory?" Sandy hadn't moved, and was waiting for my answer.

"I need some money," I said.

She did a double take. "Money? How much?"

"Enough to get me out of the city. I can't go to my bank."

She thought this over. "A hundred dollars?"

"Sure, that'd be great, that'd be fine."

"That's all you want?" she asked, amazed.

"That's a lot. A hundred bucks is a lot."

Delia had wandered over to the bed, holding her guitar case, snow melting in puddles from her feet. She scrutinized the map on the wall, Ireland dissected into colorful counties, then the bedspread, a heavy Navaho blanket Sandy had bought driving across the country a few summers ago, then the leather jewelry box she kept on her bedside table, next to the lamp with a frilly shade and the radio alarm clock that glowed numbers in the dark.

"Would you like something?" Sandy asked Delia, more than politeness in her voice, something critical, almost challenging.

Delia started. "Oh, no, no, thanks."

"I mean coffee or anything," Sandy said. "You're cold."

This she said downright condescendingly, as if cold were an idiot's problem.

Delia looked at me, not sure how to respond.

"If you could just give us the money, Sandy, we'll go," I said. "We don't want to bother you. I know this is freaky, I do, and I'm sorry."

"I don't have it," Sandy said. "Not here. I'd have to go to the bank."

She saw me wondering if I could trust her.

"Here." She held out her pocketbook. "You can look if you don't believe me."

"I believe you."

I was starting to tighten up inside, caught in this time warp, dangling halfway between what used to be and now. Looking at Sandy, I could feel nothing but the casual bond of shared intimacy, a few moments spent together that still lived simply because we'd been naked, and yet that was enough to make me want to trust her.

"Where's your bank?" I asked.

"Not far. A couple of blocks."

In the long pause that followed I could hear the snow brushing the windowpanes.

"It would be safer if Delia and I stayed here," I said.

"That's okay." Anxiousness started to animate Sandy's sentences, her gestures. "You stay here and I'll go and get it."

She was too eager, too enthusiastic, too *accepting*. "Sandy, you won't tell anyone, will you?"

"Tell anyone?" She acted as if I'd just asked her if she was a virgin. "Of course not."

"Why not?"

"Because . . . because I trust you," she sputtered, flustered by my question.

"I'll tell you what happened. I saw someone else attack that woman. I was on my way home from work. But she saw me there and thinks I did it. I didn't, but she thinks I did. In fact, all I was trying to do was help her."

Sandy was listening carefully, moving her eyes back and forth between me and Delia.

"I can't prove I didn't do it, so my only choice is to try and escape, get as far away from the city as possible," I said. "I can't hide anymore."

She nodded. "I believe you, Gregory. I'll get the money."

I had to trust her, and I did believe her. Delia was right. Anyone who knew me, except for crazies like Alex and my landlady, Mrs. Woolf, would also have to know that I couldn't possibly be the Finger Mugger. I searched Sandy's eyes for deceit. All I saw was innocence, and a struggling desire to help. Of course she was afraid. That didn't mean she'd turn me in.

"You should have come sooner," she said.

I lied, twisting guilt to my advantage. "I didn't want to involve you."

"No one will ever know," she said, shaking her head. "No one."

"Really?"

She smiled. "Really."

"Okay, then. We'll wait here."

"I'll be right back." She was wrapping her scarf around her neck. "It won't take me long."

She left her shopping bag on the floor and started for the door. I stood back and opened it for her, holding it as she stepped out into the hallway.

"Thank you, Sandy."

She paused and looked at me, confused, I saw, still scared, her hand nervously touching the banister. Then she gave me another quick smile and left, going down the stairs. I followed her progress from the top, leaning over and watching her hand descend along the banister. The front door slammed shut.

Delia was standing by the window, staring into the snow. "Do you trust her?"

"I don't know." I could feel uncertainty eating at my stomach. "I think so."

She turned and faced me, both hands clasped on the handle of her guitar case. Her eyes were sad.

"What's the matter?"

"Nothing." She glanced around the room again. "I like it in here."

To me, the room was slowly losing its charm, the feeling of a friendly sanctuary. It was beginning to feel like a trap. I tried to shake it off, pacing the place, brushing against the familiar objects, the canvas chair, the end of the bed, the bookcase, but it wouldn't go away. It wasn't just standing there that did it, waiting for Sandy to return with either a hundred dollars or an army of cops. It was the room itself, the aura of joylessness between those four walls, the loneliness I saw even in the way the books were arranged on their shelves, neatly and by author. Sandy's life became a palpable presence, and it spoke more of empty nights and long days than any kind of happiness.

"Do you trust her?" I asked Delia.

"No."

"She's a nice lady. A good lady."

Delia said nothing.

"She's loyal," I persisted. "She believed me, don't you think? And if she believed me, then she won't turn me in. I'm sure of it."

"How do you know she believed you?"

"I could tell."

"Oh."

What would I do in Sandy's position, I wondered. Would I believe her? We didn't know each other well enough to be sure of anything. She was scared. Why not call the cops? That's what any law-abiding citizen would do.

"You're right. Let's get out of here. Come on."

28

There was a narrow passageway between the art gallery and an Italian restaurant across the street, a delivery entrance for the restaurant, where we stood huddled in the snow and waited. We hadn't been there more than five minutes when the first cop car silently turned the corner and slid to a stop in front of Sandy's building. In a matter of seconds there were more, four, five, six of them lining the sidewalk, cops coming out with shotguns and pistols and hurrying cautiously toward the front door. They'd arrived without sirens, only their flashing red and blue lights on, pulsing through the snowfall, yet a crowd quickly gathered, New Yorkers' sixth sense for catastrophe serving them well.

I pushed Delia back along the passageway, past the restaurant's kitchen door, until we reached a fence and an untidy stack of empty fruit and wine crates. I climbed up onto the crates, slipping and falling a few times, and pulled myself onto the fence, straddling it sideways, my legs dangling on the other side, an alley. I took Delia's guitar and dropped it as gently as possible onto the alley floor, then reached down, taking her hand, and helped her scrabble up the fence, almost losing my balance and falling. She was heavier than I thought. I jumped down into the alley, next to her guitar, and caught her as she came down after me.

We were both out of breath, but we kept going, east along the alley, north on Third Avenue, trying to lose ourselves among the Christmas shoppers. The snow fell in waves, it had accumulated on the sidewalks now, and we had to hold each other to keep from falling. We didn't pay any attention to where we were going, we just moved as fast as we could, half trotting, half walking, farther north, then west, then south on Fifth Avenue until we found ourselves in front of the Guggenheim, Frank Lloyd Wright's spare modern building staring bleakly across the street at the snow-covered trees in Central Park.

"In here," Delia said, easing me ahead of her.

"They'll never let us," I said, remembering the Greek's reaction to seeing me at the coffee shop.

She insisted. "Come on. It's okay. I go in these places a lot when I get too cold. Painters must look as poor as me." She grinned. "The guards can't tell the difference. They never throw me out."

She was right. They didn't stop us, though the guards, officious in their snappy uniforms, gave us funny looks. We bought our tickets with money Delia had made singing and moved into the main room, up the circular ramp that loops around and around until it reaches the top, where we stopped, panting, and looked down at the crowd of small people clattering noisily across the floor far below us. Neither of us said anything, we were both too busy trying to catch our breath. Anyway, I was afraid that if I did try to say anything, it would come out as tears again. Sandy had called the cops, and I couldn't help but take it personally. Why had she done that? Had we failed so miserably together that she really could think I was the Finger Mugger? Yes, was the answer, and it hurt.

Delia, finally, was the first to speak. "Now what?"

"I don't know."

"We can't stay here."

"I know, I know."

Despite the holiday, the museum wasn't very crowded, which surprised me. Up at our end of the circular ramp, the nearest people were a middle-aged man and wife, dressed well in warm overcoats and soft cashmere scarves, doing their best not to stare at us, and what I guessed to be an art student, a young guy with a messy beard and pale skin who hadn't even noticed us. He stood hunched before a Rothko painting, a large canvas divided into two rough squares, one dark purple, the other black. His jeans had holes in them.

I looked back at Delia. She leaned against the balustrade, her guitar at her side.

"We've got to change clothes," I said. "That's the first thing. Sandy will give the cops our descriptions. They're plenty of people carrying guitars around, so that's no problem. She doesn't know you're a street singer. They won't be looking for that. And she doesn't know I'm supposed to be blind. But we've got to get new coats, and get rid of your hat."

"Where we gonna get new coats?"

I thought of Henry, but didn't want to risk showing myself again to someone I knew. Anyway, he was too far away.

"We'll switch. You take my coat, I take yours. I'll wear your hat, too."

She looked skeptical.

"It's better than nothing."

The middle-aged couple had moved away, down the ramp, and the art student had merely bent closer to the painting, studying the melancholy squares. I quickly pulled off my overcoat and gave it to Delia, then took hers, which she handed me, and slipped it on. It fit me better than mine. She was lost in the wet folds of my overcoat. She gave me her blue knit cap. I could smell her in the wool.

"Now we go out there and beg," I said.

"Beg?" she asked, taken aback.

"That's right. It's the only way we can avoid both the cops and the kids. Being a blind beggar is my best protection. The question is, where? Where should we go begging, Delia?"

She stared at me.

"Times Square," I decided. "Of course. We'll work our way down Fifth Avenue. Lots of guilt on Fifth Avenue, Delia." I took her by the arm and started leading her back down the ramp, past more squares growing increasingly depressed as we descended. "First we'll hit Madison, gob-

ble up a few bucks from all the art lovers, and then we'll
plead our way down Fifth, and then we'll end with a
grand finale in Times Square, catch us a few tourists.
What do you think?"

"I think you're going crazy."

"I think you're right. But I'm a beggar now, and I'm
going to act like one."

I was good at it, too. I assumed pathos naturally, almost
gleefully, blinder than the blind, and my cup slowly
filled. We worked opposite sides of Madison, collecting
coins, a few bills from the chastened, Delia singing well,
as usual, always getting a good crowd to stop and listen.
Watching her through my dark glasses, over the roofs of
moving cars, I felt a little less cold, a little less afraid,
though every time a cop car cruised by I practically threw
up. She was giving me a strength I didn't understand yet,
the strength simply to keep going and not let my giddi-
ness, and the panic it hid, get the upper hand. She helped
me fight the temptation to turn myself in just to make a
point: that my self-pity was justified.

Fifth Avenue was approaching the peak of its
Christmas performance, all the lights brighter, the
Christmas carols louder, the store windows more alluring
than ever, as if, in a final burst of greed, the goods themselves had started to glow. The shoppers, too, seemed
more frenetic, people hurrying in and out of Saks and
Bonwit's laden with presents, their only gaiety what they
carried in their hands, the wrappings and ribbons. I really
had become a beggar, enough to see it all from a beggar's
point of view, and what I saw didn't make me mad, it just
made me feel left out, but more intensely than it had that
morning, walking up Sixth Avenue with John. So many
things to buy in those windows, so many things to make
you warm and comfortable, things to make you feel
pretty, things to delight a child. And yet what use were
they to me, or Delia, or anyone else who couldn't afford to
buy them?

By the time we got to Times Square it was twilight, the
kind of early winter twilight that makes you want to run

indoors to a crackling, forgetful fire. Here the store windows were filled with junk, a thousand radios, a thousand TV's blinking identical, different-sized pictures out into the yellowing dark. It was too cold for the whores. They huddled in twos and threes in crappy hotel doorways, or waited for customers inside Chock Full O' Nuts and Nathan's. I wondered where Henry was, what it was like hustling on Christmas Eve. I wondered if, tonight, business was better or worse than usual. Better, I guessed. Much better. Even sex could be bought, not love, of course, but a vague physical approximation, something to hold on to for twenty minutes. And even women could be sold.

When we got to Macy's, Delia crossed the street and stood near me, her shoulders hunched against the freezing wind that suddenly sprang up, hurtling the snow into our faces. Her fingers were so stiff from the cold that it was hard for her to tune her guitar, but she got it done, blowing on them for warmth, and then started singing again, the guitar case open at her feet. She sang without much energy. She was getting tired. Things, I thought, staring around me at the windows of Macy's. They brimmed with clothes, toys, a vision of the world protected by things. Then, begging, I reached out my hand and asked for a token of the insanity that was killing me, that was killing Delia, and John, and Ezra and Frank and Ralph and McOmbie and Scissors, even the albino, killing all of us, everywhere.

"Please, a little money for a blind man on Christmas Eve."

In response, a woman's voice, to my right, a lilting voice with a heavy accent, blessed me. A bandaged hand stuffed a bill into my hand, and looking up, sharply, I saw Signora di Costini, her other hand holding a shopping bag overflowing with Christmas presents. Our eyes met, and she paused for a second, as if she recognized me.

She shook her head, still smiling, but thinking, trying to remember. "Merry Christmas."

Still she didn't move, but stood there puzzled, reflective in the gathering gloom, the bright lights from Macy's splashing across her face. I felt the same way I'd felt when I first saw her lying on the pavement, unable to act or even think. All I could do was watch her and wait for the knowledge to hit her, for that wide, kind mouth to split into a scream that brought every cop within a mile running. Finally I started to back away, taking small steps, bumping into someone, who simply nudged me aside and kept going. Signora di Costini watched me retreat.

Turning, I took four long strides and walked into Macy's, the sudden clamor of piped-in Christmas carols and the glaring overhead lights making me wince. Just inside the main door, sitting on a raised platform covered with a green feltlike carpet, a real Santa Claus, resplendently jolly in a full white beard and a clean red uniform, bent and lifted the first child in a short line of small children up onto his knee. Parents waited with the children, mostly mothers, some bored and anxious to move on, others enjoying the delight on their kids' faces. The scene was so innocent it brought back my own belief in Santa Claus, the Christmas Eves I'd lie awake in my bedroom in Springfield determined not to fall asleep, determined to hear the tapping of hooves on the roof. Of course, I always fell asleep, and in the morning there'd always be the miracle of presents under the tree, proof of the mysterious fat man's existence.

There were people everywhere, jostled together in front of counters, picking through merchandise, arguing with harried clerks, grabbing children, juggling boxes and bags. I pushed through them, trying to get away from that door, fighting my way toward the escalator I could see across the wide, crowded room. The air smelled heavy, sweet with perfume.

"What're you doing?"

Hearing Delia's voice, I stopped and looked back. She was hurrying after me through the crowd, clasping her guitar case in her arms—she hadn't had time to fasten it shut. In my fear, I'd forgotten about her.

"What're you doing?" she repeated, coming up to my side.

"Same thing I've been doing for the past three days.

Running." I kept my eye on the revolving door for Signora di Costini or any cops. "I saw the woman, the one they think I mugged. I mean she saw me. Out there."

Brushing her wet hair from her eyes, Delia secured the clasps of her guitar case with shaking red hands. Snow covered her shoulders like a short cape. Clasps snapped tight, she looked at me accusingly. "You was gonna leave me."

"No, I was just scared. I wasn't thinking. I had to get away from that woman. I'm sorry."

Many of the shoppers swirling around us faltered and stared, more disgusted than curious, their cheerfulness threatened by our appearance.

"We better keep moving," I said.

We reached the escalator, joined the line standing still yet climbing slowly upward. The woman in front of us, an explosion of yellow hair and earrings the size of Christmas-tree balls, climbed another step higher when she saw us, nearly knocking over the man in front of her. Behind us, the line had separated even more, the nearest person, a paranoid grandmother, five or six steps down and tense with suspicion, her pocketbook clutched firmly to her breasts.

I led Delia off the escalator and down an aisle of lamps, past couches and armchairs, until we came to a smaller room filled with dining room tables and chairs and crockery painted bright, primary colors. Potted plants had been strategically placed to lend the room the proper Upper West Side ambience. We crossed this room, again getting stares, and came out into the midst of a make-believe bedroom, a whole self-contained New England fantasy: brass bed, quilt, maple bedside tables, colonial lamps with fringed shades, round rag rug on the floor. Beyond this display were more, each of a bedroom in a particular style: Mediterranean, modern Swedish, Empire. "Rudolph the Red-Nose Reindeer" sounded from somewhere in the ceiling.

"Let's sit down a minute," I said, collapsing on the edge of the brass bed.

Delia sat down next to me. "What're we gonna do in here?"

"Rest."

I was suddenly, overwhemingly so tired I almost lay back on the soft bed and closed my eyes. It must have been the warmth of the store, the rich, lulling smell of new things, the very same things I'd been railing against out on the street. Now they seemed welcoming, escape from all the pain, all the fear. I rubbed my hand over the quilt.

"You really saw the woman?" Delia asked.

"Yeah." I remembered di Costini's face, the bandaged hand. "I don't think she recognized me, but I didn't want to stick around and find out."

"Excuse me, sir, I'm afraid you can't sit there."

I looked up into the face of a brittle, painted-together woman, a store clerk with a name tag pinned to her demure silk blouse. Gold sparkled on her fingers. She smiled distastefully, not even looking at Delia. "You mustn't sit on the merchandise, sir."

I could feel it coming, the petty rage, but I couldn't do anything to stop it. "How can we decide whether or not we want to buy a bed unless we test it?"

"Buy?" She blinked. "You want to buy a bed?"

"What do you think, dear?" I asked Delia, bouncing a few times. "Too soft?"

"I kinda like it." Delia stroked the quilt. "It's nice."

"Sir, I'm afraid you really will have to leave," the store clerk said, her voice a brave attempt at calm, her eyes glancing frantically around the room for help.

"I think it's too soft," I said. "I think we should try that one over there."

"Sir!"

"Come along, dear." I stood and took Delia's arm. "I'd like to look at the Mediterranean set."

The woman had caught the attention of another clerk, a prissy young man who took one look at us and picked up the phone next to his cash register. My anger had taken over, however, and I kept strolling to the garish Mediterranean bed, bulging curls of dark-stained wood. When I started bouncing on this one, Delia laughed. I'd never seen her laugh before, and it stopped me, stopped me cold, the springs still jouncing a little beneath me. Her smile was open, and her laugh a generous full-throated outburst, genuine amusement lighting up her eyes.

"Sir, if you don't leave, I'll have to call the police." The woman stood back from us, afraid we might attack her, worriedly playing with her name tag. "Do you hear me?"

There was a commotion on the other side of the room, two big men in winter raincoats pushing into the room, greeted by the other clerk and pointed in our direction.

I grabbed Delia's wrist and started running back to the escalator.

"Hold it, you!" one of the men shouted behind us.

Delia got caught up in her guitar, the thing swinging between her legs and nearly tripping her. The two house detectives were only about ten feet away. I took hold of a tall lamp and rolled it toward them, hitting them in the shins. They both yelped, outraged, and one of them, the shortest of the two, fell to his knees. Then Delia and I were running again, past the dining room tables and shelves of gleaming dishes, which I started knocking over as we ran by, bowls and dishes shattering in our wake, the shelves tumbling into the aisles, my anger finally released by simply breaking all those things. Tables, chairs, I hurtled them behind us. I could hear the detectives grunting and swearing as they came after us.

We made it down the crowded escalator, knocking into people, Delia dragging her guitar case after her, and ran toward a side exit near a display of electronic games, winking lights and noisy bleeps. Startled shoppers tried to jump out of our way, dropping presents. I could hear one of the detectives gaining on us, his wheezy, labored breathing less than a few yards back. Passing a full-sized working model of R2-D2, I grabbed the friendly robot and sent it tumbling at the detective's feet. He cursed loudly and stumbled, crashing sideways into another display booth. Shoppers screamed. Then I was outside, on the sidewalk, Delia coming out next to me through the glass door, both of us running south.

29

The sun had disappeared, dropping behind the tall gray buildings, leaving behind only a sickly yellow light. At the same time, the neon lights of Times Square beamed brighter, as if they'd received a sudden, extra bolt of electricity. The snow had stopped, and with dusk had come a colder, faster wind, hitting my face like a hand, Signora di Costini's hand, maybe, thinking I was her mugger, or the thick hands of cops trying to get me to confess. Still running, I took off my dark glasses and tucked my cane under my coat. Now I was just a bum, the dignity of blindness gone.

We stopped running after a few blocks, heading downtown, back toward the tunnel on Eighteenth and Tenth, past the last groups of people bent into the wind and plodding home for Christmas Eve. A dismal world of blackened buildings and warehouses rose to greet us as we left behind the bright lights of Times Square. Here there was nothing—nothing to expect, nothing to want. We passed small stores that had gone bankrupt years ago, others that seemed to cling to life behind their rolled-down grates, pawn shops and machine-part shops that somehow managed to pay the rent each month. Broken glass everywhere, poking up through the snow, caught what light there was, glimmering down from the few streetlights that still worked.

Human shapes, insubstantial as shadows, appeared around us, rising from the slush, drifting out of the alleys, underground people returning home, more and more of them as we got closer to the tunnel entrance. They looked like workers wearily shuffling back to drab brick houses, bodies exhausted, minds good for nothing but beer and oblivion. Smaller shadows separated themselves from the dark buildings. The kids.

They waited for us up ahead, in front of the tunnel en-

trance, which I could now make out at the end of the
street. Already people had started filing in, and I could
hear the albino's strident commands, the orders to turn
over money floating to me through the darkness, carried
by the wind. I could also hear the occasional thud of ax
handle meeting flesh. Delia unconsciously moved closer
to me. I understood her fear. The last place in the world I
wanted to go was back underground. The trouble was I
had no choice. I'd be safer there than on the streets.

Delia and I were less than a block from the tunnel entrance when I saw a familiar lumbering shape up ahead.

"John."

He stopped and waited suspiciously until he saw who it
was, and then he grinned, clutching himself in the cold,
Santa Claus with a nose like a map and eyes like contami-
nated ponds.

"I made some money," he said proudly.

"Where's Ezra?" I asked.

"He gone down already." He swiveled to Delia. "You
know what them kids did? He tell you? About cutting off
people's fingers? Little bastards. I been thinking about it
all fucking day."

He stomped his feet, chasing circulation.

"You haven't told anyone else, have you, John?" I
asked.

"Whadya mean?"

It was hard to stay patient with that man. "Have you
told anybody what I saw those kids do?"

Even in the darkness, I could see him blanch.

"John, goddammit, did you tell anyone?"

"Just Ezra," he admitted, his huge shoulders lifting in a
feeble shrug.

"Shit." I wanted to hit him again. "What if he tells
them?"

"He won't tell nobody."

"I hope not," I said, turning and starting toward the
tunnel.

"He's right." Delia moved next to me, her guitar case
swinging beside her. "Ezra probably didn't even understand what John was talking about."

John trailed along on my left, nodding as Delia spoke. I couldn't really stay mad at him. He meant no harm, and it had been a hard day for him, his first aboveground in ten years.

Suddenly a voice called to us from the surrounding darkness. "*Hey.*"

We all stopped, looking around. Across the street stood a dark brick building, boarded up. Behind us loomed another blank building, shattered windows gaping into the night.

"*Over here.*"

The whispered call came from the old, burnt-out Chevy at the curb. It sat on its empty wheel rims, stripped of all its chrome. I recognized the voice, but couldn't place it. John could, though.

"Scissors," he muttered, loping across the street to the Chevy.

Delia and I hurried after him and leaned into the windowless car. It was Scissors, all right, crouched down on the front seat, a small animal looking up at us with fear in his eyes and a face as swollen and battered as mine had looked in the mirror that afternoon.

"What the fuck you doing in there?" John was trying to open the door. It was stuck. "You wanna get your ass whipped again, boy?"

Scissors wouldn't move, except to hiss, with surprising authority, "Be *quiet.* They'll hear you."

I glanced down the street at the tunnel entrance. I couldn't see any kids.

"What the hell you been doing?" John demanded, still struggling with the door.

I saw a small proud smile cross Scissors's lumpy face. He spoke with a slight lisp, his mouth mashed by the albino's foot. "I found a tunnel they ain't guarding. They don't know about it. There ain't nobody there."

"What you talking about? Get outa there."

"Yeah, a empty tunnel." Once again, the sly smile, this time revealing missing teeth. "A *secret* tunnel."

"John, stop it." I pulled him away from the door. "Shut up for a minute."

I leaned my head into the Chevy as far as I could, close enough to see Scissors's eyes. "Are you lying? Are you making this up?"

He shook his head solemnly. "No."

"There's a tunnel they don't know about?"

"Yeah. I'll show you. I ain't lying." He swallowed, a sudden honest knowingness in his eyes.

I pulled out of the car and looked at Delia. "What tunnel did they send you out this morning?"

"One over by Penn Station."

"Do you know if they're using any others?"

"I don't think so."

That gave me a fifty-fifty chance. I had to take it. It was the first I'd gotten, and I had to take it. Nervousness and excitement fought in my throat.

I took John by the shoulders. "Now listen. I'm going to stay here with Scissors. I'll take care of him. I won't let anything happen to him. You and Delia go in there and give them your money. Whatever they ask. Don't fight them. Here." I took out some of my own earnings and poured them into John's hands. "Give them this, too. Okay. Got it?"

His big, bewildered face leaned above me. "What're you gonna do?"

"Don't worry. Just go. Get back down."

Delia stared at me, about to protest. Then she changed her mind. "Come on, John."

"Don't tell anyone where I am," I said. "Do you understand, John? Don't tell *anyone*. And remember, don't fight the kids."

The three of us looked down the length of street toward the tunnel, where the last shadowy shapes were slipping into the entrance like the tail of a snake disappearing into its hole.

"Hurry," I said.

Looking back at me, then, quickly, into the Chevy, John turned and plodded down the middle of the street, Delia at his side.

The back door of the Chevy was rusted shut, so I had to

slip my way through the window, landing on the seat, a loose spring cutting my cheek. Scissors huddled even tighter to make room for me. I glanced up over the dashboard and saw John and Delia joining the end of the line, a slope-shouldered Santa Claus and a girl carrying a guitar looking in our direction as the line moved forward and they vanished into the tunnel. Then there was only the darkness, little clouds of snow whipped up by the wind. Far away, the endless siren wailed.

I dipped back down, crouched as low as I could, curled on the painful seat, my legs jammed between the steering wheel and my chest. Something poked my side. My cane. I'd forgotten all about it. Awkwardly, wrestling with myself, I pulled it out and lay it across my knees.

Scissors watched me curiously.

"We're going to wait," I told him.

The old car smelled of moldy upholstery.

"Then what?" he asked, his high boy's voice deepening with the effort of whispering.

"Then we're going to follow them."

"Who?"

"Whoever comes out of that tunnel with the money they've just collected. That's the entrance they use, right? We're going to follow them and find out where the hell they come from."

"What if they don't?"

"Don't what?"

"Come out."

"They've got to."

We waited, side by side, while the wind howled through the open windows.

"You really found a tunnel they don't know about?" I suddenly doubted him again.

"I know the tunnels better'n anybody."

"We're screwed if you don't."

"I do." His small voice rose in defiance.

"All right then, we'll follow them, see where they go, and then make our next move. Okay? The tunnel's our backup. That's how we get back down."

"What if they don't come out?"

"Just keep an eye open for them."

The tunnel entrance was a point of light at the end of the street. Nothing moved, except the snow, swept into blasts of feathery whiteness. "Where the hell are they? My legs are going to sleep."

I shifted position, my head back against the seat, giving myself a clear view of the street, the tunnel. I managed to straighten my legs out under the steering wheel, as if I were driving. How many times had someone sat like this when the Chevy was new, not a grubby kid at his side but some young girl, her hair smelling of shampoo?

I turned to Scissors. We couldn't see each other very well. "How're you feeling?"

"Okay," he said, his lisp telling the truth. It hurt him to move his mouth.

"Don't worry, we'll get those bastards." I gazed out at the dark street.

I was talking tough but I was scared, and I'm sure Scissors could feel it in our cold, intimate quarters, fear communicated in the air, by molecules, wavelengths brain to brain. I was scared that Scissors had invented this unknown tunnel. I was scared of what would happen when the kids came out and we followed them. *If* they came out. They owned the night, even though I too had lived there so long, wandering the streets, following people. Compared to them, I was an amateur.

Scissors produced the butt of a cigarette and lit it, cupping his hands over the flame so it wouldn't show outside. The brief fire flared, and for the first time I saw how swollen and disfigured his face really was—a bruised cauliflower.

"Put that out."

"They can't see."

"*Put it out.*"

Reluctantly, he ground the cigarette to ash on the side of the door.

"You're too young to smoke anyway."

"Fuck you. I ain't too young for nothing."

He was probably right. He was certainly older than I'd

been at that age, maybe older than I'd ever be, though I was catching up fast.

"Look," Scissors whispered.

Through the splintered, shattered windshield, I saw three figures emerging from the tunnel. One of them was carrying what looked like a small suitcase, or a briefcase. They stood huddled together for a second, tightening their collars. Cold air plumed from their mouths. I couldn't be sure, but I thought one of the kids, the one carrying the briefcase, was the albino. The three kids talked among themselves, shuffling their feet in the cold.

"What're they waiting for?" Scissors asked.

"Shh."

He was right, though. They didn't seem in any hurry to move. The only light at that end of the street came from within the tunnel, a lackluster patch of yellow that didn't stretch three feet beyond the entrance. Only when the kid holding the briefcase turned and stepped back to the tunnel, looking in, was I sure it was the albino. The other two kids moved a little farther out into the night, staring about them, up at the dark buildings, down the silent street toward us.

"For Christsake don't move," I whispered.

"I ain't moving."

There was something strange going on, some guarded ritual I didn't understand. I followed their gazes up to the buildings. Nothing moved.

Suddenly the albino stepped back and out of the entrance trooped a double line of kids, some twenty of them marching in order. They split into two groups as they exited, one line moving to the left, the other to the right, forming a corridor through which the albino now strode, swinging the briefcase at his side. The other two kids who had come out with him moved on ahead, at least thirty feet in front, like scouts. I heard the albino give an order, and then the double line of kids started forward, behind the advance kids, the albino leading the group but securely protected within its ranks. Feet crunched lightly on the snow.

The silent army disappeared.

"Okay. Let's go."

I had to slide out the window, head first, walking my-self all the way out on my hands. Scissors crawled out be-hind me, dropping noiselessly to the ground.

"Ready?"

He nodded, excited.

30

The wind was like an extra coat of ice, slipping around us as soon as we reached the corner. There didn't seem to be any more kids inside the tunnel entrance, but we moved fast, just in case. Up ahead, I could make out the kids marching into the darkness. In couples, a few had left the main group and now walked on either side of the street, covering the flanks, point men.

Keeping a good distance back, we followed them three or four blocks downtown, then west, past more ware-houses. Soon we were under the West Side Highway, dodging from pillar to pillar, the roar of cars and trucks above us vibrating down to our feet. Scissors let me lead the way. I knew just how far back to hang, just how close to get, I knew how to use the cover of the trash cans and broken-down cars that littered the underside of the high-way. I was in my element now.

Above us, cars streamed to New Jersey and Long Is-land. No one in those cars knew we were here, though they might have suspected that rats and killers crawled through the destroyed city they could see through their windows. I saw loading cranes and ship berths on our right, the dark Hudson, and lights blinking across the water. Broken glass, bottles tossed away as fast as they were emptied, crackled and clinked under our feet. Up ahead, the kids moved methodically, scouts in front, flank-ers at the ready. A tugboat hooted on the river. Chain-link fences topped by barbed wire surrounded empty parking lots, blackboards in reverse, tire tracks scrawled in criss-crossing curlicues across the surface of snow. Here and there, lights wearing little white caps cast funnels of light from the corners of buildings. Silent trucks, parked for the night, looked like sleeping animals. Scissors plodded quietly at my side, and I suddenly realized how much he resembled John. He had the same dark, thinking eyes, the same heavy jaw.

The kids stopped. Scissors and I crouched and waited while they regrouped, the thunder of wheels reverberating down the concrete column next to us. I couldn't see what they were doing.

"We've got to get closer," I whispered into Scissors's ear.

He nodded, earnestly, but when we looked back they were gone. All of them. There was just an open space where they had stood, a desolate stretch of road, a bleak, yellow light, and the snow. Except for the traffic rumbling above us, there wasn't a sound in the night. Even the wind stopped for a moment. I didn't move, and I held Scissors down, firmly.

"We're gonna lose them," the boy complained.

I kept staring at the spot where they had been, as if I expected the hallucination to end and for them to reappear. "Something's wrong."

Maybe they had somehow seen us and were now waiting up around the next corner, waiting with their ax handles, hidden in the shadows. Their disappearance had been so quick, so efficient. The street had the uneasy tension, the false peacefulness, of a battlefield before a battle. Looking behind us, I saw another street, parallel to the one they must have taken.

I grabbed Scissors. "This way. Stay low."

We scurried, doubled over, across to the next concrete column. I paused here, because there was nothing left between us and the street corner, nothing but open space brightened by a glowing light high on one of the buildings. We'd have to cross it, exposed.

"Ready?"

Scissors nodded.

"Now."

We ran, not bothering to crouch. I could hear his lighter footsteps behind me, my own fear racing with me. We both slipped a few times on the snow, skidding sideways, and I was out of breath halfway across, a cramp tightening in my gut. Finally we made it, flinging ourselves into the street and pressing back flat against the first building we reached. I closed my eyes and worked on controlling my breathing.

The street was empty. Snow ran like a runway into the darkness. We started along the sidewalk, keeping close to the buildings, our footsteps quiet on the snow. I should have been cold but fear kept me warm. Behind us, cars and trucks whooshed by on the elevated highway. I couldn't get rid of the feeling that we were being watched. I glanced uneasily at the buildings. They were dark, silent. Nothing moved, except the wind, and then a small black shape, a shadow within the shadows, on the roof of the building across from us.

I stopped, Scissors bumping into me. He didn't say anything. He stood next to me, motionless, not even breathing, as we saw, or half saw, more dark shapes scurrying along the rooftops like plump, soundless rats. But they weren't rats. They were human figures, crouched low. At the same time, I looked down the length of the street toward the next streetlight and saw the kids, all twenty of them, marching silently across the intersection, the albino's white hair clearly visible in their midst, small warriors patrolling the night, ax handles, their lances, raised at their sides.

I didn't have time to be confused. All along the far side of the street, dark figures were hurrying down the fire escapes on the fronts of the buildings. I could hear harsh scraping noises, a rattle and creak as the last lengths of fire escape were lowered and the figures dropped onto the sidewalk. Two of the figures suddenly appeared from an empty doorway across from us, two tall figures in long leather coats and leather boots. Their heads were abnormally large, weirdly shaped, and for a second I wasn't even sure they were really human. Then they started toward us, and I realized they were wearing Nazi helmets.

I ran back toward the West Side Highway, Scissors in front of me. The clump of boots chased us. I was tackled, fell down rolling onto my side and kicking, screaming, I think, though what I remember hearing is the sound of one army attacking another, the helmeted gang pouncing on the albino's gang, the crack of clubs and bones breaking. I heard the kids crying, squealing, and almost felt sorry for them. But a booted toe was bruising my balls, and my own scream took over, drowning out everything else. One of the guys went for my face, and I was still gurgling in pain, when there was a brief, bright crash and the Nazi above me crumpled, clutching his head.

The other one tightened his grasp on my ankles, at the same time struggling to get me with a knife. The blade cut my leg, I felt the steel and then the warm sting, but out of some atavistic memory, a thousand movies and daydreams of revenge, I found the skills to fight him, reaching down and poking at his eyes with my fingers, grabbing the hand that held the knife and beating it against the snow-covered pavement. Before I knew it I was up, free of his grasp, and kicking him as hard as I could, as hard as the albino had kicked Scissors. It was his turn to scream. Not just because I'd kicked him, but because Scissors, who stood over the other fallen Nazi with a brick in his hand, now stooped and picked up the knife and without a second's hesitation drove it straight into my attacker's chest.

There came a startled shriek. The helmet fell from his head and rolled clattering across the sidewalk.

"Drop it." I shook Scissors's hand. "Drop it."

The knife fell too, and then we were running, under the shelter of the West Side Highway, north. The night had exploded.

31

Somehow we made it all the way to Fifty-eighth and Fifth. I don't remember how we got there. I don't remember anything but the pain in my leg, repeating itself over and over again. It wasn't a deep cut, though. I managed to stop the bleeding by ripping off a piece of my shirt and tying it around my leg.

And now here was the Plaza, brilliant in the winter night, the windows lighted, people moving comfortably up and down the wide stone steps. The whole building seemed to smile, placid and unconcerned. I kept ending up here. The place taunted me with its luxurious façade, its vision of a safe and happy world. Some college kids in evening dress and white scarves playfully chased each other around the fountain, laughing and stumbling. Don't you know what's going on? I wanted to shout. Don't you see what's happening?

A police cruiser slid by in the slush. I lowered my face. Scissors didn't flinch. I don't think he saw it. He was already halfway across the street before I caught up with him.

He knows what he's doing, I told myself. I trusted him the way you trust someone you've known a long time. His short, exhausted stride was too purposeful, too determined to lead us anywhere but to safety. He no longer had that eager, excited gleam in his eyes. He was shaken, scared, withdrawn into his small, tight body. He'd just stabbed a man, maybe killed him—even he wasn't used to that. I wanted to say something, console him, thank him for saving my ass once again, but his silent demand for privacy was too strong, so I kept my mouth shut and followed him west on Fifty-ninth Street, through the line of waiting taxis and then along the side of the Plaza, past the

Oak Room entrance, more intimations of mahogany-paneled paradise leaking out high, warm windows.

Scissors stopped, staring at the hotel. There was nothing there but a brass water main, bent like a thumb, and what looked like a large brass plaque.

"What're you doing?"

Scissors didn't answer me. Instead, he looked around, up and down the street. An elderly couple, sleek, European, floated past us, turned to each other in intimacy, ignoring us.

"Scissors, we can't just stand here. We've got to get to that tunnel."

He looked at me, sideways, and smiled, not the old, impish smile, but a smile. "We're here."

"What do you mean?"

Once again he checked the sidewalk. It was clear in both directions. Quickly, he stooped, grabbing the edge of the brass plaque and pulling. It swung away from the wall, a small door.

"This is it?"

Scissors nodded.

I looked up at the Plaza windows, the warm lights glowing within, then down at Scissors scrabbling through the door, his pale face disappearing into darkness.

"Hurry," he whispered.

I had to squeeze to make it, and then I was underground, on a path leading downward through the heart of the city, a secret, hidden maze of water pipes and furnaces and electrical wires supporting the elegance above. Bare lights ebbed on the damp walls, and the shadow of a huge elevator shaft lay across the concrete floor like the shadow of a slumbering guardian. In the corners, forgotten leather suitcases and heavy steamer trunks stood stacked and dressed in dust and cobwebs, dreaming of ocean liners.

Scissors scrambled back behind the furnaces to a long empty room, past fuse boxes and closets to a door marked MAINTENANCE. Beyond it, of course, stretched a steam tunnel, the familiar dry warmth and flat, dusty air, the dim bulbs glowing weakly at fifty-foot intervals, the clanking and hissing, as if someone, maybe the slumbering guardian, were protesting our entry.

Scissors had marked the turns we had to make with yellow chalk, little slashes, clues in a treasure hunt. What was the treasure? The underground people, bag ladies and beggars? The albino? Delia? Following the sound of Scissors's softly slapping sneakers, my skull tightening, the air squeaking in my lungs, I felt the weight of the city as if it were my own failure pushing down on me. Gone the brief exhilaration of solving a problem. Gone the fear that had made our trip from Tenth Avenue to Fifty-ninth Street a gray blur whistling through my eyes, a tormenting inner vision of endless violence and survival in the streets. Now there was just the weight, the failure. I was defeated. Nothing left but the tunnels, unfolding before us.

This pointless despair was the worst, the weight that got heavier and heavier as we sank lower and lower through more tunnels, along wobbling catwalks, down slippery metal ladders, until finally, when Scissors stopped, I could barely breathe. If I'd known how, I would have gotten down on my knees and prayed, because I really didn't believe I could save myself. I gasped for air, for hope, anything, even the brief faith I'd felt being a beggar, the surrendering comfort of accepting fate. Instead of climbing out, I was falling deeper. I wasn't ever going to get out.

Scissors watched me nervously, his mangled face attentive, curious—no, sympathetic, for he laid his small, grubby hand on mine.

"You sick?" he asked.

"No. I'm not sick. Just tired. I'll be all right."

"We go through there." His solemn eyes rose to one of the steam pipes.

Unlike the others, it crossed the tunnel laterally, disappearing into the tiled wall. Maybe a foot of dark air surrounded the wide pipe, a hole small enough to give Tinkerbell claustrophobia. Scissors nimbly scrambled up onto the pipe and straddled the thing, hugging it.

"Like this." He looked down at me. "Okay?"

He started inching his way along the pipe, his head going into the wall, then his shoulders, his legs. By the time I'd climbed up I could only see his sneakers, tucked around the sides of the pipe. I crawled in, my shoulders bumping the top of the hole, my knees scraping the con)crete. Pushing my cheek against the pipe, hugging and squeezing, I pulled my way into the close darkness. It was hard to breathe, and a couple of times I almost got stuck, but fear kept me pulling with my arms and pushing with the pressure of my knees until I dropped out into the dead-end tunnel near Delia's lean-to. In fact, that's the first thing I saw, her plaid blanket hanging in the doorway, and a light inside, her kerosene lamp and its jittery shadows. The thought of her there to welcome me made me feel a little better.

"You go find John," I said to Scissors. "Make sure he's all right."

He stared at me for a second, deciding something, then took off down the tunnel, his footsteps echoing softly as he disappeared toward the other lean-tos.

I limped to Delia's shack. My leg hurt, a vague throb where I'd been stabbed.

"Delia?"

"Who is it?" She sounded frightened.

"Me. Gregory."

She drew back the blanket, a strange look on her face, half the indifferent defiance of her earlier self, half a new friendliness. But when she saw my wound, the blood, she quickly pulled me inside and sat me down on her mattress.

"What happened?"

I told her about following the albino, and about the older kids in helmets slithering down the buildings. She cleaned my wound, ripping the hole in my jeans wider and washing away the dirt and dried blood with a piece of cloth and water from her Coke bottle. Her pale strong hands, marbled with blue veins, worked easily, efficiently, the same way she played her guitar. When she was finished, she wrapped another rag around my leg and tied it off. I poured myself a glass of water and drank it all. She moved onto the mattress, sitting next to me.

"The kids were looking for you," she said.

"What for?"

"I don't know. They didn't say."

That scared me. Had they somehow learned who I really was? I couldn't figure out how, unless John had told them, or Ezra, now that he knew. Delia rubbed her tired eyes and moistened her dry, chapped lips. I remembered her laughing in Macy's. That seemed so long ago. I wondered again how she could take it, living down here in the tunnels.

"Delia, I want to thank you, for helping me today."

Startled, she blushed. "Too bad it didn't do no good."

"You blush very easily, you know that?"

Her face grew even redder, and flustered. "What do you mean?"

"Nothing. I'm sorry, just teasing. You seem embarrassed to have helped me."

She didn't know what to say. Silence stretched between us, broken only by the sound of our breathing and the rattling steam pipes out in the tunnel. I guessed that she had spent so many years defending herself that the idea of helping someone made her feel too vulnerable to be comfortable. Then it occurred to me, a slow-witted revelation, that she liked me, that she had helped me simply because she had wanted to, and that she had blushed because she thought I knew it.

She suddenly looked toward the tunnel and said, "What's that?"

"What?"

"That. Listen."

Then I heard it, too, a low murmuring sound that seemed to grow in strength without getting louder. It reminded me of the slow, heavy-footed gathering of people for church. Delia was already up and moving toward the plaid blanket. I left the mattress and followed her.

Looking out, I could just see the shapes of people leaving their lean-tos and newspaper beds and shuffling in the direction of the station like a ghostly funeral procession. No one spoke, there wasn't a sound except for the scraping of their feet on the concrete floor.

"Where're they going?" Delia wondered aloud.

"I'll see." I edged her back into her shack. "You stay here."

"Why should I stay here? I wanna see for myself. You don't have to protect me, Gregory."

It was the first time she had used my name, and it made me happy, as if she'd said something intimate.

32

The station was packed, underground people crowded together around the fountain, most of them sitting on the floor, all of them staring up at Frank, the old blind man. He had perched himself on the edge of the fountain, his back to the yellow subway car. The idiot Ralph crouched next to him, looking worried, as usual. More people limped in through the main entrance, as if a secret message had somehow been sent through the tunnels, commanding them there. They joined everyone else in a large semicircle around the fountain, the implicit power of their numbers intimidating the kids on guard, I guess. The few that I could see had stepped back into the shadows along the walls.

"The boy was sixteen years old." Frank started to speak, his quiet voice filling the station. "He had to take care of his younger brother, on account of the fact that their mother and father was both killed that spring. Murdered, you understand. Killed dead and cold for no reason, just that they was out walking along the street at the wrong time. He was only sixteen, and taking care of his brother. He didn't want to go to no orphanage."

Frank's blank eyes stared out over the raised faces. I

saw McOmbie, still bruised, chin resting on his closed fists. An old woman's puckered red face rose out from the crowd for a moment, then disappeared as she leaned back on her haunches, hidden by someone else's shoulder. Closer, I saw John and Scissors, squatting together near the fountain, listening attentively.

"It was December," Frank went on. "And it was cold, so cold they spent most of their time in the picture palaces." He smiled to himself. "They really loved them pictures. For a dime you could spend the whole day and whole night in a warm place."

They all listened, and breathed in unison, a soundless vibration that spread from wounded face to wounded face, just as the message to gather had spread through the tunnels. They had defied the kids by coming here, by gathering together in the first place, and now they defied them even more with this weird feeling of restfulness, this quiver I responded to with a slight, hot blush. I could feel it in myself, and only later realized it was the first stirring of rebellion.

Frank's face was vivid in the darkness behind him, the high walls and rafters of pipes. "There was a hill in those days. May still be there, for all I know. Anyway, this hill was next to the graveyard. Every Saturday, around Christmas, when there was snow on the ground, they'd go over to that hill for sliding. Cardboard boxes and the tops of trash cans worked the best. On those, they could slide all the way to Clinton Avenue."

Again, Frank paused. He swallowed and seemed to wait for something, as if he were listening to the inside of his head, another voice telling him what to say.

"On December the twelfth, nineteen hundred and thirty-seven, sliding down the hill on a flattened-out cardboard box from Sears, his younger brother got up such a good speed that he couldn't stop. He went right onto Clinton Avenue, where he was killed by a truck. The truck was carrying vegetables to New Jersey. It weren't the driver's fault. It was an accident. Fate. It was what happened. Things like this get worked out someplace else first. Then you come walking along and it happens. Nothing personal."

Frank lowered his face for a second. "But the older brother didn't understand." Tapping his temple, he tried to smile. "He was kinda stupid. So he thought it was his fault. He felt bad. He cried. He almost stepped out in front of another truck to make things even. He'd failed, you see. He couldn't take care of his own flesh and blood. He didn't think he shoulda been allowed to live, and he punished himself, he didn't eat and he didn't sleep, he just sat in the cold, he didn't even try to stay warm, or get himself another coat. He was *stupid.*" Frank hesitated for emphasis. "And you know why? You know why he was stupid? Because he thought it happened to *him.* He thought *he* was dead, when in fact it was his little brother that was dead. He took it *personal.* Well, shit, it weren't personal. It was an *accident.*"

Frank took a deep breath. "But then you know what happened? He got hungry. His empty stomach told him he needed a job. He didn't really want to die, you see. That's the whole point. When he got hungry enough, he become his hunger. He was just a stomach needing something in it. So he got a job. He got a job working for Mr. Harold Barker, and his job was cleaning out the subway cars over at Grand Central. He worked at night, and he liked that, the whole city being asleep and him up, moving through them empty cars, sweeping up cigarette butts and candy wrappers. He didn't change his mind about his killing his brother. He just stopped thinking about it. He swept, and he cleaned the seats, and he cleaned the toilets, his face down in the smell of shit, and he didn't think. Like pure air. He wasn't there. So he couldn't change his mind until he started thinking, and he couldn't start thinking until he thought he was there. And that didn't happen until he met the girl. *Her* job was to clean all the ladies' rooms. She worked nights, too, you see. That's how they met. She put out her Thermos bottle and said, 'Would you like some coffee?' Just like that. And he blinked, you know, and looked at the Thermos, and suddenly he smelled the coffee, it went through him and woke him up, I guess, because he said, 'Thank you,' took the coffee, and drank some, and looked at her, and his hand holding the Thermos, and then he started talking to her, asking her where she come from and all that, and by the time it was morning and he was walking home—"

"*Who called everybody together?*"

It was the albino, hovering in the entrance, his face twisted with frightened rage, a fresh gash on his cheek.

Frank just kept right on talking. "He was walking home and he'd never felt so *alive.*"

The albino started wading through the sitting bums, a phalanx of kids behind him. He'd brought most of his army back down. They quickly circled us, ax handles and pool sticks in hand, filing out of the tunnel and taking up positions around the station walls. They, too, had wounds from their recent brawl: welts, ugly bruises, open cuts. Delia gripped my arm, hard. I was pretty numb, stupid with Frank's voice, stupid with a dreaminess that had settled over me, invaded me, released me, until the adrenalin started cutting through it, racing from nerve to nerve, and I woke up, like the man in Frank's story. Someone—the Viking, not far behind his leader, eager to please—had gone to get the albino. The threat, implicit until now, had become real. We were gathered, together, one. We had challenged the albino's authority, the pink greedy eyes. Frank had thrown down the gauntlet.

"He couldn't explain it to himself," the blind man continued. "He didn't know what he was feeling, he just knew it was different."

The albino had reached Frank. He slapped him across the face. "Shut up! I said shut up!"

Someone screamed. Delia's fingers tightened on my arm. John rose to his feet, roaring, and started toward the albino. Two kids hit him, and his head jerked back, blood running from his nose and a cut above his eye. He reeled. Scissors steadied him and lowered the huge man down next to him on the tile floor. More kids pushed through, swinging their ax handles, forcing us away from the fountain. I couldn't do anything. I stood there helplessly, jostled by rancid bodies.

Ralph had jumped, terrified, when the albino slapped Frank. Now the deaf-mute was trying to drag the old man away, tugging at his arm, but Frank wouldn't budge, and he still wouldn't stop talking. "When he slept he dreamed of her lips. He dreamed of kissing them."

The albino stared at Frank in disbelief, his white, mottled skin reddening as anger filled his cheeks, his pale pink eyes.

"I said shut up!" he sputtered, slamming Frank's face, with his fist this time.

The old man's head recoiled, like a rubber ball, but he kept talking. "He took her to Coney Island. He showed her the boardwalk."

"*Shut up!*"

Again, the fist. Blood dribbled from Frank's mouth.

"They had their picture taken." He spoke slowly, thickly, a painful breath between each word.

Ralph gave up pulling at Frank and tried to protect him with his body. The albino easily swatted him aside, then hissed into Frank's face. "You gonna shut up?"

The kids had formed a barricade between us and the fountain.

"No one breaks the rules!" the albino screeched into Frank's unblinking eyes. "*No one.* You understand me?"

He was acting the street tough, the boy with knuckles, daring Frank to defy him again, sneaking a glance around the station at the other kids and throwing them a quick, coy smirk. I could feel the tension growing, the test of wills intensifying, and I finally understood why Frank had once more started telling stories, and why, now, he wouldn't stop. He was taking a stand. He was doing what he thought he had to do. He turned his bloody face to me, searching me with his blind eyes. He couldn't possibly see me, yet, as before, I had the feeling that he did.

"We went for rides on the roller coaster, even though it scared me," Frank said, his voice so low I could barely hear him, his eyes still staring at me. In the confusion, in his befuddlement, in the agonized chaos of his old head, he'd changed the story to the first person. Or—and this is something I've often wondered since—was he telling us a story about himself? "We ate ice cream, just like little kids. We *was* little kids."

The balance had shifted, power had slipped to Frank's side, and the albino knew it. Fighting panic, he looked around for something to hit Frank with, his eyes coming to rest on McOmbie's Bunsen burner near the edge of the platform, a battered coffee pot on top.

"Where was I?" Frank asked haltingly. "Oh, yeah. Ice cream. We was eating ice cream at Coney Island. But it's the picture I remember best, because that's all I had of her after we was separated, that's what I carried with me and what I looked at and what I remembered her by—"

The albino took three long strides to the Bunsen burner, kicked off the coffee pot, sent it clattering across the tiles, spilling black liquid.

"—and later it was something I lost, another accident, I just lost my jacket in some whorehouse in France and with it I lost my wallet and I lost the picture."

Unscrewing the cap, the albino carried the Bunsen burner back to Frank and started shaking the kerosene out onto the old man's head, his shoulders, dousing him until he was a dark stain of kerosene. I finally realized what the albino was going to do. I didn't really believe it, but I knew it, and so I struggled through the bodies around me and tried to charge, but the other kids got me first, whacking me with their ax handles and shoving me back. I could hear Delia behind me, screaming, "*No!*"

Frank sniffed, smelling the kerosene, but he didn't stop talking. "And so I lost a thing. That's all it was, a thing. I shouldn't of needed it, but I did, even though it was only . . ." He felt the air with his fingertips. "A thing."

The albino pulled a pack of matches from his pocket. Once again, I tried to get to him, but I couldn't. He lit one of the matches, the flame rushing up, dropping to a steady flicker, before he tossed it, lightly, carelessly, the way you might toss a cigarette out a car window, onto Frank's head. The hair caught first, immediately flaring into a bright orange flame which spread like running fire over Frank's face, over his shoulders, down the front of his shirt and pants. In a second, he was a torch.

Everyone was screaming now, even some of the kids, especially the younger ones—even they were horrified. I flailed at them, trying to get to Frank and smother the flames. Scissors and John hit at the kids, flinching and falling back when the clubs hit their heads. Ralph's smooth idiot face had changed completely, horror turned it to rubber, pulled at it and stretched it into a grotesque mask. I saw one of the kids drop his ax handle and start to cry, forgetting his duties, forgetting that he was supposed to enjoy such things.

The albino had jumped back from the flaming body and now stood watching, calmly, his arms crossed, as Frank slapped at himself, trying to beat out the flames. Frank started screaming when the pain hit him, when the flames had eaten through his clothes and reached his skin. I could smell him burning. The stench of burning flesh seeped into my nostrils, making me gag. Frank fell from the fountain onto the floor, rolling, kicking at the flames, but he couldn't fight them, they'd already merged with his skin, his nose burning, his lips burning, his fingers burning. The pitch of his scream rose higher and higher, and then, suddenly, stopped.

His body was still, lying on the floor. The flames crackled and hissed. They burned and they burned. It takes a long time to burn through a human being. First there's the skin, and then the muscle, the veins and blood spitting like burning grease, and then there's the bone. The fire finally ran out of fuel and began to falter. Frank's shape remained intact, sculptured ash, a black, almost featureless statue of a man caught by surprise, lying on the floor, his knees bent, his arms hugging his legs, his head down. The flamed flickered, simmering. Smoke puffed up from the motionless corpse.

I didn't have much time to react, because the next thing I knew Ezra was pointing his finger at me and screeching, "That's h-h-him! He's the one!"

I hadn't noticed him before. He was standing across from me. Most of the screaming had died, with the flames, into a muted whimpering. We stared at each other over the smoking body on the floor. The albino had retreated a bit. Even he, I think, was amazed by what he'd done. He tried to prod his expression into its customary sneer, but he couldn't quite do it. Now he raised his cold eyes from what was left of Frank to me. Ralph hovered uncertainly near the blackened corpse, his head cocked to one side. He didn't seem to understand that the blind man was dead. Like a faithful dog, he sat down next to the still smoking body and waited for Frank to rise.

"H-h-he's the one!" Ezra was practically jumping up and down in deranged excitement, jabbing his scabby finger in my direction. "It's him! It's him!"

The albino's gaze held me. We were both dazed. Slowly, like a memory, my mind began to work again, and I remembered that John had told Ezra what I knew about the albino, and that Delia had said the kids were looking for me earlier, and I realized that Ezra must have gone straight to the albino with his priceless information, as eager to please as the Viking. This was a leisurely series of connections. I was too stunned to understand that my life was at stake. I simply stared back at the albino, wondering if it was Ezra who had shown him how to get down there in the first place. That would explain Ezra's getting Delia's begging spot.

Casually, like a man ordering food at a restaurant, the albino turned and said to the other kids, "Get him."

Someone grabbed me and started pulling. It was Delia. At the same time, I became completely lucid. I was running before I knew it, pushing through bodies back toward the entrance into the subway station. I heard a commotion behind me, John's voice calling, "Help him!" Glancing over my shoulder, I saw the big man lift two kids off their feet and fling them against the wall. Delia was beside me, and when we cleared the throng and saw three kids waiting anxiously for us at the tunnel entrance she put her head down and charged. So did some others, howling their rage. I got one kid with my fist. Another kid caught me across the shoulder with a pool stick. Panic and rage had given me strength. I grabbed the stick from his hand and belted him, then turned and let the third kid have it. He crumpled, his ax handle, raised above Delia's head, slipping from his fingers and falling to the floor. A gun went off in the station. I could hear John bellowing, the scramble of running feet.

Delia and I squeezed into the steam tunnel that led to her shack, running as fast as we could. I was thinking now. It only took us a few minutes to reach her place, but by the time we got there I knew what I had to do. I don't know why, but I realized, at that moment, pulling back Delia's plaid blanket and hurrying into her room, that I really did have to get rid of the albino for her as well as for myself, for McOmbie and John and Scissors and Ralph, for Frank dead back there in the station. I had to help them, if I could. They'd been hurt by so many people so many times that the pain had become something inevitable, something they had no control over, a brute merciless force that had picked them out to flatten over and over again, until finally they were like those moving targets in shooting arcades, thin, dented, chipped, flat tin people pitching backward and then springing macabrely upright, ready to continue their journey before the bullets.

I opened Delia's guitar case and lifted out her guitar, laying it on her homemade mattress.

"What're you doing?" she asked, panting.

"I'm going to do the same thing I tried to do before." I fastened the clasps on her guitar case. "Only this time it's going to work."

I wasn't at all sure that was true, but I said it anyway.

"You're gonna follow them?"

"Yes."

"And call the cops?"

"In one hour you get to McOmbie and tell him to give the kids his Bible."

"Bible?"

I took her by the shoulders. "Just listen. McOmbie has

a Bible he found, with gold on it. He'll know what I'm talking about. He's got to let the kids find it. Okay? Don't give it to them, make them think they found it. And if he can, let it be that redheaded kid who gets it. You know the one I mean?"

She nodded.

"Better make it an hour and a half," I said. "You got it?"

If I'd known that was the last time I'd see her, I might have said more. I would at least have thanked her. Voices filtered up the tunnel outside, voices and footsteps. I picked up her guitar case and drew back the plaid blanket. I didn't even have time to look back at her. Crouching, I ran to the steam pipe I had crawled out on with Scissors. I reached up, balancing the guitar case on top, and then hauled myself up next to it, pushing it ahead of me into the hole around the pipe and sliding in after it just as the kids reached Delia's shack below me. I hoped they wouldn't hurt her. I hoped to God they wouldn't hurt her.

33

This Side of Paradise—the pink neon sign blinked demurely, a tasteful Deco scroll writing itself in the dark, snowless air. I stood across the street, Delia's empty guitar case in my left hand, and watched a taxi stop and deposit three boisterous drunks onto the sidewalk, young men in Abercrombie overcoats who let out some kind of football yell before shoving each other through the door and into Alex's club. They were the first people I'd seen since leaving the tunnels. All the way over from the Plaza, I'd seen nothing but empty streets and closed stores. I began to wonder if there had been a war while I was underground. Maybe the whole city was deserted now, the millions burned to little evaporating crisps by neutron bombs. It was like walking through a ghost town. Then I remembered. It was Christmas.

I shifted Delia's guitar case to my other hand and shoved my cold hand into my pocket, wishing I had a cigarette. The glowing red ash would have cheered me. Lighting a cigarette and contemplating cancer would have given me something to do. I hadn't let myself think yet about what I was going to do. I'd climbed up through the tunnels, following Scissors's yellow chalk marks, I'd slipped out the brass door in the side of the Plaza and walked the six blocks to Alex's seeing nothing, as if I were simply acting out somebody else's script, a movie written just for me, a harmless part I'd memorized with great detachment.

But once I got there, dread had returned, larger and larger in my throat, and all I could do was stand in the shadows staring across the street at Alex's inane pink sign, wishing I didn't have to go in there. But I did. I needed a weapon. I wasn't going to let what happened to Frank happen to me. I knew now what I'd tried hard before to convince myself wasn't true. Those weren't *kids* down there. They were brutal and remorseless, especially the albino. I had to meet them on their own terms, and their terms were as grotesquely demanding as any I'd ever encountered.

It was bad enough that my plan was so fragile. I had to get back to the Chevy before McOmbie gave the Bible to the Viking. I had to hope that the Viking's desire to please the albino was greater than his greed, and that he'd take the Bible straight to him instead of waiting until the next day or, even worse, keeping it for himself. I also had to hope that McOmbie would be able to bring himself to part with his precious treasure, his hoarded secret. He'd already lost his necklace. Would he be able to give away the rest? No, I couldn't take more chances than that. I was ready to fight, and I wasn't going to do it unarmed. I'd carry the gun in the guitar case.

A black limousine nosed slowly up Fifty-fourth, pausing outside the club, dark heads inside twisting to get a look. A decision was made, the limousine picked up speed, turned the corner. Once again, the street was empty.

I looked around for someplace to hide the guitar case. The best I could find was underneath a front stoop. I pushed the case in and then moved a trash can over to hide the opening. If I was lucky, it would still be there when I got back. If I got back. I had no doubt that Alex would gleefully shoot me with his Magnum when he caught me, and I had no doubt that he would catch me. As I said, I'm not a hero.

I looked up and down the street. No cars. A few lights. The windows of most of the brownstones were dark. *This Side of Paradise* waited. Pink light from the sign dribbled down the brick and onto the door. I fixed my eyes on that door and started toward it.

It was heavier than I remembered, and the music, once I got the door open, much louder, a screeching thudding noise that practically pushed me back out. I let the door close behind me, sticking to the left wall. I knew Alex couldn't see me there, his view from the bar was cut off by another wall, a dark, varnished wooden wall that formed the back of one of the booths. Coats hung from pegs, dozens of tweed overcoats and down jackets. Right across from me was the cigarette machine. I almost pulled out some of the change I'd begged that afternoon and bought a pack. As if I could stroll in and sit at the bar, have a smoke and a whiskey, watch the girls, chat with the bartender. As if I was a normal person. The glowing red cigarette machine had nothing to do with me. Nor did the black-framed photographs above it of baseball players and theater celebrities.

My immediate problem was getting upstairs. I knew Alex kept a key behind the PRIVATE: DO NOT ENTER sign he had tacked to the stairway door. But to get there I had to cross maybe twenty feet of open nightclub. The only time I'd be hidden from him would be when the '48 Ford was between us. Otherwise, I'd be completely exposed. A stinky, disgusting Frankenstein. Even if Alex didn't see me, Sandy might, and if she didn't, I still had to

work my way through those sweet, fleshy dancers without starting a riot.

The front door opened, a blast of cold air, and in stumbled two kids in tight leather pants and black leather
jackets zipped up to the neck. They each wore a pair of
scuffed black boots with pointed toes and Cuban heels,
they both had a gold earring in the left earlobe, and they
both had short, spikey hair that had been dyed blond and
skunked purple. One was a boy and one was a girl. I felt
like Theodore Roosevelt standing next to them. They
stomped their feet as the door settled closed behind them,
whacked their hands against their leather jackets, the girl
muttering, "I hate this place."

They saw me at the same time, but it was as if I weren't
really there, or presented just a blurred outline, because
they both squinted slightly and peered *through* me.
Whatever they saw bored them. They went back to im-
proving their circulation. Their eyes were weary and
bloodshot.

I walked in with them, on their right, keeping them between me and the bar. They didn't even glance at me. I
don't think they could smell anything anymore.

Beyond them, over the dark bobbing heads of the dancers, I could see Alex pouring drinks at the bar. His hook
glistened in the flashing strobes. Two stood crouched
over his controls in the Ford, baseball cap in place,
dark glasses masking his eyes. He was playing the Talking
Heads.

I looked for Sandy but couldn't see her. I did see
George and Lewis, making their way among the tables
carrying trays of bottles and glasses. Everything seemed
the same: the music to drown consciousness, the yakking
faces and spastic hands, the smell of sweat and perfume
and beer and grass.

The leather kids left me when we were halfway across
the floor. I didn't think Alex could see me, the wheelless
truck was in the way. I turned sideways and side-stepped
my back to the dance floor. I had to sidle past a row of
round tables. No one looked up, they kept their faces low

and close to the rippled glass candle bowls, mouths moving wildly, nervous smoke streaming to the ceiling, bracelets bright, teeth bright. They wouldn't have noticed King Kong.

I reached the hallway, ducked inside and hurried past the ladies' room. Then came the men's room, which was crowded, the door opening as I passed and a young professional type stepping out. Over the shoulder of his brown suit, I saw that the bathroom was crowded. Men bent studiously above pieces of tin foil, straws in their noses. The coke snorters. I'd forgotten about them. The man moved on down the hallway toward the music, straightening his coat, running a hand back through his perfect hair. He hadn't seen me any more than the leather kids had. I really might as well have been invisible. Were they all so stoned they thought they were hallucinating me?

There was no one else around, though I could hear the boys talking Super Bowl talk as they snorted coke in the bathroom. Drums and bass reverberated in the door. I fumbled with my fingers for the key behind the sign. It was there, hanging on a small nail, a bronze Yale key that didn't want to go into the lock. My hand was shaking. I had to hold it steady with my other hand and guide the key into the lock. The key fit, turned, and I quickly yanked open the door and stepped into the stairway, closing the door behind me and dropping the dead lock. All I could do was hope that Alex didn't decide to come upstairs. Odds were he wouldn't.

The stairway stretched up into the darkness of a second-story hallway. Since it was the back stairway, there wasn't any banister. The plain wooden steps creaked under my feet as I climbed. I hurried, taking the steps two at a time until I'd reached the hallway.

The hallway lay parallel to the stairs, a simple oak half-wall to the left, three closed wooden doors to the right. Then the hallway made a sharp left turn and met the next set of stairs rising to the third floor. The hallway wasn't as dark as I'd thought. Squares of light fell through marbled glass windows in two of the doors. Beyond the doors were offices, rented out by Alex to small businesses on the make. They fronted on the main hallway on the other side of the building. I listened hard. The hallway was quiet. No one seemed to be in any of the offices. The lights must have been for security. There was a slight, high-pitched rattle it took me a few seconds to place: the windowpanes vibrating because of the rock and roll shivering up the bones of the old house. When I put my hand to the glass I could feel the *thump-thump-thump* of a bass guitar.

I climbed to the next floor. Alex's floor. I lit a match. In the quick, flaring light, I saw a simple hallway, shorter than the one below, and a single door. A window at the end of the hallway caught the reflection of my match and made me jump. Then the flame burned my fingers. I dropped the match, stomping it out with my toe, and felt my way to the door. It was locked. Tightly. It didn't even rattle in its frame.

There was a little light filtering through the window at the end of the hallway. I moved slowly toward it until I was staring out at rooftops, an alley, some hunched, shadowy shapes that could have been parked cars. And a fire escape. It ran along the side of the building, just outside the window.

I unfastened the twist latch, which wasn't easy. I don't think anyone had opened that window in a long time. Then I had to push the window up, dragging away a skin of old paint and coagulated dust. I really had to put my shoulder to it, and had almost decided to give up and try the door again when suddenly the flesh ripped and the window gave, sliding up about sixteen inches before sticking again. But that was enough. I put my leg out into the cold, reaching until my foot had found the fire escape, then contorted myself and squeezed through the narrow space.

The stars had come out. Hundreds of clear, trembling stars. I couldn't remember the last time I'd seen the stars. Incarnations ago. Lying on my back in a field, the buzz of crickets filling the dark night, gazing up at the stars so intensely I sometimes would feel myself rising toward them, accelerating faster and faster, catapulted into space. Now real wind bit at my face, and the crickets were replaced by the overlapping cries of distant sirens. Looking down through the metal slats of the fire escape, I gasped. It was a long way to the ground. I could see myself falling, I *felt* myself falling, end over end as I plummeted to the alley, broken glass and garbage cans rushing up to smash me.

I straightened and embraced the wall, pressing my cheek against the brick. Opening my eyes, I saw the stars, pinpricks of yellow quivering above the buildings. As I watched, blinking airplane lights slid noiselessly between me and the stars. I wasn't so high. The trick was to pretend that I stood on firm ground, that the fire escape was earth. If I could believe that I'd be all right.

I crawled to the first window, never looking down. It was the same kind of window as the one off the hallway, a large, old-fashioned window, six panes to each casement. Shading my eyes with my hand, I peered inside. There was nothing to see. The place was dark. A flurry of icy snow, thrown by the wind, stung my face.

The window wouldn't open. I pushed up with the flats of my hands, straining to use my legs as springs. It wouldn't budge. I didn't exactly have a lot of strength left, but it was clear that the window was locked. I tried the next one. It, too, was locked. So was the next one. Then the fire escape ended. No more windows.

I took off my shoe, wrapped it in my scarf, and punched it through the middle pane of the last window. The sound of shattering glass roared in the still, cold air. Bits of glass fell to the alley, a tinkling, spattering noise far below me. I waited for the floodlights to pin me to the wall, the loud honking alarms, or a poison-tipped arrow, Alex's booby-trap, to hiss toward my throat. Nothing happened. I could hear mice playing football in my heart, and banshees whining in the wind, and the slow, heavy squeak of a witch riding a TV aerial across the roofs. Sniffing, I smelled incense.

I shook the glass out of my shoe and put the shoe back on, my fingers thick and spastic with the laces. Shaking more glass from my scarf, I wrapped it back around my neck. I reached in through the broken pane and found the latch. It unfastened easily, and I slid the window open and stepped into the room.

34

The overwhelming smell of incense made me gag. I lit another match, looked around, and saw that I wouldn't have to worry about making any noise. The carpet was at least six inches deep. Thick, white, wall-to-wall, it drifted like snow all the way to the other side of the room. Alex had ripped down the secondary walls and turned the third story into a huge single room—larger than most lofts, more like an art gallery, except there weren't any pictures on the bare, white walls. Track lighting. A long glass coffee table in front of a low black leather-and-chrome couch.

I treaded my way soundlessly over the soft pile toward the far corner, looking for Alex's bed. There wasn't a sign of life in the place. Not a magazine, not a glass, not a shoe or a dirty sock, no shirt draped over the back of a chair, nothing to indicate that anyone lived here. Except the incense. I couldn't tell where it was coming from. I passed the front door and then my match flickered out, instant darkness.

I lit another one and saw the bed, directly ahead of me. It was one of those fake Spanish frames. The purple satin sheets looked as neat and unslept in as hotel sheets. Pink neon light blinked at the front windows, not quite enough to see by. Except for the bed, and a squat bedside table, this corner of the apartment seemed to be empty.

Alex had said he kept it by his bed. So he could reach it fast and blast out the brains of some intruder like me. I knelt down and looked inside the table. There wasn't enough room in there for a rifle. On top I found the source of the incense, a brass dish covered with a well-fitted porcelain cap, ventilated to let the sickening scent escape. I lit a third match and looked under the bed. Nothing. I felt with my free hand, patting the carpet. Even under the bed, it was clean. It had to be here somewhere. Everything depended on that. I'd *believed* Alex. It hadn't occurred to me that he might just be one of the world's all-time great bull-shitters, crazier, in a way, then I'd thought. I singed my finger again and gave up with the matches. I went by touch, bringing my fingers up to the bottom of the mattress, as far in as I could reach, and then out in wide sweeps. I got to the frame. I danced my fingers along the inner ledge, where the slats rest on the sideboards.

The M-16 was taped under the right sideboard, up near the head of the bed, within easy reach, if he slept on his stomach, of his one good hand. It pulled away easily, heavier than I'd expected, cold black steel with a wood stock. Alex had strapped three full clips to the gun with the same surgical tape. I ripped them off and stuffed them in my pockets. Then I carried the M-16 over to the window and studied it in the pink light. I found the safety catch, and convinced myself that it was on. I found the slot where the clips fit.

I tested the trigger. It rested perfectly, hard, taut, dangerous. I squeezed it a little, felt the subtle resistance, a temptation to keep going, to keep testing, until suddenly, of its own accord, it would snap back as the hammer fell and the gun erupted. I'd never held a gun in my hand before, not that I could remember, and I think that's the kind of thing I would remember. It looked evil in the pulses of pink light.

I thought I heard footsteps, outside in the front hallway. Mice started playing sports in my heart again. If the door opened and Alex walked in I was a dead man. Crouching, I scuttled out of the pink light. I climbed through the window and ran along the fire escape to the hallway window.

Once I was back inside, I opened my coat and stuffed the M-16 under my arm, the barrel facing the ground along my right side. I buttoned the coat up. As far as I could tell nothing showed except a lumpish growth, a bulge in my coat. Keeping my right arm pressed tight against my side, holding the gun in place, I practically ran down the two flights of steps. As I raced lower the music grew louder, until it was vibrating in the walls again, heartbeat and anger greeting me when I opened the bottom door and carefully glanced out into the hallway. Empty, it ended in darkness, candlelight, the even louder noise of the dance floor. The bathroom doors were closed. I stared at the fire extinguisher clamped to the wall. I counted to ten. The hallway stayed empty.

I slipped out the door, closing and locking it behind me, returning the key to its nail behind the sign. I don't know why I was so meticulous about that. I seemed to need to make an orderly departure, as if, by slowing down and moving nonchalantly, I could control things. I couldn't, of course. Far from it. But I wanted to believe I could. So I hung the key on its nail and then sauntered down the hallway and then, without stopping, stepped right out into the raucous rock and roll. I kept going, past the eager couples leaning over their orange candlelight. Why didn't someone look up from one of the tables, see me, and start shouting? Why didn't the dancers shrink in horror? I was beginning to feel invincible as well as invisible. I allowed myself to look toward Alex once, quickly. He had his back to me, bent over as he searched for fresh bottles.

I reached the dark vestibule between the main room and the front door just in time to see a woman straighten from the cigarette machine and turn to me with a pack of Camels in her hand. It was Sandy. She was wearing her thick-soled working shoes and an apron, and she looked tired. For a second she merely stared at me, blankly, as if we'd never met, her weight on one foot. The music clashed behind us, the cigarette machine sent its red glow up onto the side of her face. Then she licked her lips, and slowly, inevitably, her mouth started to open into a wide, terrified scream, fear so intense it came out a strangled stutter before gaining strength and rising above the music.

I brushed past her, yanked open the heavy front door, and hurried out into the night. I was greeted by a barrage of whirling blue police lights.

Nothing strains the mind like shock, sudden surprise, any almost imperceptible transition from one world to another. It's like flying to another country, that disorienting sense of having traveled a great distance without moving at all. Finding myself caught, handcuffed and slammed into the back seat of a squad car between huge, angry cops, I nearly turned to one of them and asked, "Is this really happening?" I can imagine what he would have said. I couldn't believe that I was there, anymore than I'd been able to believe, first waking up, that I was underground in an abandoned subway station with fifty or sixty derelicts and long-gone street people. It was as if I'd moved from days of just talking to myself to the unexpected company of a crowd. Yet the cops said nothing as they sped me through the empty streets to a precinct station on East Seventieth Street. Even this part of my nightmare seemed too much my own.

Detective Malone arrived after I'd been fingerprinted and photographed by more curious cops who stared at me as if at someone, or something, disgusting. I recognized him. He was the pot-bellied detective I'd seen climbing the steps to my apartment. He came into the plain room where I had been deposited, a room of green walls, no windows, an old office desk, and a few scarred wooden chairs. Closing the door behind him, he also gave me a curious look, but more openly than the other cops. He wasn't afraid to gaze into me. Then he cleared his throat and moved to one of the chairs across from me. Sitting down, he pulled out a pack of Pall Malls and lit one. He didn't offer me any. He dropped his match into a chipped glass ashtray on the desk, inhaled deeply, gratefully, coughed and grimaced.

"You know you have the right to remain silent." He

took another painful drag on his cigarette. "And all that shit."

Dark circles hung like sacks under his blue eyes. His face had a flat, imperturbable quality, matching his tired eyes. He was used to dealing with scum. In his forties, well built, he wore a rumpled blue suit, nothing expensive, and black shoes. His hands were oddly graceful. I must have dragged him away from home, his sleeping house and the dark Christmas tree in the corner of the living room. Absurdly, wanting to please him, I apologized.

"For what?" He waited thoughtfully.

"It's Christmas Eve."

He stared at me some more, trying to translate my comment.

"You're Gregory Hartz, right?"

"Yes."

"You live at one thirteen West Seventy-third Street?"

"Yes. Is this being recorded?"

His eyes flickered. "Yeah."

"Do I have the right to have a lawyer here?"

"You do," he admitted, a little reluctantly. "Want one?"

"No. Not yet."

"Okay. Let's get on with it then. What were you doing with that M-16."

"Trying to defend myself."

"You stole it. That's a crime right there. You don't have a license. Another crime. We haven't even gotten to the good stuff yet and you're already in trouble." He studied his cigarette, burning slowly between his slender fingers. His nails were long, carefully shaped, and I noticed a thin gold chain around his right wrist. "Defend yourself against what?" he asked.

"You won't believe me."

"Try me."

"A bunch of kids. Homeless kids, I think. A gang of some kind." I tried to look honest. "They're the ones you want. They're the Finger Mugger."

He smiled to himself, stubbed his cigarette out in the

ashtray. "You're right. I don't believe you." His voice assumed a steady, deadly patience, and his blue eyes looked right into mine again, daring me to lie. "Gregory, we're checking your fingerprints out right now against the fingerprints on a certain pair of very bloody scissors. Want to bet they match?"

"They will."

"And we've got certain good friends of yours who can place you in the vicinity of a certain crime."

"I know."

"And finally we've got some law-abiding citizens who can identify you on the spot of the crime, including a certain distinguished woman who was the *victim*. Are you following my drift, Gregory? Do you see what I'm getting at?"

"That's why I was hiding. That's why I ran."

"What I'm getting at, Gregory, is that your ass is fried. You're a punk, Gregory. And you're going to go to punk heaven. Know what I mean? It's throw-away-the-key time, Gregory. Bye-bye daylight. Hello four walls. Are you still with me? You're fucked, and the more bullshit you give me, the more you're fucked, because I take these things very personally. Being lied to, I mean. By greasy psychos like you. That gets me mad. So don't make me mad, Gregory. Tell me the fucking truth."

"I did."

"Right. Right you did."

He was good. He had me scared, and if I had been guilty I might have confessed, anything to rid me of his vengeful and penetrating rage, the rage of injured society scorching behind those eyes. He either really was furious, or a very good actor, a better actor than I'll ever be. His rage was so convincing, in fact, that he almost had me believing I was guilty. Part of me wanted to confess. The words struggled in my mouth. I had to will them silent.

I was tired, and in a strange, luxurious way, grateful to have been caught. "How did you know where I was?" I asked.

His smile was malicious. "Your former employer saw you. Gave us a call."

"I'd like that lawyer now."

"Why not just save us all a lot of time and money and tell me why you did it? Why, Gregory? Hmm? Did you enjoy it? Need the money, did you? Come on. What's the story?"

"I want to sleep."

"Oh you'll sleep, all right. You'll sleep. But first just give me a little clue. Was it *satisfying*, Gregory? Is that it?"

"And I'd like to wash," I said. "I'd like a shower."

Distaste formed ridges around his mouth. "You don't even feel guilty, do you? You little prick. You don't even feel guilty."

Oh, but I do, I almost said. More than you'll ever know. Without another word, Malone stood and left the room, his big shoulders hunched in anger. Seconds later, two regular cops came in and took me out into the hallway, each holding one of my arms firmly. They led me along past closed office doors, over a linoleum floor pitted by cigarette butts and the sharp heels of heavy shoes.

"Jesus, this asshole stinks," one of them said.

"You don't have to kiss him," his partner replied.

They escorted me down to a dimly lit room, a cagelike place where an older cop, sipping coffee from a paper cup, collected my shoelaces and the little money I had and stored them away in a metal box. I had to sign a receipt, and then the journey continued, downward again, as if I were fated always to descend. Thick doors, grinding mechanisms, like vault doors, opened up onto the jail. I was given my own cell.

The two cops left, and I was alone in the darkness, light from the hallway outside revealing the thin slab of a bed, a toilet, a sink. The single tap sputtered cold water. I splashed it across my face, trying to rub away the dirt. I couldn't find any soap, or a towel. I dried myself with the thin blanket on the bed. I sat down, wrapping the blanket around me, shivering, not because I was cold—I wasn't— but because I had lost all control of my body. I might as well have had a fever. Maybe I did.

I couldn't sleep. That's all I wanted to do, swoon and

sink into sweet oblivion. But I couldn't. I sat there shivering and listening to the strange noises around me, noises of men in other cells, turning uncomfortably in nightmares, snoring and calling obscenities, a fitful, invisible crowd. I wondered what they had done to get themselves down there. How many of my neighbors were murderers, rapists, muggers, and how many were merely drunks, like John, picked up and thrown into jail for a night? I had never been in jail before, never even seen one. It was no better than the tunnels. The same claustrophobia, the same terrible feeling of being trapped in a shrinking box.

The albino had won. He had defeated me.

35

The next morning two more cops woke me, both young. They led me to a shower, where I stood for a long time under the hot water, washing away three days' worth of dirt. Then they gave me some starched gray clothes, prisoner's clothes, and led me back upstairs. I was put in a room divided by a glass wall. On the other side of the wall, facing me through the glass, sat a young man my age. He looked up at me as I entered, eyes lost in memorization. A few seconds passed before he seemed to see me, and when he did, he smiled. He wore a spiffy Pierre Cardin suit and tassle loafers. He must have owned a blowdryer. He held a slim gold Cross pen poised above his yellow pad. The smile stayed motionless, just one more thing he'd put on that morning. I think he was nervous. I doubt he'd ever had to defend a mass murderer before.

"Gregory Hartz?" His voice drifted through the grate in the glass.

I sat down opposite him, in one of the chairs lined up along the glass.

"My name's Duncan Chandler," he said. "I've been sent over by the public defenders office to represent you."

He consulted some papers before him. "Brown, huh? I went to Williams. Class of 'seventy-five." He was watching me, I realized, the way you watch someone to see if they're crazy or not—warily, condescendingly, already more than half convinced. He glanced back at his papers. "An actor? You know, I did some acting once. In high school. Good training for law, standing up in front of all those people."

Why did he keep talking about himself? It was as if we were just having a friendly chat, two like-minded Ivy Leaguers with plenty of time on our hands.

"I didn't do it," I said, so matter-of-factly I startled myself. The statement lacked conviction.

"Well, now that's what I'm here to talk about. I've looked over the situation and it seems to me it's not as bad as it could be. There is absolutely nothing except circumstantial evidence to connect you to the other, uh, crimes. I mean there's a case, a *psychological* case, a probable pattern, a syndrome—but nothing hard. The only *real* evidence they've got is your connection to ..." His eyes checked the yellow pad. "This di Costini woman."

"I was trying to help her."

"What?"

"She'd been mugged and I was trying to help her."

"Oh."

He didn't believe me any more than Malone did. They'd probably already talked about me, come to conclusions, arrangements with the DA's office. He twirled the end of his gold pen. The ball point retreated. He set the pen down on his pad and folded his hands. Talking, he didn't look at me. He looked at a space somewhere above and beyond me.

"Gregory, their evidence is pretty solid. You're not stupid. You know that. But I think we can do all right. Yes, I really do. I've been giving this some thought and I see a way to do it."

"I'm innocent."

"Of course you are." He said it too quickly. "My point is that *they've got you.* It's all there. The scissors. The witnesses. The victim. You ran away, Gregory. An innocent man doesn't run away. I mean, that's the way *they* see it. That's the way the judge will see it. You don't have an alibi, do you?"

I shook my head.

"So there we are. That's the problem. No alibi, a lot of heavy evidence. But—but." He raised his finger, a lecturer making a fine distinction. "We can plead temporary insanity."

"I'm not crazy."

"*I* know that. Look at it this way. You've been under a lot of strain recently. You've been looking for work. You couldn't find any. You want to be an actor. You're a waiter. You're ambitious, you want to be a good actor, a *great* actor. You're frustrated. You went to *Brown*, Gregory. You're an overachiever. You're not used to failure. You *hate* failure. You hate *yourself* when you fail. I know. I'm the same way." He flashed me a smile. "Anyway, you cracked up, Gregory. That's all. You cracked up. You took out all your rage against life, against this goddamn city, against your failure, against yourself. But that's all. *Just that once.* Just against that di Costini woman. And do you know why, Gregory? Do you know why? *Because you're an actor.* In a moment of frantic confusion, no longer yourself, you *became* the Finger Mugger. I mean, like all of us you knew about him, you'd been reading about him, what he did, and then you *acted* him, Gregory. You played a role. You're not the Finger Mugger. You copied him, on a stage. At least you thought it was a stage. In your confusion, you thought it all was a play. You never meant to *really* hurt anyone. You were just . . . temporarily insane."

Finished, he leaned back in his chair, so pleased with himself he grinned. As far as I was concerned, *he* was the crazy one. Yet I both admired and detested him for this twisted bit of logic. Like Malone, he was only doing his job. As a defense, I suppose it might actually have worked. Though he clearly thought me guilty, he wasn't going to let that stop him. Anyway, what choice did I have? My being innocent meant nothing if I couldn't prove it. And I couldn't.

"The arraignment's tomorrow." He stood, pad in hand. "We'll enter our plea. Then we have to wait for the preliminary hearing. God knows how long that'll take." He gave me a little wave. "See you tomorrow then."

The same two cops came for me later that day and brought me back to the room with a glass divider. There, standing anxiously on the other side, were my parents, both looking out of place, embarrassed.

"We drove down," my father said, as if explaining an intricate maneuver. "When we heard."

Just seeing them, I was close to tears.

"That's all right son," my father said. "Everything's going to be all right. I'm getting you a good lawyer. Don Martell knows a couple of real powerful lawyers on Wall Street. We'll fix this thing up."

Even in her agitation, my mother stayed calm. "Are you sick? Do you need a doctor? Are they treating you well?"

She might as well have been asking after my accommodations at summer camp. That's as real as she'd let that jail be. And my father, with his big, earnest hands, he somehow thought that his friend's hotshot Wall Street lawyers could save the day. He couldn't help it. He believed in the power of money, no matter what the situation. It had treated him well, flowed into those hands in exchange for long, hard work, built him a million-dollar dealership, gained him membership on the board of the local bank. He had the blind faith of the successful convert. He wanted to help me, and that's the only way he knew how.

"What happened, son?"

I still felt as if I'd traveled to another country. I couldn't find the words to tell them about it. I just stared, mutely.

"You should have come home for Christmas," my father said, the closest he's ever come to making a joke, though I don't think he meant it as one.

Then my mother did start to cry, her calm dissolving. "Why, Gregory? Why?"

I realized they thought I'd done it. They thought their son was a killer—our family had no more meaning than that. They didn't know me, or themselves, enough to trust me. That hurt so much I turned away. I just wanted to be alone, I said. They finally left.

I was lined up with five other men my age, our eyes staring into white light that blurred and trembled while behind a one-way mirror that I could only half see Signora di Costini undoubtedly scrutinized my face, trying to be sure, trying to remember what she could of that night. If she'd already identified my photograph, there wasn't much chance she'd miss me in the flesh. A mechanized voice, not Malone's, issued orders through a speaker on the wall: turn left, turn right. I was beginning to feel more and more like a specimen on display, a curiosity, a freak. It made me angry. The lights were hot, burning into me. Sweat prickled on my forehead. Who else was out there? The outraged coward leaning from his window above me, calling down encouragement to di Costini like a junior high school coach? One by one, the bricks were being mortared around me. Daylight was disappearing.

Next came Malone and Duncan Chandler. They were waiting for me in the room with a desk and an ashtray. Malone seemed to be wearing the same clothes and the same brooding Irish expression of sad resentment. He looked at me closely when I came in, examined me with his blue eyes. He was a better man than my lawyer, who stood near the window looking out, then graced me with his phony smile and motioned to Malone to begin. We all sat down on the hard wooden chairs. Malone clawed a Pall Mall out of a crumpled pack and lit it, immediately succumbing to paroxysms of coughing, a grating sound deep in his chest.

"Well, Gregory, your goose is cooked," he finally said. "The lady picked her man, and the man is you."

The anger I'd felt in the line-up had stayed with me. "Listen, you creep, I didn't do it. I don't care what she says. I don't care what anybody says."

Malone smoldered. I was probably lucky slick Duncan

was there, or otherwise Malone might have given me a slug or two. He wasn't in the mood to take grief. His free hand, delicate as a woman's, reached up and massaged his neck.

"What I'm trying to do," he said, "is save everyone a lot of pain. Okay? I want you to confess."

"Don't," Duncan said quickly. "I mean, you don't have to."

"I know that."

"So?" Malone raised his eyebrows.

I decided to try one last time. "Those kids I told you about, they live somewhere around Tenth Avenue, in the warehouse district, below Fourteenth Street. Right now they're most likely in the steam tunnels beating the hell out of all the bums down there. You know about the steam tunnels?"

For a while I didn't think Malone was going to respond. He kept staring at me, the way he had when I'd come in. He nodded. "I know."

"Last night I saw them burn an old man alive in those tunnels."

Malone shifted weight in his chair. The legs creaked under the strain. Duncan kept his eyes on his gold pen, revolving it idly in his fingers.

"They use an entrance over by Eighteenth Street when they come out of the tunnels," I went on. "They've got half the beggars in the city working for them. They take their money every night. Then they go out and mug people on the streets."

Malone lit another cigarette, while Duncan gazed at me with cynical admiration. He thought I'd made up a good story.

"Your father says he's looking for a top-flight lawyer to represent you," Malone said.

Duncan reacted, his pride wounded. "I think we'll do just fine, lieutenant."

"But no matter what kind of lawyer you've got, it won't change anything." Malone ignored Duncan. "This is what's known as a closed case. Cooperate and the judge might go a little easy on you. Don't, and he'll kick your butt to Oyster Bay." I'd noticed that Malone's language was considerably cleaner with Duncan there, but he was having a bad time restraining himself. "All I want from you is the truth. Tell me what happened. Confess, you son of a bitch."

"No." Duncan was curt, angry himself now at Malone. "He won't confess. He has nothing more to say. Let him go back to his cell."

Malone didn't move. He gazed at me thoughtfully.

They arraigned me in a bleak courtroom that was empty except for me, a lawyer from the DA's office, Duncan Chandler, the judge, and the court recorder. The judge was the Honorable Dorothy Household, a tight-lipped woman in her sixties who looked down at us from the bench through thick glasses. On the wall behind her was a framed picture of Mayor Koch. Duncan fussed with his papers. Though my father had in fact finally located and hired what he was assured was one of the best criminal lawyers in the city, I had decided to go with Duncan. I didn't believe it made much difference whether or not I was found sane or insane. Either way, I was going to spend a long time behind bars.

I don't remember the proceedings very well, except for the hot buzzing in my ears, the sweat dripping down my arms. The judge asked for the charge, and the DA's lawyer announced, as Duncan had predicted, that I was only being accused in the di Costini case. Then he said, "Your Honor, the defendant, Gregory Hartz, is charged with one count of assault with intent to murder, one count mayhem, and one count of assault with a deadly weapon."

"How do you plead?" the judge asked me.

My throat was dry. I practically whispered, "Not guilty."

All I could see was the last brick being mortared into place, the sunlight disappearing forever.

It was hard, after three days of trying to solve a problem, to just sit in a cell and do nothing. I made no attempt to communicate with the other prisoners. Nor did I think, exactly. My mind wandered. It occurred to me that I'd felt guilty all my life. I felt guilty for existing. Now here I was, accused, practically convicted. It seemed to me, at my worst moment, that I deserved that cell. It's what I'd always wanted, the way I'd always lived anyway. A follower is someone who thinks someone else can make him feel alive. A follower is someone who is afraid of himself, afraid to do anything except hide and watch. A follower is someone who can only take, never give. Had I ever, in my whole life, felt anything for another person, I mean really *felt* it?

Ten days later Malone came to my cell.

He stared at me, poker-faced, then said, "You can go."

I thought it was a joke, a sick joke, and said so.

"We caught the kids. You're free." He stood there watching my reaction, waiting for me to say something. "I never thought you did it. Not since we brought you in. Not since I saw you. Shit, kid, you never hurt anyone." He handed me a folded newspaper. "Here."

I took the newspaper but didn't look at it. "If you didn't think I did it, why'd you treat me like that?"

He shrugged. "I wasn't sure. I never am."

I opened the newspaper. There, on the front page, was the story. Undercover cops, one of them masquerading as a rich woman out alone, had arrested the albino, whose name was given as Johnny King, as well as ten other kids. Photographs showed an abandoned warehouse full of juke boxes and pinball machines, pool tables and TVs, racks of fur coats, a tableload of jewels.

"They lived there," Malone said. "Like fucking rats. Collected the damn stuff. I don't think they even tried to sell it. Just kept it like it was gold."

"What about the other kids? In the tunnels?"

"We're looking." He pulled out a cigarette and lit it, took a drag, fought a huge cough and won. "I'm killing myself, for Christsake."

36

I went back to Mosby's the other day. I was in the neighborhood, uptown for an audition at a theater on Fortieth Street, so I wandered over to see if Henry was still holding court among the phone booths. I'd always wanted to thank him again for the coat. He wasn't there, but I took a seat at the counter anyway and ordered coffee. The blue-haired waitress still called me honey as she asked for my order and scribbled it onto her pad. I don't think she remembered me. It was a warm, spring day, sunlight slanting through the big glass windows. I sat there basking, sipping coffee, remembering the day I had left the drugstore and followed Delia toward death.

"Well, well, if it ain't Mr. Mean."

I turned, staring into Henry's prehistoric eyes, marbled and glazed. He stood back and appraised me, clucking, wagging his head from side to side, then slid onto the stool next to mine. He'd changed his uniform, discarding the old pimp's image for a more demure classicism. He wore a baby-blue suit, dark blue turtleneck, tan shoes. The hat was gone.

"Where you been, man?" His fingers drummed across the counter. "Where the fuck you been all this time?"

"Around," I said. "I moved. New job."

"Going up in the world, is that right?"

"Mostly in circles. Want some coffee?"

We sat and talked for a while, the bright sunlight exposing Henry's exhausted face. It was as if the tissue of his skin had been stretched too tight, turning gray in dark rooms, gray and thin and dry, starved for some essential vitamins. He blinked in the light like an old cat.

"Do you remember that coat you got me?" I asked him.

He smiled. "Henry don't forget nothing. Your sweet white ass was deep in shit, I do believe." He couldn't help grinning at the ludicrious memory. He chuckled. "Mr. Killer. Mr. Bad Man."

He punched my arm playfully and laughed. His hands shook when he picked up his cup of coffee and took a sip.

"I'd like to pay you back," I said.

He peered at me over his cup. "How?"

I hadn't expected that. "Money?"

"I told you, I don't want no money. Anyway, that coat didn't cost me nothing, if you know what I mean." He patted his coat pocket. "I got plenty money, boy. Don't you worry about me. See, I been thinking. What's amusing about this predicament is there ain't no way you can pay me back. What you got that I want? What you got that I need? Understand my reasoning? There ain't nothing to *exchange*. Unless you suddenly real rich. You real rich?"

"No."

"You got some rich friends want themselves a nice girl for the night?"

"No."

"Well then, we just leave the debt outstanding, I guess, huh?"

There was a trace of mockery behind Henry's smile, and it made me uneasy. Of course he was right, and maybe he just felt a little superior because he'd known it and I hadn't. Unless I lived in Henry's world, I had nothing to offer him, and he had nothing to offer me. We lived that far apart.

"Girls." He sighed, squinting out the window at the hurrying passersby, New Yorkers scurrying about their business. "Got so many girls now don't know what to do with them. Poor girls." He seemed genuinely distraught. "Poor girls."

He straightened and clutched my arm. His small fingers were frighteningly strong. "Know what I think? I think we fucked. Know why?" He pressed closer, that jaunty conspiratorial expression rising to clear his face for a moment. "Because God's losing patience. That's right. I talked with him the other night, and he says, 'Henry, I'm losing patience with you. I give you what you want, I helps you out now and again, but, nigger, you got to start *living right.* Hear me? *Start living right.'* " Henry released my arm, grinned. "Trouble is, how am I gonna start living right?"

When I first got out of jail, when I first walked out onto the street and looked around and realized that no one was chasing me and that I didn't have to spend the rest of my life in small dank holes, I laughed aloud, startling a few people on the sidewalk. For about ten intense seconds I knew what it was like to be fully alive, much as I'd felt when I stepped out of the tunnels into the soft falling snow, yet even more strongly, more completely, because I was truly free. I could do anything I wanted to do. I was simply me. Now time has passed, more than a year, and that freedom, the deep thrilling sense of it, has submerged again, lost in dailiness. But I remember it, enough to know that it's there.

I moved to an apartment on Eleventh Street, a fifth-floor walkup with lots of light and smooth wooden floors. I rented a van, went up to Springfield, and came back with books, prints for my walls, the old leather couch from my father's office, pots and pans my mother gave me. It's been difficult for them to forgive themselves, they know they betrayed me by thinking me guilty, though they feel worse about it now than I do. I'm not sure what I would have thought in their place. We judge ourselves badly, and it's a mistake to take other people's judgment too personally. I make a point of talking to them more often on the telephone, and visiting when I can. After all, I'm their only son.

Six nights a week these days I play one of the ghosts in *Our Town.* The theater, a small one, isn't far from my apartment. The rest of the time I spend going to auditions, or working in a bookstore over on Eighth Street. I've made some friends there, as well as in some of the theaters around town. I've never told them about what happened to me. It would make them afraid of me. But I still think about it, and wonder why the albino kept going, why, when he knew the cops had caught what they were sure was the Finger Mugger, he risked going out and revealing himself. He must have been jealous of all the attention I was getting. Maybe he wanted to be recognized. I can understand that. It's not so different from what I wanted—to feel a part of life instead of like a Martian just passing through.

I followed the trial closely. With all the evidence the cops found in the warehouse, including Signora di Costini's necklace and fur coat, as well as the pathetic confessions of some of the kids, the DA didn't have too much trouble getting convictions. The albino was tried as an adult. I'm not sure that was fair. Even so, they knew they couldn't send him to a regular prison, they knew he wouldn't last a week, so they shipped him north to some high-tech reformatory near Albany. He'll probably spend the rest of his life in jail. All the other kids were also sent to reform schools, and for a few weeks there was a lot of noise in the *New York Times* about curing the grave social problem of homeless children and youthful violence. The cops cleaned out the tunnels, they said, and found more kids. They didn't find the deserted subway station, though.

I've looked for Delia. I've gone to her favorite spot on the corner of Thirty-ninth and Sixth. I've waited outside Grand Central for hours at a time. I've looked for her all over the city. I once even stood before that door on the side of the Plaza, knowing where it led, but I never went down. I couldn't. I didn't have the courage. Anyway, I doubt that Delia was there. I would have seen her by then, at least once, somewhere up on the streets. Maybe she's moved back to Chicago.

I did think I saw Scissors a couple of months ago. It was twilight. I was walking downtown from a theater off Columbus Circle when I passed an alley. I heard a noise, as if the bottom of a paper bag had broken and thirty bottles had fallen shattering to the ground. There, among the usual litter of cans and dumpsters, I saw what looked like Scissors scrambling away though the garbage. I called his name. He didn't stop.